Dead-Stick

Also by L. J. Washburn

Wild Night

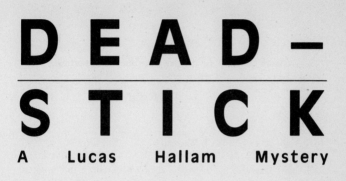

DEAD-STICK

A Lucas Hallam Mystery

L. J. WASHBURN

TOR

A TOM DOHERTY ASSOCIATES BOOK
NEW YORK

DEAD-STICK

Copyright © 1989 by L. J. Washburn.

A TOR BOOK
Published by Tom Doherty Associates, Inc.
49 West 24 Street
New York, NY 10010

First edition: July 1989
0 9 8 7 6 5 4 3 2 1

ONE

Against a cloudless sky so blue and bright the eyes hurt to look at it, four airplanes swooped and twisted in a dance that was beautiful and deadly at the same time. Fragile constructions of wire and wood and canvas, they darted here and there, flames flickering from the machine guns mounted on them. It seemed that at any moment, the sheer strain of the maneuvers they were going through would tear them to pieces, dooming their luckless pilots to plunge earthward to their deaths.

Lucas Hallam had never seen anything like it.

He stood well back, away from the director's position. It was hard for anyone as tall and broad as he was to be unobtrusive, but Hallam was trying. He had worked for Danby Swan as an extra on a couple of pictures, and he knew that any interruption during shooting would send the man into a downright fit.

Hallam wondered if Swan would remember him. Carl McGinley, the producer of *Death to the Kaiser!* and the man who had called him in the first place, knew that Hallam split his time between movie work and an occasional case as a private detective. Hallam doubted that Swan knew that, though.

Swan crouched beside one of the cameras, urging the cameraman to stay with the planes. A tall, lean man with dark blond hair, Swan wore boots, jodhpurs, and a white shirt open at the throat. Hallam thought the outfit was a little ridiculous, but he had to admit that Swan wore it well. He had quite a reputation among the leading ladies of the film colony, and Hallam suspected a lot of it was deserved.

Hallam heard a step behind him and turned his head to see Carl McGinley approaching. McGinley put a smile on his pudgy face and said, "Hello, Lucas. Glad you could come out."

"Howdy." Hallam nodded. "Sounded like you were havin' a mite of trouble."

McGinley nodded, his smile disappearing. "You could say that. So much trouble that I'm starting to wonder if this picture is ever going to get made."

McGinley was a small, round man with brown hair and a perpetually worried expression. He had been producing pictures here in Hollywood almost from the first, and that was enough to make any man stay worried. Hallam had met him in 1915, not long after he had arrived in Hollywood himself, and had worked in a few of his pictures before McGinley made his way out of Poverty Row and quit grinding out two-reel Westerns. Now he did prestige pictures with well-known directors like Danby Swan, but evidently the headaches had just increased over the years.

Hallam himself had never left Poverty Row, not where the movies were concerned. The little independent studios down on Gower Gulch were home to him now, and the men who made the Westerns were his family.

A man had to eat, though, and Hallam's old aches and pains wouldn't let him be a riding extra all the time. His PI ticket let him take up the slack, and those jobs could send him anywhere.

In this case, the studio's location ranch north of town was supposed to be France, and the planes looping around in the sky declared the time to be 1917 again. The Great War was still on, and the battle in the air was as fierce as ever.

"Danby should be through with this scene pretty soon," McGinley said. "If you don't mind, Lucas, I'd rather wait until all three of us can speak together. Danby might remember some things that I don't."

Hallam nodded. "Fine with me."

"Danby wasn't crazy about the idea of hiring a private detective in the first place," McGinley went on. "He said that if there was anything going on that studio security couldn't handle, we should call in the police. I convinced him that wasn't the kind of publicity we needed."

"If I take the job, I'll keep it as quiet as I can."

"I know you will, Lucas. That's why I suggested that we call you. You understand how the movie business works."

Hallam's wide mouth twitched in a suppressed grin. He wasn't sure he'd go so far as to say that. He'd been born in a little community in Texas called Flat Rock in 1870 and had seen a hell of a lot of strange things since then, but he wasn't sure he'd ever run across anything stranger than the movie-making industry.

This was the first time he'd been around an aviation picture; he'd worked on a couple of war films, playing German cavalry troopers, of all things. Like most of his breed, Hallam regarded a job you could do from horseback as a job worth doing. But until today, he had never been this close to an airplane.

In addition to the four in the air, there were two more parked on the flatland a couple of hundred yards away. They were brightly painted, and one was decorated with the Iron Cross of Germany while the other bore the concentric circles that signified it was British. Two men and a woman were standing near the planes, but Hallam couldn't tell much about them at this distance.

Much closer was the little knot of people around the camera, including Danby Swan. Besides the director and the camera operator, an AD, a script girl, and one of the screenwriters were hovering nearby. The assistant director and the script girl were conferring in low voices, being careful not to distract Swan. The writer, like most of the rest of the cast and crew scattered around the location, had his head tilted back and was watching the planes, his gaze drawn by their daring acrobatics.

There were two other cameras set up to either side of the principal one where Swan was. The fact that the studio was willing to commit that much equipment to this production told what high hopes they had for it. Hallam had been on plenty of locations where only one camera was used. Battle films had suffered a slump following the end of the Great War, but if what he read in the industry papers was correct, they were making a comeback.

From the looks of things, *Death to the Kaiser!* was going to be a box-office success. It had plenty of action, and though Hallam wasn't overly fond of Danby Swan, he had to admit that the man could handle action sequences. Swan's touch was just as good with love scenes, too, which was somewhat unusual. And this picture had beautiful young Vesta Quist as the female lead and handsome Rodger Kane as its male star. Their presence certainly wouldn't hurt ticket sales.

Kane was standing near Danby Swan, costumed in high boots, whipcord pants, and a leather flying jacket that had to be hot and uncomfortable. He held a flying helmet and goggles in one hand. One of the pilots now circling above was portraying Kane's character in these flying sequences, but evidently there were some close-up scenes on the shooting schedule, as well. Those would require Kane's presence in costume.

There was no sign of Vesta Quist. She probably hadn't been called for today's shooting.

Behind Hallam were several large, barnlike buildings. At one time, they had in fact been barns, but now they had been converted into an Allied aerodrome in wartime France. They were only used in exterior shots, though. All the interiors would be shot at the studio back in town.

"How about something to drink?" McGinley asked from beside Hallam.

"Reckon I wouldn't mind. That sun makes a man thirsty."

"Let's go over here to the trailer."

Hallam turned and followed McGinley toward one of the little trailers parked nearby. Not much drinking went on during the shooting of a picture, regardless of what the public might think about what degenerates movie people were. The work was just too damn hard to put up with that. But it wasn't unusual to find a keg of bootlegged beer around a location, either.

Hallam knew that he and McGinley made a pretty unlikely pair, the little roly-poly producer and the tall, rawboned man who somehow looked like a cowboy even in street clothes. Hallam's shaggy gray hair and thick moustache made him look even more out of place anywhere but on the set of a Western picture.

They were only halfway to the trailer when a shout made them stop suddenly. Hallam looked back over his shoulder as Danby Swan cried in alarm, "Dammit, what's happened?"

Hallam lifted his eyes to the planes, sensing that if there was trouble, that was where it would be. He had been listening to the roar of the engines ever since arriving on the location and had ignored it for the most part, but now it sounded different. And one of the aircraft was listing to one side, seeming to spin more than it had been.

Its engine had died. Hallam realized that with a little shock of horror. He had faced down a lot of dangerous situations over the years, but the thought of being several thousand feet in the air in some sort of gimcrack contraption that had suddenly gone balky . . .

Hallam loped forward, his stiff right leg slowing him down. He knew there wasn't a damn thing he could do to help, but he couldn't just stand still and watch, either.

The plane continued to lose altitude in a wide spiral. By the time Hallam reached Danby Swan, the three people who had been standing near the parked planes had also arrived at a run. Swan gripped the arm of one of the men and said, "My God, Mackey, what's wrong? Has he lost power?"

The man nodded grimly. "His engine's failed for some reason."

"Can he pull out of it?"

"I don't know, Mr. Swan. Lord, I just don't know."

The man was wearing an aviator's costume much like Rodger Kane's, but he was no actor. Just under medium height, he was stocky, dark-haired, and had a pleasant ugly face. One of the stunt flyers, probably, Hallam thought.

The other man could have been an actor, but Hallam had a feeling that he wasn't. His face was a little too lean, his profile a touch too hawklike. He wore the same type of outfit, though, and that marked him as another of the pilots.

Standing close by his side was the woman. Hallam hadn't gotten a good look at her until now, but he could see a resemblance between her and the second aviator. Her features were fuller, lacking the harshness of the man's. In fact, she was downright beautiful, Hallam thought, though this sure as hell wasn't the right time or place to appreciate that beauty. Her raven hair and flashing dark eyes gave her something of a mysterious look.

Now, however, as she stared up at the disabled plane, she looked like a horrified spectator.

Just like everybody else on the location.

The stocky pilot called Mackey was watching the plane intently, muttering something. Hallam edged a step closer and heard him saying, "That's it, Hank. Jockey that baby in easy!"

Hallam glanced back up at the aircraft. "He goin' to be able to land that thing?" he asked.

The pilot never took his eyes off the plane. "Maybe," he replied, though his tone of voice said that he didn't hold out much hope. "A dead-stick landing's not that hard under good conditions. Those old Spads glide pretty well. But it's windy today, and the struts and the canvas have already had to take a lot of strain . . ."

The other three planes had turned and flown off to the north, and they were now circling a couple of miles away. Hallam figured they were just getting out of the way, giving the pilot of the disabled plane plenty of room to try anything he wanted to try. There was nothing else they could do to help him.

With the sound of their engines being carried away by the wind, that left an eerie silence to settle down on the fields that were supposed to pass for France. No one on the ground was talking now. There was nothing left to say.

Suddenly, the little biplane seemed to straighten somewhat and level off. A whoop went up from the pilot standing next to Hallam, and as he thrust a fist into the air, he shouted, "That's it, Hank! Don't let her nose come up too much now!"

Hallam was sure the pilot in the Spad couldn't hear his comrade over the rush of the wind, but he could have seen the upthrust fist. The plane wasn't far off the ground now, settling closer and closer to the surface of a field two hundred yards away. The ground didn't look too rough from this distance, but Hallam knew how deceiving that could be.

And all it could take was one bad bump to wreck the plane and turn this day's shooting into a fiery catastrophe.

Just like this picture had been fouled up several times before . . .

Hallam supposed that was just instinct, thinking like a detective at the very instant the pilot was fighting for his life. But the fact remained that he had been summoned by Carl McGinley and Danby Swan because they were afraid someone was trying to sabotage their picture. What more effective way to slow down or ruin an aviation film than to wreck a plane and kill a pilot?

A gasp went up from the watching crowd when the wheels of the landing gear touched down for the first time and bounced back up slightly. The pilot rode the plane on down with an easy, expert touch. The tail slewed to one side as the front wheels encountered some obstruction, but somehow the craft held together. Dust billowed up, hiding all sight of it for a moment, but then as the wind caught the dust and shredded it, the plane came back into view, on the ground, stopped, all in one piece.

Cheers went up, ragged at first, then stronger, fueled by relief. Several of the crew started running toward the plane, including the flyer who had been calling encouragement to the pilot.

Danby Swan blew out a long breath and said softly, "Damn." He looked over and noticed Hallam for the first time, standing nearby with Carl McGinley. He strode over, extending his hand. "Mr. Hallam, isn't it?" he asked. "Glad you could make it."

Hallam returned the grip. "Looks like you're havin' some trouble, all right." He nodded toward the downed plane.

Swan glanced at it and then shook his head emphatically. "Let's not jump to any conclusions," he said. "There are a great many things that can cause a plane's engine to go haywire."

"Yeah, and one of 'em's sabotage, and you know it, Danby," McGinley said. "We can't keep denying it. Somebody wants to put us out of business."

"Keep your voice down, Carl," Swan hissed. "We don't want to panic the cast and crew any more than they already are. What say we find a quiet spot and discuss this like gentlemen?"

Hallam had never considered himself a gentleman, but he thought Swan's suggestion was a good idea. He glanced past the director and saw that the pilot was climbing out of the disabled plane. As Hallam watched, the man leaped to the ground and held out his arms in a grandiose flourish, as if taking a bow for bringing the kite in on a dead stick. Judging from the way the other men crowded around him and pounded him on the back, it was something to be proud of, all right.

Swan and McGinley headed for the trailer, and Hallam fell

in beside them. The three men were silent until they got inside, out of the sun. The trailer was rather spartanly appointed with a threadbare sofa, several chairs, and a table. There was a miniature bar at one end of the single room, with the keg of beer sitting behind it.

McGinley drew mugs of beer for Hallam and himself, then looked inquiringly at Swan. The director shook his head sharply.

"Danby thinks he's too good for beer," McGinley said with a hollow laugh. "He's strictly a champagne man."

"And if this ungodly Prohibition ever ends, perhaps we'll be able to get some champagne worth drinking again." Swan gestured for Hallam to sit down.

Hallam took the mug from McGinley, swung one of the chairs at the table around backward, and straddled it. The beer was warm and not particularly good to start with, but Hallam sipped it and then licked a fleck of foam from his moustache. "Things like that happen often?" he asked, a nod of his head indicating the open door and the downed plane several hundred yards away.

"Too often," McGinley grunted, sitting down across the table from Hallam. Swan had taken the chair at the head of the table. "How many little *accidents* have we had since we started this picture, Danby?"

"I'm not convinced that this episode today had anything to do with our other misfortunes," Swan said stubbornly. "But to answer your question, this is the fifth or sixth time we've had something happen to slow down production."

"How much is this accident today goin' to hold you up?"

Swan rubbed at the corner of his right eye as he thought. "Assuming that there's not much damage to the plane, it won't cause much of a delay. We'll probably get a few more shots in today, in fact. But if it had crashed and Hank had been killed . . . Well, it could have taken us several days at least to replace the machine. And there could have been some bad publicity along with it."

"What were them other *accidents* that happened before?"

McGinley said, "Nothing as major as what could have happened today, but they were bad enough. We've had cameras fail, film accidentally exposed, sets damaged—annoyances, but they've got us worried."

"I still think you're seeing a conspiracy where none exists, Carl," Swan said. "I prefer to believe in bad luck. And it appears we have plenty of that."

McGinley slammed his palm down on the table, an unusual display of violence from the producer. "Bad luck, my foot! What about Garrettson?"

"He's a nuisance, I'll grant you that, but he's just a blowhard. You know that as well as I do."

Hallam leaned forward. "Who's this Garrettson fella?"

"B. W. Garrettson," McGinley said, looking like the name left a bad taste in his mouth, "is a dyed-in-the-wool bastard."

"He's the leader of the local Ku Klux Klan," Swan added. "I don't remember what absurd title it is that he holds, but that's what it amounts to. He's been trying to stir up trouble for the studio ever since we started production on *Death to the Kaiser!*"

Hallam frowned. "Never had any run-ins with those Klan boys, but I always thought it was colored folks they didn't get along with. Why would they have it in for a war picture?"

"You saw the reason outside," McGinley said. "When they heard that we'd hired Wolf von Ottenhausen as a pilot and technical adviser, they said we were traitors."

"The tall fella with the good-lookin' sister?"

"You're very observant, Mr. Hallam," Swan said. "You picked up on the family resemblance right away. But don't tell me you've never heard of the Steel Wolf?"

"Reckon maybe I saw the name in the newspapers, but I don't recollect any of the particulars."

"Count Wolfram von Ottenhausen was one of Germany's leading aces during the war," McGinley said. "He had over sixty confirmed kills and flew in the same flying circus as the

Red Baron, Von Richthofen. When we decided we wanted someone to make sure we portrayed the German side of the war accurately, there was no better choice than Wolf."

"What about that Von Richthofen fella?"

Swan smiled thinly. "That would be a touch difficult, Mr. Hallam. You see, the Red Baron went down in flames before the end of the war. Count von Ottenhausen was the leading German ace to survive the fighting, in fact."

"How the hell'd he wind up in Hollywood?"

"He made some pictures for UFA a couple of years ago and evidently became quite interested in the film business. He claims that he came to America because there were more opportunities for him here."

"You don't believe him?" Hallam asked.

Swan shrugged. "I suppose he could be telling the truth. Actually, though, he's not a very good actor. I suspect that he was starting to find it difficult to get work in Germany."

"How's he been doin' over here?" Hallam didn't have any concrete reason for asking these questions about Von Ottenhausen, other than the fact that he was still trying to get a handle on this situation. He hadn't even decided yet whether there was a case for him to take.

"Wolf is cooperative, takes direction fairly well, and looks good in costume," Swan replied, again smiling faintly. "That's all we're asking of him. Lorraine has been more of a problem than her brother."

"She in the picture, too?"

"We've used her as an extra. Quite a comedown for her, from the spoiled daughter of a noble Prussian family to a bit player in Hollywood. That's not an uncommon occurrence these days, however."

That was true, Hallam knew. He had run into a couple of crown princes at the various studios, though their paths didn't cross often. Former members of European royalty didn't make too many Westerns. But most of them were glad for the work they did get.

"So this Garrettson fella thinks you're doin' wrong by hirin' Germans to work on the picture," Hallam mused.

McGinley nodded. "He and the rest of his sheet-wearing yahoos have paid us more than one visit. Garrettson's threatened to shut us down if we don't stop employing agents of the foreign menace, as he calls them."

Hallam finished off the beer and set the mug on the table. "Sounds to me like that's your answer. Garrettson must be behind all the fuss you've been havin'. Why don't you just get the cops to handle him?"

"For one thing," Swan said, "I'm not sure that the police in this town don't agree with Garrettson. For that matter, the whole country has a long memory when it comes to things German."

Hallam couldn't disagree with that. He'd made a few pictures over at Fox with Charlie Gebhardt, who was a former cowboy from the 101 Ranch and a decorated veteran of a couple of wars. But now he was calling himself Buck Jones because the executives at Fox didn't want to put a German name on a marquee or a lobby poster. Hallam remembered, too, how folks back home in Texas felt about the Alamo and Mexicans. There was no getting around the fact that people had long memories when it came to bad things.

"You could put a stop to what Garrettson's doing, Lucas," McGinley urged. "He's a bully, just a lot of hot air. I know you could take care of him."

"Might be I could put the fear o' God into him," Hallam agreed. "But I don't know if that'd stop a fella like him for very long. Some folks, you can't really change their minds."

"I don't care what Garrettson *thinks*. I just want him to leave us alone."

Swan was looking at Hallam with a thoughtful expression on his face. Now, he leaned forward and said, "Don't I know you from somewhere, Mr. Hallam? I mean, I know that you're a private detective, but is it possible that we've met in some other capacity?"

Hallam grinned. "I do a little picture work now and then. I was a ridin' extra in that Foreign Legion movie you made last year and did a bit in your Revolutionary War picture the year before that."

With a nod of recognition, Swan said, "I remember you now. I must say, Mr. Hallam, you didn't make a very convincing Arab. You handled your mount very well, though." Swan hesitated, then went on. "Were you on the set when I had that little disagreement with Bill Roland?"

Hallam's grin grew wider. "I was one of the fellers who held you apart and kept you from killin' one another. Reckon that day was what they meant by *creative differences*."

"Yes. Well, what do you say, Mr. Hallam?" Swan hurried on. "I'm still not convinced that we're being harassed by Garrettson and his cronies, but I suppose it's possible. Will you look into the matter for us?"

"Twenty-five dollars a day and expenses, though I reckon there won't be many of those," Hallam said, making up his mind.

"Done," Carl McGinley replied quickly, extending a hand to seal the bargain before either Hallam or Swan could back out. "I'll write a retainer check for you."

Hallam shook his head. "We'll just settle up when the job's done, if that's all right with you."

"Whatever you say, Lucas."

The three men stood up, and Hallam said, "While I'm out here, you mind if I poke around a little, ask a few questions of the cast and crew?"

"It's all right with me," McGinley said, looking to Swan and getting a nod of agreement. "I don't really understand why, though. B. W. Garrettson is our problem."

"More'n likely. But happen it turns out he ain't. That means you got trouble closer to home."

"You mean someone actually involved in the production could be trying to sabotage it?" Swan asked.

"I've seen it happen," Hallam assured him.

"Oh, that's very unlikely, I think."

"You didn't think we had a problem to start with, Danby," McGinley pointed out. "You handle this investigation any way you like, Lucas. We won't try to tell you your job."

"Just be sure that your job doesn't interfere with mine," Swan said, a touch of coolness in his voice. He'd cooperate to keep McGinley happy, Hallam knew, but only up to a point.

They stepped out of the trailer and looked toward the field where the plane had made its forced landing. Several men were rolling it back toward the mock aerodrome. The other airplanes had landed not far away, and all of the pilots except for Wolf von Ottenhausen were clustered together, talking excitedly, no doubt trying to figure out exactly what had gone wrong.

"Uh-oh," McGinley suddenly said. "Look."

He pointed a pudgy finger toward the south, where a cloud of dust was boiling up along the dirt road leading to the location.

"Who the devil could that be?" Swan muttered.

Three cars drove up, stopping behind Hallam's old flivver. The doors of the vehicles popped open, and men began to climb out. All of them were pretty hefty, Hallam saw. Somehow, he wasn't surprised at McGinley's next words.

"It's that bastard Garrettson," the producer said. "And it looks like he's brought the whole damned Klan with him."

T W O

When all the men had gotten out of the cars, they stalked forward, toward Hallam, McGinley, and Swan. They had spotted the producer and the director and had angry looks on their faces.

The man in the lead was only medium height, but his thick arms and massive shoulders told how powerful he was. His broad face was flushed a brick red, but whether that was from heat, anger, or heavy drinking, Hallam didn't know. His features were sullen under a thick mass of curly brown hair. He wore the khaki clothes of a laborer.

The men with him were physically imposing, some of them taller than others but all heavily muscled. Some of them wore suits, but most were dressed like their leader. They looked around the location with glares on their faces, ready for trouble.

Hoping for trouble, in fact, if Hallam was any judge.

The leader stopped in front of McGinley and Swan. He

ignored Hallam as he scowled at the two moviemakers and snapped, "You boys changed your minds yet?"

"Look, Garrettson," McGinley began hotly, "I'm getting tired of you and your goons coming in here and trying to intimidate us!"

Garrettson smiled, but it was a shit-eatin' grin if Hallam had ever seen one. "We're just trying to show you the error of your ways, McGinley. You were the one who started it by hiring those Heinies. When we heard you were making a picture called *Death to the Kaiser!*, the boys and me thought you knew what you were doing."

"We're attempting to make a film about the realities of war," Swan put in. "That requires some small balance in the points of view involved. Though I suppose I'm wasting my breath explaining subtleties like that to you, Garrettson."

Garrettson's big hands clenched into fists. "You calling me stupid, you faggot?" The men waiting behind him stirred, sensing violence and blood.

Swan started to take a step forward, but Hallam's big hand came down on his shoulder and stopped him. If it came to a fight, Garrettson would take Swan apart. "Just hold on there," Hallam said quietly to the director.

"I won't allow that man to speak to me in that fashion," Swan replied, his voice shaking slightly with anger. "I can take care of myself, Mr. Hallam."

Hallam glanced past Swan at McGinley and saw the producer give a quick, minuscule shake of his head. McGinley knew the same thing Hallam did—Swan was no match for the big Klansman.

"Reckon you can," Hallam told him. "But why don't you let me start earnin' my money?"

Swan considered for a few seconds, then nodded abruptly.

Hallam turned to face Garrettson, who was watching him with an appraising stare. The stare turned into a smirk as Garrettson looked past Hallam. "Who's this old geezer,

McGinley?" he asked. "Did you decide to hire a bodyguard for you and Swan?"

Hallam hooked his thumbs in his belt and stood easy. "Name's Lucas Hallam," he said to Garrettson. "You'd be this fella B. W. Garrettson?"

"That's right. What's it to you?"

Hallam leaned his head toward the movie company. "You been botherin' these folks. I'd be obliged if you'd stop it."

Garrettson's eyes narrowed. "Oh, you would, would you?"

"In fact, I reckon you had something to do with a little accident they had out here a little while ago. Nearly got a man killed."

"You're mighty free with those accusations, mister." Garrettson took a step closer. "What're you going to do about it?"

Hallam had seen a lot of bullies in his time, men who thought they were something special with fists or guns. Some of them would back down when they saw you weren't afraid of them.

Others had to be shown.

Hallam reached up and rubbed his jaw with one bony-knuckled hand. "Reckon I'll have to pound some sense into that ugly skull of your'n, Garrettson," he said.

Garrettson's face got even redder. He snarled a filthy name at Hallam and launched a punch, a long, looping blow that would have taken Hallam's head off if it had connected.

Hallam moved smoothly to the side, feeling the wind of the fist's passage beside his ear. He snapped out the hand he had been using to rub his jaw, driving a wicked jab into Garrettson's face. The punch was more of a distraction than anything else, enraging Garrettson even more. He howled and threw another wild punch.

Dodging that one, Hallam stepped in and buried his other fist in Garrettson's stomach. Breath puffed out of Garrettson's lungs as he doubled over in pain, but the burly Klansman had the presence of mind to lunge forward. His head butted into Hallam's middle, shoving him backward. The two men's feet tangled, and Hallam felt his balance going.

Both of them sprawled in the dirt.

Hallam rolled to the side as Garrettson's hands grabbed at him. He didn't want Garrettson getting those arms around him in a bear hug; Garrettson looked like he could squeeze the life out of a man in a matter of minutes. As he eluded Garrettson's grasp and surged back onto his feet, Hallam saw that they were surrounded now. The cast and crew of the picture were watching from one side of the battle, while Garrettson's men waited eagerly on the other side. Hallam was a little surprised that the other Klansmen hadn't turned this into a full-scale riot, but he guessed they were holding off until they saw what their leader was going to do.

Garrettson climbed to his feet and charged like a maddened bull once again. Hallam felt a twinge of pain in his right knee as he spun out of the way. That knee had given him trouble for years, but it had never stopped him from fighting when he had to.

Right now, he had to. This fight had gotten personal in a hurry.

Hallam was waiting when Garrettson lunged at him again. He ducked under the punch the other man threw, put his shoulder into Garrettson's middle, and heaved up. Garrettson flew through the air over Hallam's back, landing with a crash in the dirt. He rolled over almost immediately and came up on all fours, but then he had to stop, head hanging, his torso heaving as he tried to catch his breath.

Garrettson lifted his head after a moment and hauled himself to his feet. As he did so, one of his men stepped forward and pressed something into his hand. Hallam's eyes narrowed as he saw the metal tire tool gripped tightly in Garrettson's fingers. The weapon changed things.

"You come at me with that thing and this ain't a friendly fight anymore, son," Hallam rasped.

"It never was friendly, you goddamn old fool!" Garrettson started forward, lifting the tire tool.

It was funny how loud the click of a pistol being cocked could be, even in the middle of a fight.

Count Wolfram von Ottenhausen leveled the German army revolver at Garrettson and said, "I believe you should drop that and leave, before I'm forced to shoot you."

Garrettson stopped in his tracks, obviously torn in his emotions. Caution warred with rage, and he shook from the internal struggle.

"I can handle this," Hallam said sharply to von Ottenhausen. "I fight my own fights."

"Be my guest," the count said coolly. "If this barbarian is foolish enough to continue once he's dropped his weapon, so be it."

Garrettson looked at his men, then at McGinley and Swan. "You bastards want a bloodbath, you're liable to get it!" he said hoarsely.

Hallam had felt this kind of near hysteria in the air before. If the German shot Garrettson, his men would go crazy and attack the movie company, and then a lot of innocent people would wind up getting hurt. He muttered, "Oh, hell," and stepped forward.

The move put him between Garrettson and von Ottenhausen. Before Garrettson could move, Hallam swiped his left hand at the tire tool, driving the weapon to the side. His right fist shot up, the knuckles crunching into Garrettson's jaw and snapping his head to the side. Garrettson's eyes rolled up, his knees buckled, and he pitched forward onto his face, out cold.

Shaking his throbbing fist, Hallam glanced over his shoulder at the count and growled, "Put that damn gun up!" Without watching to see if von Ottenhausen did as he was told, Hallam turned back to the Klansmen, who were moving forward threateningly.

Hallam bent over and grabbed Garrettson's collar, hauling

the man to his feet and shoving him toward his followers. "Get him out of here," Hallam told them in cold tones. "This's all over."

Two of the men caught Garrettson before he could fall again, and one of them said angrily, "The hell it is!"

"You push it and somebody's goin' to get killed." The menace in Hallam's voice was simple and direct.

The Klansman who had spoken glared for a moment longer, then jerked his head toward the cars. "Let's get out of here," he said to the others. "B.W. may need a doctor."

They piled back into the cars, taking Garrettson's limp body with them, and a moment later the big vehicles disappeared into clouds of dust, just as they had arrived.

Hallam examined his right hand, hoping he hadn't broken a knuckle. He had about decided that he hadn't when McGinley and Swan came hurrying up to him.

"Are you all right, Lucas?" McGinley asked anxiously.

"Yeah, I'm fine. That fracas didn't amount to much, not when you think about how it could have turned out."

"You see now the type of lunatic we're dealing with," Swan said.

"He did seem a mite touchy," Hallam allowed. He was disappointed that the confrontation with Garrettson had turned into a fight, even more disappointed that he had had to knock the man out. He had hoped to do a little more digging about the near crash of the plane and the rest of the supposed sabotage.

In the brief time he had had to study Garrettson's reactions, he had gotten the feeling that the man didn't know what he was talking about when he mentioned the trouble today. On the other hand, why else would Garrettson and his men have shown up *now,* if not to find out the results of their handiwork?

Hallam supposed he might know a little more when he'd had a chance to talk to the pilots. He wanted to know exactly what had happened up there in the sky.

"I think you should file charges against Garrettson," McGinley was saying. "We all saw how he swung at you. He started the fight."

"No argument there," Hallam said. "But I ain't one to go pressin' charges over a ruckus like that. We'll settle it between ourselves, some other day."

"If that day comes, I'd watch my back if I were you." Count Wolfram von Ottenhausen stepped up to Hallam. "That man has no honor and cannot be trusted. By the way, I apologize if I offended you by stepping in when I did. I will not tolerate a man who does not fight fairly, though."

Hallam gestured at the pistol which was now holstered in a military rig around the count's waist. "That gun loaded?"

Von Ottenhausen's thin lips curved in an ironic smile. "As a matter of fact, it is not."

Hallam grimaced. He had stepped in and disarmed Garrettson on account of a bluff, then. There was no point in saying anything about it, though. He had a feeling von Ottenhausen wouldn't understand.

The girl appeared beside her brother and took his arm. Hallam remembered that her name was Lorraine. With a frown on her face, she said in a peeved voice, "Please, Wolf, can we not get out of this awful sun? It will dry out my skin."

"Of course, *Liebchen*. Come along." He nodded to Hallam, giving the gesture a military look, then turned and strolled away, arm in arm with the girl.

"You can see why he was called the Steel Wolf," McGinley said. "His Prussian attitude doesn't make things any easier when you're dealing with a man like Garrettson. And the girl doesn't help matters."

"She didn't seem too happy to be here," Hallam commented.

"They've had some bad experiences since they arrived in this country. This isn't the first time they've run into trouble from people who remember the war."

The members of the movie company had gathered around

after the end of the fight, and now one of the men in a pilot's outfit stepped forward and extended a hand to Hallam. "That was quite an exhibition," he said with a friendly grin.

He was a young man, no more than twenty-one, with unruly blond hair and a handsome, open face. The leather flying jacket he wore gave him an undeniably dashing air. His voice had an accent that was familiar to Hallam.

"I'm Hank Schiller," he went on as he shook hands with Hallam. "And despite the German name, I'm a Texan born and raised."

"Schulenberg?" Hallam asked, knowing there was a good-sized German settlement in that central Texas town.

Hank Schiller shook his head. "New Braunfels. You must be a Texan, too, to know about Schulenberg."

Hallam returned the grin and said, "Ate sausages and black bread there many a time, there and in New Braunfels, too. I was born up Fort Worth way, in a little place called Flat Rock."

"Afraid I never heard of it." Hank glanced at the men standing with him and went on. "Reckon some introductions are in order."

"Of course," McGinley said quickly. "Lucas, these are the men who are handling the piloting for us. You've met Hank here. These other fellows are Simon Drake, Art Tobin, Mackey Russell, and Pete Goldman."

Simon Drake was a tall, thin man with eyeglasses and slicked-down hair. His face wore what seemed to be a perpetual solemn expression. Art Tobin was a redhead with a broad, freckled face. Pete Goldman had dark, curly hair and intense dark eyes that held a hint of humor. Mackey Russell was the pilot Hallam had stood near while the disabled plane was coming in for its forced landing. Hallam shook hands with all of them, meeting their curious gazes. They had to be wondering who he was and what he was doing here, besides waltzing around with B. W. Garrettson, that is.

"Men, this is Lucas Hallam," McGinley went on. "He's a

private detective, and he's going to try to find out who's been causing us so much trouble."

"It's about time," Tobin said, his voice angry as he looked at McGinley. "We've been telling you all along that someone was out to ruin the picture. It's just sheer luck that someone hasn't been killed so far."

"Luck and awesome piloting ability," Hank Schiller said with his friendly grin. "Don't forget who brought that plane in on a dead stick."

"That was you?" Hallam asked. He had expected that one of the other pilots had been the man in the cockpit of the downed plane. They were all older, obviously more experienced than the youthful Hank Schiller.

"That's right," Hank said, pride in his voice.

"Mind tellin' me what happened up there?"

"Sure. You know anything about airplanes, Mr. Hallam?"

Hallam shook his head. "You could put what I know about them contraptions in your little finger, boy. I just know they go up in the air and then come back down."

"Well, something happened to my oil pressure," Hank said. "It's just like the engine in a roadster—when there's no oil pressure, the engine heats up and shuts down."

"I want to take a look at that engine, Hank," Mackey Russell cut in. "I know damn well it was fine when we went over it before the flight. It must have sprung a leak somewhere."

"Or someone cut the oil line," Simon Drake said dourly. "That would fit right in with all the other trouble we've been having."

Hank shook his head. "Who'd want to do a thing like that?"

"Somebody who wants this picture to shut down production," Russell told the younger pilot. "And who doesn't mind killing somebody to do it." There was a savage anger in his voice and on his face, an anger mirrored on the features of the other pilots. Hallam could tell they were a close-knit group.

"Is there anything else Danby and I can do for you right now, Lucas?" McGinley asked.

Hallam shook his head. "Reckon not. I thought I'd hang around here a little longer, maybe talk to a few of the folks in the company."

"Feel free to do so, Mr. Hallam," Swan said. "In the meantime, Carl and I will see about setting up a few more shots." His tone became bitter with frustration as he went on, "We might as well try to get *something* done today."

As Swan and McGinley walked away, Hank turned to the other pilots and said, "I don't know about you fellas, but I could sure use something to drink."

"That's not a good idea, Hank, and you know it," Drake said stiffly. "You saw just moments ago how important it is to have a clear head when you're flying. If you were drunk, you might not have been able to bring down that Spad."

"Maybe so, Simon, but I would have been singing all the way down." Hank's grin was infectious, and all of the pilots except Drake smiled. They started toward the old barns that had been converted into an aerodrome.

Acting on impulse, Hallam fell in beside Hank and said, "Mind if I go along?"

"Hell, no," Hank said with a shake of his head. "I don't think I've ever met a private detective before. My daddy used to read the Magnet Library stories with Nick Carter. Are you that kind of detective, Mr. Hallam?"

Hallam had read a few of those stories himself, and their fanciful disguises and melodramatic menaces were pretty far removed from reality, as far as he was concerned. With a grin, he said, "Don't reckon I could hold a candle to ol' Nick when it comes to detectin'. But I plug along at it and do what I can."

"If there's anything I can do to help you, you just let me know. The detective business must be a lot of fun."

Hallam made no reply. He was wondering if Hank Schiller had any nerves in his body at all. Less than an hour earlier, the boy had come damn close to dying, and he didn't seem to be having any reaction to it. Hallam supposed he had been shot at on over a hundred occasions during his career as a lawman and detective. There had been the early years, too, when he had hired out his gun as long as the money was right and the cause wasn't too dubious. In those days, the West had still been plenty wild, and he had traded lead with some pretty salty characters. After all that, he could look death in the face and never flinch.

But he felt it later, when things were all over. Lordy, yes.

Not Hank, though, from the looks of it.

Goldman and Tobin swung open the big door that was supposed to lead into a hanger for the planes. Hallam didn't know if they ever used it for that purpose or not, or if the craft were flown out from the city every day during the location shooting. Inside, though, it was just a barn, and Hallam had been in plenty of those. He watched as Tobin went into a little cubicle that had probably been a tack room at one time and came out with a bottle in his hand. The bottle was made of thick brown glass, and liquid sloshed in it.

"Hand it over," Hank said. "I'm the one who was nearly pushing up daisies, so I should be first."

"Obnoxious youngster, ain't he?" Tobin asked no one in particular. But he passed the bottle to Hank. "Leave some for the rest of us, kid."

Hank pulled the cork from the bottle with his teeth and then spat it into his hand. He lifted the bottle to his lips and tilted his head back, swallowing long and thirstily. Then he passed it on to Mackey Russell.

When he did, his hand shook just slightly. Maybe the bootleg booze was hitting him already, Hallam thought, or maybe the reaction to almost dying was just slow in coming.

The bottle made its way around the circle of flyers, with even Simon Drake taking a drink, despite his earlier protests. And then Pete Goldman extended the whiskey to Hallam.

He had known, almost as soon as he shook hands with these men, that they felt a certain kinship with him, that they accepted him. He wasn't necessarily one of them—Hallam doubted that anyone except a fellow pilot would qualify for that honor—but it was plain they thought enough of him already to share their stashed liquor with him.

Because he had knocked out B. W. Garrettson, the man who had been causing so much trouble for everyone involved with *Death to the Kaiser!*?

If that was the case, then the whole fight and his aching hand might have been worth it after all. He had a feeling these men might turn out to be a good source of information.

He took a long swallow of the fiery hooch and then gave the bottle back to Hank Schiller. "That's good whiskey," he said.

"Fella I know runs it in from Mexico," Hank replied as he stuck the cork back in the neck of the bottle. He glanced at Drake and went on. "See, Pa, I didn't get drunk."

"I suppose you do have some sense, after all," Drake said.

"Mind if I ask you fellers a few questions?" Hallam wanted to take advantage of the feeling of camaraderie and the fact that they were alone. The pilots might say some things to him that they wouldn't if the producer and the director were around.

"Why don't you come along with us while we take a look at Hank's plane?" Russell asked. "I want to dig into that engine."

Hallam agreed, and they left the barn, trudging through the late afternoon sunshine toward the field where the disabled plane still sat. Off to one side, Swan had the cameras set up again and was filming a scene with Rodger Kane and several other actors who were playing officers in the flying corps.

"You fellers do a lot of flyin' in the movies, do you?" Hallam asked as they walked along.

"More now than we used to," Drake answered. "War films haven't been popular for several years, but I believe they're going to make a comeback."

"We've been barnstorming," Art Tobin added. "That's how Hank here got bit by the flying bug. He saw a show we put on while we were touring Texas."

Hank grinned somewhat sheepishly and suddenly looked even younger. "I'm afraid I made a pest out of myself until the guys agreed to teach me how to fly."

Pete Goldman snorted. "Pest is right. It's a miracle we were able to turn a farmboy with shit on his shoes into a competent pilot."

"I always cleaned off my shoes before I got into the planes," Hank protested.

"Only because we made you."

The good-natured gibes only reinforced the feeling Hallam had gotten earlier that these men shared a special kind of friendship. He had the same sort of relationship with men like Jack Montgomery, Neal Hart, Bill Gillis, the young man called Pecos, and all the other stuntmen and riding extras he worked with on the Gower Gulch Westerns. It was a trust and affection born of the knowledge that your companions would do to ride the river with, no matter what the circumstances.

"Sounds like you men go back a ways," he said.

"Back to the war," Simon Drake replied. His voice suddenly sounded far away as he went on. "Back to France."

Hallam saw the somber expressions that abruptly appeared on the faces of Drake, Tobin, Russell, and Goldman, and he had the feeling that he had brought back some memories they would have just as soon forgotten. He should have known better, he thought. He wouldn't have dreamed of asking a bunch of cowboys about their pasts, and these pilots obviously had the same sort of code.

"Reckon I was gettin' too personal," he rumbled. "Sorry, gents."

Drake waved a hand. "No, Mr. Hallam, you've nothing to apologize for. We were just remembering. You see, we were all in the same fighter squadron during the Great War, all except for Hank, of course."

"He was still having his didys changed at the time," Tobin said with a broad grin at Hank.

"Now, dammit, that's not true and you know it!" Hank exclaimed in his defense. "Maybe I was too young to get into the war, but that don't mean I didn't want to!"

"It's probably a good thing you were too young," Drake

went on. "Pilots were just as much cannon fodder as the ground troops were. The Germans were good, damned fine pilots. And they had better planes for the most part. We did what we could with what we had, though. I was a captain, one of the squadron leaders."

"And the bloody Boches didn't have any better officers than you, Simon," Goldman told him. Despite the fact that Drake seemed rather stiff-necked, the other men obviously respected him. Goldman continued the story. "The rest of us were lieutenants. Our squadron was a damn good one. We had a lot of kills, and we'd even managed to fight old von Richthofen's *Jagdstaffel* to a standstill a time or two." He sighed heavily. "Until one morning west of Pont-à-Mousson."

They had reached the disabled Spad, and as Hallam looked the craft over, seeing an airplane close up for the first time, he said, "I don't reckon that's any of my business."

"Yes it is," Russell said. "If you know the story, then you'll understand why we watch out for each other." He turned to Hank Schiller. "You've heard it often enough. Why don't you tell Mr. Hallam about it while we have a look at your engine?"

The youthful exuberance had disappeared from Hank's face and been replaced by a serious expression. "You're sure about that?"

"Quite sure," Simon Drake said.

Russell raised the cowling of the Spad's engine and began delving into it, with the other three pilots leaning over his shoulder and watching. Hank looked up at Hallam and said in a low voice, "Their squadron was ambushed. The Germans knew they were coming, and they had a whole circus of Fokkers waiting. Our pilots didn't have a chance. There were only four survivors, and their planes barely limped back across Allied lines."

The stunt pilots didn't appear to be paying any attention to Hank's words, but Hallam knew they were listening. They had to be.

"A lot of good men went down in flames that day," Hank went on. "It was a miracle four men made it back."

"It was damned good flying," Mackey Russell said as he straightened from the engine, his florid face grim. "Just like it was damned good flying that got you down when somebody had cut your oil line, kid."

Hank frowned. "You mean—?"

"Yeah. It looks like somebody tried to kill you."

THREE

Hallam leaned forward. "Can I see that?" He was no mechanic, but he still wanted to see the damage for himself.

"Sure," Russell said. A couple of the other men moved back so that Hallam and Hank could get closer to the engine and take a look at it. Russell indicated a length of thin metal tubing with a blunt finger. "You can see where it's cut. Whoever did it didn't saw all the way through the line, but that slash was enough to do the job."

"Damn," Hank said softly. "We really are being sabotaged. I was hoping it was just Mr. McGinley's imagination."

This case had gone beyond imagination, Hallam thought. He asked, "How long would it take for all the oil to leak out from a bunged-up line like this?"

"Under the pressure of a hot engine, not long," Simon Drake replied. "While the engine was off, the leak would have been much slower, of course."

"Was this plane flown out from Hollywood this mornin'?"

"That's right. Von Ottenhausen brought it out."

"No trouble along the way?"

"You'd have to ask him about that to know for sure," Drake said, "but I didn't notice anything wrong. How about the rest of you lads?"

The other men shook their heads.

Hallam rubbed his jaw thoughtfully. "Reckon that means whoever did this had to've done it here on location."

"You mean somebody in the company?" Hank asked. He sounded as if he didn't believe that for a minute. "I thought we had decided that Garrettson and his Klansmen were behind the trouble."

"That's what McGinley thinks," Hallam pointed out. "I ain't made up my mind about anything yet."

He was thinking rapidly, though, and the others evidently hadn't yet arrived at the conclusion he found to be the most likely—someone here on the location was working with B. W. Garrettson.

From the first, Hallam had suspected some kind of inside job. It was all very well for McGinley and Swan to believe that Garrettson was the source of all their problems, but Hallam had thought all along that the Klan probably had some sympathizers among the cast and crew. One of them could well be following Garrettson's orders concerning the disruption of the filming.

If that was the case, it had become even more important to discover the identity of that inside man. Today's events were ample proof that things were getting uglier. Hank Schiller could have easily been killed by this little bit of sabotage.

"You said this Von Ottenhausen feller brought the plane out from Hollywood. What do you think about him, anyway?" Hallam was asking primarily to satisfy his own curiosity. He didn't think it was likely that the German had had anything to do with sabotaging the plane.

"Wolf's all right," Hank said. "He and I have gotten along just fine. Oh, I reckon he's a little standoffish, but that's just the way he is."

"He's a Prussian," Drake added. "We ran into his sort quite a bit during the war. Noblemen to whom piloting a Fokker was somehow akin to dueling at Heidelberg. War had rules for his kind, a code of honor, if you will."

Hallam had sensed that the American pilots felt the same way, though they probably wouldn't admit it. He said, "You ever run up against von Ottenhausen himself during the fightin'?"

"He was a member of the *Jagdstaffel* that attacked our squadron near Pont-à-Mousson," Drake said, his voice flat.

Hallam frowned. "And you're able to work with him now?"

"That was years ago. Besides, he was just doing his duty as a pilot and an officer."

The other flyers nodded in agreement with Drake. Hallam supposed he could understand. During the years when he had been a star packer, he had hunted down men on the other side of the law who he could feel some respect and even liking for.

"I'll talk to him," Hallam said, "see if he noticed any problems with that engine on the trip out. Way it sounds, though, it looks pretty sure whoever messed with it did it here on location."

He said his good-byes to the pilots and started back toward the aerodrome. They stayed clustered around the plane, all five of them bending forward to study the damaged engine. From the looks of things around the buildings, Swan was wrapping up the day's shooting. Some of the equipment was already being loaded back in the trucks.

Hallam scanned the area for Wolf von Ottenhausen and spotted the German leaning against one of the cars parked near the company trucks. The car was a low-slung, fast-looking Bugatti, and Hallam had a feeling it was the count's personal vehicle. He wondered for a moment why someone who could afford a car like that would be working as a stunt flyer, but then he decided that flying was probably in von Ottenhausen's blood. This might have been the only flying job he could get. Hallam knew more than a few cowboys who could have done something else and made more money at it, but they stayed in the picture business because it gave them the opportunity to ride.

He saw as he came closer that Lorraine von Ottenhausen was sitting inside the car and talking with her brother. Both of them fell silent as he approached, regarding him with a touch of suspicion in their eyes.

"Howdy," Hallam nodded. "Mind if I ask you a few questions, Mr. von Ottenhausen?"

"You should address my brother as Count von Ottenhausen," Lorraine said coldly.

"Shush, Lorraine," von Ottenhausen said with a slight smile. "We are in America now. Americans have no use for titles."

"I do not care, Wolf. You are still due some respect from commoners."

Von Ottenhausen looked at Hallam and shook his head. "Please excuse Lorraine, Mr. . . . Hallam, is it? She is not yet accustomed to life in your country."

"And I never shall be," the girl said. "This is a barbaric place, and I shall not be happy until we return to Germany, Wolf."

"Reckon our ways might be a little upsettin' to a lady like you, ma'am," Hallam said, grinning at her in an effort to be friendly. "We are a mite rough around the edges sometimes, I'll grant you that."

Lorraine sniffed and looked away.

"What can I do for you, Mr. Hallam?" the count asked. He had his helmet and goggles in one hand as he leaned negligently against the Bugatti, and a thin cigar was in his other hand.

Hallam jerked a thumb toward the field where the other pilots were still working on the plane. "Those boys said you were the one who flew that crate out from town. Is that right?"

"That is correct. We have several airplanes that we can use in the film, but we can only bring six of them to the location at a time. There are only six of us pilots, after all."

"You notice any problems with the way it was runnin'?"

Von Ottenhausen shook his head. "It seemed fine. Why? Have my American comrades found out the cause of its trouble?"

"That's right," Hallam said, watching the count closely as he went on. "Somebody cut the oil line. It was sabotage, all right."

He saw the sudden exchange of glances between brother and sister, the frowns that played over their faces for an instant before they smoothed them out.

"Really," von Ottenhausen said, his voice carefully neutral. "How interesting."

"Wolf, you know—"

"I am shocked that someone would do such a thing," von Ottenhausen went on quickly, overriding whatever his sister had started to say. "I knew that Mr. McGinley had suspected that someone was trying to ruin his production, but I thought we had simply encountered some ill luck."

Seemed like everyone involved with the production knew something was going on, Hallam thought, but none of them wanted to admit that maybe it was deliberate. No one except McGinley, that is.

If he'd had his druthers, Hallam would have come in here and maybe worked undercover, tried to get a job on the film as an extra. It hadn't worked out that way, though, mainly because McGinley had blurted out why he was really there. He had felt like the American pilots were shooting straight with him, but the von Ottenhausens were either lying or holding something back.

The count had to be around the planes quite a bit. He might have the opportunity to slash the oil line. If there was more friction between him and the other flyers than any of them were letting on . . .

Hallam let that thought play around in his mind for a

moment and knew that he couldn't discount that possibility. At this stage of the game, he couldn't be content to blame the sabotage on Garrettson and let it go at that. He just didn't know enough yet to positively eliminate anyone from suspicion.

"Well, I appreciate you talkin' to me," he said. "Hope I didn't bother you too much, ma'am."

Lorraine glanced at him again, but she didn't say anything. Her face, normally pale, seemed even more so now.

She was worried, all right, Hallam thought. Could be she and her brother knew more about what was happening than they were letting on.

Hallam left them there and headed toward the trailer that was serving as the production's unofficial office. He had a feeling he'd find McGinley and Swan there, and he wanted to talk to them a little more before everyone started back to Hollywood.

He rapped knobby knuckles on the door and McGinley called for him to come in. The producer and the director were sitting at the table inside the trailer, looking glum.

"More problems?" Hallam asked.

"The other scenes went badly," Swan explained. "I'm not surprised. I didn't really expect anyone to be able to work well after what happened earlier. Everyone was remembering how close Hank came to dying."

"Reckon that would make it hard to concentrate on actin'. I been talkin' to your pilots. They found out what went wrong."

"What?" McGinley asked, his expression a mixture of eagerness and anxiety.

"It was sabotage, all right. Somebody cut the oil line on the engine. Had to've happened since y'all got out here this mornin', too."

McGinley frowned. "But I thought Garrettson—"

"Could've been an inside job, somebody in the company workin' for Garrettson."

The producer shook his head. "I can't believe it. I know all these people, I hired them."

"You don't know what all of 'em think," Hallam pointed out. "You couldn't. But if you could work up a list of everybody who's out here today, I can do some checkin', maybe find out if any of 'em have any ties to the Klan."

"I believe you're right, Mr. Hallam," Swan said. "If I'm going to admit that we have a problem, I think we should be logical about it. Garrettson has been around a great deal, both out on location and back in Hollywood at the studio. We've given strict orders that he is to be kept out of the studio compound, but somehow he keeps turning up. Still, I think it would be very difficult for him to carry out the sabotage personally. One of the company is a much more likely possibility, much as I hate to admit it."

McGinley shook his head wearily. "Lord, when we first started on this picture I had such high hopes for it. I sure as hell didn't figure on being jinxed like this."

"The jinx'll go away soon as we find out who's doin' what," Hallam promised. "And we will find out."

"I certainly hope so."

Hallam changed direction. "Is there anything else you can tell me about them two Germans?"

"Wolf and Lorraine?" Swan looked puzzled. "Surely you don't think they've been to blame for the problems. They'd hardly be working with a man like Garrettson."

"No, but they might have reasons of their own for seein' the production shut down. I was just talkin' to them outside, and I got the feelin' they knew more than they were sayin'."

Swan shook his head. "Wolf has been no trouble at all."

"You didn't say anything about Lorraine," McGinley pointed out. "We've had problems with her from the first."

Swan waved a hand. "She's just not used to this country," he said, echoing the comments that Wolf von Ottenhausen had made earlier. "She is a bit overbearing, but you have to realize where she comes from, the kind of life to which she is accustomed."

"She's a royal pain in the ass, if you ask me," McGinley said. "I'd fire her in a minute, but I'm afraid her brother would walk out if I did. And him we need. He's a good pilot and a decent actor if the part doesn't require too much." He sighed. "I knew I shouldn't have hired her, after all those stories I'd heard about her."

Hallam leaned forward. "What stories?"

"About what she did during the war," McGinley explained. "She was a spy, Lucas. The girl was a regular Mata Hari."

Hallam frowned. "That pretty little gal?"

"Carl is right," Swan said. "I was in Paris a few times during the war. Lorraine von Ottenhausen was the rage of the city. She put on quite a pose as a flighty society type, but the rumors had it that she was actually a German intelligence agent." Swan lifted one eyebrow. "It was said that she would do practically anything in order to get whatever information she was after. One thing is certain: she made many men happy during those times."

Hallam shook his head. "She sure don't seem like the type." Not that he was any expert on spies, he thought. His only experience with them had come on a case during the Spanish-American War, not long after he had started working for the Pinkertons on a part-time basis.

"I don't think she's changed a lot, either," McGinley said. "I've heard that she's running around with some pretty unsavory characters these days, too."

"Who might that be?"

"Do you know a man named Wayne Burke?"

Hallam's craggy brow furrowed. "Wayne Burke?" he echoed. "You mean the feller they call Jocko?"

"I wouldn't know about that," McGinley said. "All I know is his name and that he's rumored to have some shady connections. He runs a nightclub—a speakeasy, actually—called the Pimlico."

That was Jocko Burke, all right. Hallam's face became more

grim. To say that Jocko Burke had some shady connections was an understatement. Burke himself was a shady connection for a lot of other folks.

"That's downright interestin'," Hallam mused. "Don't know that it has anything to do with the problems you've been havin' here."

"Is this Burke some sort of gangster?" Swan asked. "I think we've got a right to know, Mr. Hallam, if one of our actresses is associating with someone she shouldn't. There is a morals clause in Lorraine's contract, you know."

Given Jocko Burke's background, just being in his speakeasy was probably grounds for invoking a morals clause, Hallam thought. But he didn't want to say anything like that just yet. It was more than likely that Burke didn't have a damn thing to do with this case. A little sabotage on a picture was probably too small potatoes for a guy like him. His connection would do with some looking into, though.

"I wouldn't say anything to Lorraine just yet. Let me do some pokin' around first."

Swan nodded. "Whatever you say."

Hallam stood up and pulled the turnip from his watch pocket. "Reckon I'll be headin' back toward town. Got some things to do and you folks probably do, too. I'll be in touch."

McGinley and Swan shook hands with him again and said their farewells. Hallam left the trailer and strode toward his flivver, moving with the rolling gait of a horseman which would be with him until he died. He noticed that everything was packed up in the trucks and ready to go. The airplane in the field was gone, which he supposed meant that the pilots had been successful in their efforts to repair it. All the other planes were gone, too, no doubt being flown back to Hollywood, to whatever airfield they were kept at. He hadn't heard their engines when they left, but he had been concentrating on what Swan and McGinley were telling him. The story about Lorraine von Ottenhausen being a spy was surprising enough, but the connection with Jocko Burke on top of that was too much. Hallam couldn't see how it tied in with the picture's troubles, if indeed it did.

Well, he'd think about it later, he decided as he pointed the flivver south toward Hollywood. He had another appointment now, an appointment he didn't want anything to delay him in reaching.

He was going to meet a redheaded woman.

"I don't know, Lucas," Elizabeth Fletcher said dubiously. "I just don't know if I'm doing the right thing."

"Sure you are," Hallam assured her. "Hell, Liz, once you get used to the big city, you won't never want to go back to Chuckwalla."

Liz looked around the empty sitting room of the apartment. There was a big rug on the wooden floor, but that was the only furnishing. Bare this way, the flaws were more glaring, the patches where the paint on the walls was peeling, the sag in the ceiling, the sheer cheerlessness of it. With furniture, something to give it a feel of occupancy, the place might not be so bad. Right now, though, it was more than a little bleak.

"I guess I'll have to take your word for that, won't I?"

"You'll see," Hallam said.

This apartment was on the floor below his in the big old adobe house in the hills overlooking Hollywood. Hallam liked the building with its Spanish architecture, red tile roof, balconies with wrought-iron railings, and thick walls. When he had found out that this apartment was going to become vacant, he had immediately headed out into the desert, to the ghost town of Chuckwalla, to see Liz Fletcher and renew his campaign to get her to move into town.

He had first seen Chuckwalla, and Liz, a few months earlier while he was running an errand for a friend who was a film producer, scouting locations for possible use in Western pictures. There had been some shooting that day. Hallam shot to kill. The same thing had happened in Chuckwalla a few days after that, as one of his cases came to a bloody, unexpected climax. Both times, Liz Fletcher had been in danger. It was time, Hallam had decided, that she give up her fantasy and move into the city.

Liz owned Chuckwalla, lock, stock, and barrel. At first she had only owned the saloon there, but as the town's residents moved away following the failure of the mines in the nearby hills, she had bought up their property by paying the taxes on it. Several years went by, years that she spent as the sole occupant of Chuckwalla.

Until the day when the big, rugged-looking man called Lucas Hallam had arrived. Something had happened to both of them that day, and neither of them knew what to make of it.

If Hallam didn't know better, he would have said that he was falling in love.

Liz was a beautiful woman, he thought as he looked at her now, even in surroundings like this. She was somewhere between forty and fifty; Hallam wasn't sure just where. Her red hair was piled on top of her head in an elaborate arrangement, but he had seen it when it was taken loose and let down, and he knew how thick and luxurious it was, what a sweet fragrance it had. The first time he had seen her, she was wearing a saloon dress that showed off just how trim her figure was. He didn't doubt that she could have worn the same dress when she was twenty. Today she was wearing a simple linen frock and a lacy little hat, and Hallam thought she had never looked lovelier, not since he had known her, anyway.

She kept staring around at the vacant apartment, and he could see the doubt growing in her green eyes. "I don't think this is a good idea, Lucas," she said slowly. "I'm going to be a fish out of water."

He shook his head. "I won't let that happen."

"Oh? You're going to be personally responsible for my happiness?"

"Damn right," Hallam growled. He took her in his arms and cupped her chin, looking down at her for a long moment.

She kept her eyes open while he was kissing her. That threw Hallam off. He released her and stepped away, waited a moment and then said, "Reckon I'd better start bringin' your gear in."

"Yes. Maybe that'll make the place look better."

There was a truck parked at the curb outside, and it was loaded with furniture and trunks and all the odds and ends Liz had brought with her from Chuckwalla. Hallam had brought her into town the day before, and she had rented the truck and driven it back out to the desert herself. She had handled all of her packing herself, too. That was the way she had wanted it, and Hallam had sensed that he shouldn't push her on the point. Today, she had driven back in and met him here after his return from the location where *Death to the Kaiser!* was being shot.

As the sun disappeared and full night fell, Hallam spent the next hour carrying in the items from the truck. Liz offered to help with the furniture, but Hallam declined. He knew that she had gotten the stuff on the truck by herself some way, and he was damned if he couldn't *unload* it without assistance. Liz worked in the apartment, unpacking her clothes from the trunks and arranging the furniture the way she wanted it.

"That's the last of it," Hallam finally announced as he carted in the big mirror that went with the dresser he had brought in earlier. "You got a whole passel of trappin's, lady," he went on with a tired grin.

"I'm old," Liz explained. "I've spent a lot of years accumulating *things*. I've accumulated more *things* than anything else."

Hallam spotted a framed picture sitting on a little spindle-legged table. It hadn't been there earlier. He reached out with a long arm and picked it up. "What's this?" he asked.

Liz was across the room almost before he knew what was happening, snatching the picture out of his hands. "You just leave that alone, Lucas Hallam!" she snapped. "It's no business of yours."

Hallam shrugged his broad shoulders. "Sorry. It was sittin' in plain sight, and I reckon I was just curious."

Liz looked down at the picture for a moment, a faraway expression on her face. Then, abruptly, she thrust it toward him.

"Hell, you might as well look at it," she said. "It's just part of an old memory."

Hallam took the photograph, handling it with an unexpected gentleness in his big, rough hands. It obviously meant a lot to her, and he didn't want to hurt it.

The picture showed several young women standing on a wooden sidewalk. All of them wore fancy gowns with bustles and carried parasols. There were tall feathers in their hats, and the gowns were tight and rather low-cut. From the dusty street in front of the sidewalk and the hitching rail that showed on one side of the picture, Hallam guessed it had been taken in some frontier town, around the turn of the century. He studied the faces of the four girls and saw right away that one of them was Liz.

"That was in Durango," she said softly. "I was working in a place called the Wagon Wheel."

"I remember it," Hallam said. "When was this taken?"

Liz smiled ironically. "That question might be considered an indelicate one, Lucas. But to answer it, the picture was taken in 1899. I was . . . just a girl, as you can well imagine."

"A damned pretty girl. That was after I was in Durango. I trailed a feller there back in ninety-five, when I was workin' for the U.S. marshal. Recollect it was in the Wagon Wheel where I caught up to him, too."

"I remember the story. The bartenders were still talking about it four years later. One of them showed me the bullet holes. We've seen a lot of the same things, Lucas."

Hallam nodded solemnly. "That we have."

"But you don't understand." Liz's voice took on a new urgency. "You've been able to change, to accept the way things are now. Oh, I know that underneath you're still the same old cowboy you always were, but you can at least make your way in the world the way it is today. For me, it's . . . it's all changed too much. The war, moving pictures, automobiles—I drove that truck today, Lucas, but it scared the hell out of me, I'll tell you that."

"You managed," he said. "You did right fine."

"I feel like I ought to be back in Chuckwalla, though. Back there I had my memories, all my memories of the fine times and those girls I worked with back then." She took the picture out of his hands and replaced it on the little table. "I know I can't turn the clock back—"

"You can't stop it, either," Hallam said.

"Maybe you're right." She moved into his arms again, and before she rested her face against his chest, he saw that her eyes were wet. "I guess I should give all these newfangled things a try," she went on, her voice muffled now.

Hallam just held her silently for a few moments, then said, "Reckon what you need is some cheerin' up, some lights and music and dancin', maybe some dinner and a little bootleg champagne."

She looked up at him. "Oh, that does sound good, Lucas. I haven't been to a saloon in a long time, at least not one that had somebody there besides me and the rats."

"Place I had in mind ain't strictly a saloon. It is a speakeasy, though, and from what I hear it's a humdinger. How about it?"

Liz nodded decisively. "Yes," she said. "I'd like that."

"All right," Hallam said as he kissed her lightly on the nose. "I'll go upstairs and take a bath and get all duded up, then we'll go out and paint this here town the brightest red you ever did see."

Liz laughed, and Hallam liked the sound of it. "Whatever

you say, Lucas." As he reached the door of the apartment, she called after him, "By the way, what's this speakeasy called that you're taking me to?"

"The Pimlico," Hallam said.

FOUR

Though Hallam wouldn't have believed it was possible, Liz looked even better when he came back downstairs to pick her up an hour later. She was wearing a gown of dark green silk that went well with her red hair and fair skin. Hallam didn't know how fashionable it was—Liz had been out in the desert for a lot of years, after all—but he had to admit that she looked stunning in it.

"What did you say the name of this speakeasy was again?" she asked as they drove away from the apartment building in Hallam's flivver.

"The Pimlico. It's named after a famous race track back East. The feller who owns it used to be a jockey, so I've heard tell."

"I haven't seen a horse race in a long time. They used to have quarter-horse races at some of the rodeos."

Hallam nodded. "I've lost a dollar or two bettin' on quarter horses."

"So have I."

Hallam glanced over at her. "I never thought you was the bettin' type, Liz."

"I'm taking a gamble right now, Lucas."

He knew what she meant and didn't make any reply. He just hoped she would give life in the city a fair chance. She had her mind made up she wasn't going to like it, though. So he'd just have to change her mind . . .

Maybe he was meddling in something that was none of his business, he thought. She had a right to live wherever she wanted. But it was dangerous for a woman to be living alone in a ghost town, even a woman like Liz who could take care of herself better than most men. And Hallam wanted her where he could see her more often, without having to drive a hundred miles.

Traffic on the Hollywood streets was heavy, as usual. Hallam maneuvered the flivver through it with a skill acquired over the years. He could understand how driving the truck had made Liz nervous. He still got a little nervous himself when he had to dodge all the other cars. It was as crowded as Abilene and Dodge must have been when the trail herds had come in. He had heard stories about those days from his father, but the era of the great cattle drives was already coming to an end by the time he was born.

"Lordy, I never saw so many people, Lucas," Liz said as they drove down Sunset, past Gower Gulch and Hollywood Boulevard. "Where are they all going?"

"Reckon most of 'em are on their way to places like the one where we're goin'. There're dozens of speaks around here, and they all do a boomin' business."

Liz grinned. "Prohibition doesn't seem to have worked, does it?"

"Not hardly. But it's made rich men out of a lot of fellers like Jocko Burke."

"Who's Jocko Burke?"

"Feller who owns the Pimlico. Remember, I said he used to be a jockey. Reckon that's how he got his handle."

Hallam wheeled the flivver into a side street that led through a quiet residential neighborhood. The houses began to get a little larger, the lawns broader and more sweeping. Palm trees lined the road and cast deep shadows that the occasional street lights did little to dispel. Hallam knew roughly where the speakeasy was, but he had to slow down and lean forward to watch for the turn.

A narrow driveway angled off to the left through a gap in a tall hedge. As Hallam veered onto the little asphalt path, the headlights of his car flashed briefly on the high iron fence behind the hedge. There was a small gatehouse beside the driveway, about twenty feet inside the estate, though there was no fence and no gate here.

A man in a tuxedo stepped out of the gatehouse as Hallam slowed to a stop beside it. The light from inside the little building threw him into silhouette, and it was a damn big silhouette, Hallam saw. The man's shoulders stretched the monkey suit almost to the point of ripping.

"Howdy," Hallam said through the open window of the car. "You open tonight?" He already knew the answer to that; the Pimlico never closed, according to what he had heard.

"You must have the wrong place, bud," the tuxedoed guard answered. "This is a private residence."

Hallam knew that two things would be required for entrance to the speakeasy. He slipped one of them out of his billfold and let his hand dangle out the window, a corner of the bill showing in the glow from the light inside the gatehouse. "Tom Mix told me to drop by some night," he said.

The combination of the money and the name of a regular customer did the trick. The bill disappeared in a deft movement as the guard stepped back and waved a big hand. "Go ahead," he told them. "And enjoy yourselves."

Hallam put the flivver in gear and let it roll toward the

massive house at the end of the curving drive. As he pulled away from the gatehouse, he resisted the impulse to nod to the second man, the one watching through the peephole to the side of the gatehouse door. There would be a shotgun in his hands, ready for any sort of trouble. Let them think he hadn't been spotted.

"This is some place," Liz said, a touch of awe in her voice. "I don't think I ever saw a house so big."

The house was a mansion, all right. Hallam had never seen it close up, though he had driven by before and caught glimpses of it through the hedge. There were three stories to it. On the first floor, a broad porch ran the entire length of the building, lined with thick pillars that supported a balcony on the second floor. The design made Hallam think of a plantation house in the old South. The flower beds dotting the lawn added to that image. Only the palm trees around the house were out of place.

"Feller who made a fortune directin' pictures had it built back around 1912 or '13," Hallam said. "He died a few years back, so Jocko Burke bought the place and turned it into a club. Burke lives up on the third floor, from what I've heard."

"What happened to the director who had the house built? What did he die of?"

Hallam grimaced. "Wore himself out with booze and women. I worked for him once, back in '19, and he was already in bad shape then. Had to have a few drinks 'fore he could even get started in the mornin'. Damn shame, too. He was a pretty fair picture maker when he put his mind to it."

The narrow driveway widened out into a big parking area at one side of the house. There were already a great many cars parked there, even though it was still early in the evening. There were Marmons and Rolls-Royces, a Bugatti similar to the one driven by Wolf von Ottenhausen. Hallam's battered old flivver was going to look more than a little out of place. No wonder the guard had looked so dubiously at them at first.

He parked next to a Rolls and got out to go around and

open the door for Liz. She wasn't used to such treatment, though, and was already halfway out of the car by the time he got there. He held the door for her anyway, then closed it and linked arms with her. As they strolled toward the house, Hallam glanced over at her and saw the way the moonlight cast a silver glow over her lovely face.

He shouldn't have lied to her, he thought. He should have told her that he was working tonight.

There was no real reason to suspect that Jocko Burke had anything to do with the trouble that McGinley and Swan had encountered. But all of Hallam's manhunting instincts were telling him to at least check out the little ex-jockey. There might be some connection between him and the movie that even its producer and director didn't know about.

Death to the Kaiser! was expected to be a big success. The studio could certainly use the money that a box-office smash would generate. If Burke was somehow tied in with a rival studio . . .

Hallam knew he was just speculating, theorizing in the dark. But it wouldn't hurt to try to talk to Burke, see what he could find out.

There were tables on the verandah, and people were sitting at most of them, drinking openly. Burke would have the local cops paid off so that his patrons wouldn't be bothered. That kind of thing went on all over town, much to the disgust of officers like Hallam's friend Ben Dunnemore, who worked on the Homicide squad. Violations of the Volstead Act weren't any of Dunnemore's business, but he hated to see otherwise good cops taking payoff money from the likes of Jocko Burke. Hallam had heard him grousing about the subject plenty of times, even though Ben himself liked to take a drink now and then.

The payoffs didn't bother Hallam. What he didn't like about Jocko Burke was the reputation that the man had for being utterly ruthless. If anyone got in his way, Burke would do his best to ruin them.

Failing that, well, there were several unsolved murders in this town that Hallam wouldn't have hesitated to lay at Burke's feet.

Music floated through the open windows of the mansion, and some of the couples on the verandah were dancing. Hallam saw quite a few movie people he recognized, and some of them nodded greetings to him. He spotted one cowboy star, a fellow from the East who couldn't even ride a horse in real life. The actor ignored Hallam, which was no surprise and which was also just fine with Hallam. The real cowboys didn't have any use for the man.

Big double doors in the center of the verandah led into the house. They were open, but two more men in tuxedos stood to one side to keep an eye on who was going and coming. As Hallam and Liz started inside, one of the men put out a hand and laid it heavily on Hallam's arm.

"Wait a minute, Pop," the man said. "Where do you think you're going?"

Hallam glared at the man. "I think we're goin' inside to have a good time," he said. "So why don't you just move your carcass out of the way?"

"Lucas . . ." Liz said warningly. Hallam knew she didn't want any trouble tonight. She already had enough to worry about, what with moving into town from Chuckwalla.

The second man moved in. He was as big as the first one, but he had a smoother attitude as he said, "Look, mister, I'm not sure this is your kind of club. Why don't you and the lady try somewhere else?"

Hallam looked down at his suit, glanced at Liz. She looked beautiful, and he figured his own outfit was at least acceptable. "What's the matter, ain't we dressed fancy enough for you?"

"That's not it, mister. I just think folks your age would be happier with a place that's not quite as fast as this one, you get what I mean?"

Hallam got it, all right. The man was calling them old, both of them. Well, he'd admit he was no spring chicken, but to call Liz old . . . Hallam reminded himself he was there for a reason and tried to force down the anger that was threatening to boil over inside him.

The first man, the one who still had his hand on Hallam's arm, sneered and said, "Sure, you understand, don't you, Gramps?"

Hallam glanced at Liz, saw the tautness of her features, knew that she was trying to hold in her anger, too. In a quiet voice, he said, "Get your hand off my arm, mister."

"Or what?" Suddenly, the man's voice was low and dangerous. He wanted an excuse to get rough. "What'll you do if I don't, you old geezer?"

"Harry . . ." the second man said. He didn't want a fight, not right out here where so many of the speakeasy's patrons could witness it.

Hallam ignored the second man. His gaze bore into the piggish eyes of the one leaning close to him, the one whose face was twisted in an arrogant mask. In a voice little more than a whisper, Hallam rasped, "Happen you don't let go, I'm goin' to make you eat that monkey suit, boy, startin' with the cummerbund."

The man's eyes widened in anger and his face flushed. He snarled, "Why, you—" and started to launch a punch with his free hand.

The fingers of Hallam's left hand hooked behind the man's fancy red cummerbund and jerked him forward. At the same time, Hallam tore his right arm out of the man's grasp and shot a short, vicious punch straight up. His knuckles cracked into the man's chin, snapping his head back. The man sagged forward, suddenly out cold.

The fight, such as it was, had taken only a second, and some of the people on the verandah hadn't even noticed it. Hallam shoved the man toward his companion, who caught him and kept him from falling.

"Didn't want to do that," Hallam told him. "Your pard don't know when to back off."

"He never did," the man replied. "Sorry, mister. I can't let you do that to Harry and get away with it, though." He let the unconscious man sag into a wicker chair behind him, then turned back toward Hallam. His hand went into a pocket of the tuxedo and came out with a pair of brass knuckles.

"Forget it, Jess," a new voice said from the doorway. "It was Harry's fault. Anyway, if you push it, this gentleman will almost certainly make you wish you hadn't."

Hallam glanced at the newcomer, saw a tall man with smooth dark hair and a sardonic smile. "Reckon you'd be Nate Farraday," Hallam said.

"That's right. And you're Lucas Hallam. I see we've heard of each other." Farraday turned his head slightly and snapped at the man called Jess, "Get Harry out of here. Take him to the back and pour some whiskey in him. And tell him he's off door duty until he grows some brains." Farraday stepped back, the smile reappearing on his face as he gestured expansively at Hallam and Liz. "Please, come in and enjoy yourselves. Welcome to the Pimlico."

Hallam linked his arm with Liz's once more and walked into the mansion. "Much obliged," he said.

Nate Farraday was wearing a tuxedo, like the guards, but he looked right at home in his. Hallam had seen him around town a few times, enough to recognize him, and knew him to be Jocko Burke's chief lieutenant. Farraday's main responsibility was the running of the Pimlico, but Hallam felt sure he had fingers in all of Burke's other crooked pies.

"I'm a mite surprised you'd know who I am," Hallam said.

"Oh, we've got some mutual acquaintances." Farraday turned his smile toward Liz. "I don't believe I know this lovely lady, however."

Hallam made the introductions, and Farraday took Liz's hand in both of his, murmuring, "So happy to meet you, my dear." He waved to indicate the merriment going on around them. "I hope you have a wonderful time this evening. I can assure you there won't be any more unpleasantness."

"I'm sure there won't be," Liz said. "My, this is some place you have here, Mr. Farraday."

"Oh, it's not mine, Miss Fletcher. I just work here." He caught Hallam's eye and said, "If I could have a word with you in private, Mr. Hallam . . . ?"

Hallam's first impulse was to tell him to go to hell. He already didn't like Nate Farraday. Not only did the man work for Jocko Burke, he was just too damned slick. But curiosity got the best of him, and Hallam said, "Sure. Be back in a minute, Liz."

He followed Farraday to an alcove a few feet away, leaving Liz to watch the band playing at the other end of the big room. When they were out of earshot, Hallam said, "What can I do for you, Farraday?"

The suave facade fell away from Farraday. As his lean face tightened, he said, "What the hell are you doing here, Hallam?"

"Came to show my lady friend a good time," Hallam said. He grinned. Farraday was acting more like himself now. "That all right with you?"

"Listen, the only reason I stopped Jess from going after you was that I didn't want a fight out there on the porch. You'd already caused enough of a commotion." Farraday poked a slender finger against Hallam's chest. "But I know damn well you're a private dick, Hallam, and I want to know why you're here."

Hallam glanced down meaningfully at the finger prodding his chest, and Farraday jerked it away. "Already told you the truth," Hallam rumbled. "I ain't here to cause trouble for nobody. The lady's a little down in the mouth, and I figured a night on the town might cheer her up."

That much was true. Hallam was taking advantage of the opportunity to perk Liz up while he did some poking into Burke's affairs. But nobody had to know about that last part.

Farraday studied him with narrowed eyes. "I'm not sure I believe you. But I suppose I can give you the benefit of the doubt, Hallam."

"Thank you most to death," Hallam said, unable to keep the sarcasm out of his voice.

"But I'll tell you this much," Farraday went on, his voice low and intense. "You cause any more trouble around here tonight, and we won't go easy on you. I never like to embarrass a lady, but that won't stop my men from beating the hell out of you, you understand?"

"I understand," Hallam said, his own voice grim now.

"All right." The smile reappeared as if by magic on Farraday's face. "Shall we rejoin Miss Fletcher?"

"I can find my way back," Hallam said. "No need for you to go."

Farraday nodded. Hallam walked over to Liz, but he could feel Nate Farraday's eyes on his back all the way.

"What was that about?" Liz asked. "I thought for a minute you and Mr. Farraday were going to start arguing."

Hallam shook his head. "Reckon he just had a burr under his saddle. We took care of it, though." He grinned. "With this ol' leg of mine, I don't do much dancin', but it'd be a downright shame to let all this music go to waste. You reckon?"

Liz laughed. "All right, Lucas. You talked me into it."

He took her in his arms and swept her out onto the dance floor, moving with unusual grace for such a big man.

The Pimlico was doing a booming business. The dance floor was crowded, and through a big arch, Hallam could see that the bar was packed. A doorway on the other side of the big room led into a candlelit area with booths and tables where meals prepared by an authentic French chef were available. A large staircase at the back of the room led to the second floor. Hallam had heard about the games of chance operating up there, all of them high stakes and all of them supposedly honest. The house would always have the edge, though, there was no getting around that. There was a steady flow of traffic up and down those stairs, so the tables would be getting quite a workout.

Hallam enjoyed the feel of Liz in his arms as they moved around the floor. She leaned against him as they danced, giving him the opportunity to study the other people here tonight. Most of the men wore evening clothes, and the ladies sported the most expensive, exclusive gowns. Many of them were draped with jewels, and Hallam didn't want to even think about the amount of money represented here. And the customers were spending it hand over fist.

If Jocko Burke hadn't already been a rich man when he opened this place, he would be by now.

Hallam felt a twinge of pain in his bad knee, and as the band finished a number, he said, "How about we find a place to sit down and get something to drink?"

"Of course, Lucas." Liz looked up at his face. "Is your leg bothering you?"

"Ain't nothin' to worry your pretty head about, Liz. Come on."

He led her over to a vacant table next to a large potted plant. It was the only vacant table he saw around the dance floor, in fact. They had been seated less than a minute when a waiter showed up from somewhere.

"Could I get you something, sir?" the man asked politely. He wore a red jacket and a ruffled white shirt, and he looked somehow familiar to Hallam.

"Reckon we'll have some champagne," Hallam told him. "You pick the bottle yourself, son."

"Of course, sir. Very good."

The waiter started to turn away and head back to the bar to fill the order, but Hallam stopped him by saying, "Excuse me, son, but don't I know you?"

The waiter grinned broadly, but only for a second before he put the look of carefully polite interest back on his face. He said, "I believe we may have worked together on a few films, sir."

Hallam squinted and said, "Goddamn. Is that you, Johnny?"

"Damn right," the waiter said. His expression gave away nothing as he went on, "How are you, you old horse thief?"

"Horse thief, is it? Well, hell, at least I could stay on one to steal it. Last time you tried to fork a bronc, I recollect he pitched you clear into the next county."

"I'll learn," the waiter said earnestly.

"I know you will, son," Hallam told him. "Now go get us that champagne, and pick a good bottle."

"You bet, Lucas."

When the waiter was gone, Liz leaned closer to Hallam and said, "You've got friends in the oddest places."

"Johnny? He wants to be a stunt man. He's learnin', but right now he's just doin' some extra bits. Guess he's havin' to make ends meet by workin' here."

The young man returned with their champagne a few minutes later, a big bottle chilled in a bucket of ice. He poured it in delicate crystal glasses and then said, "I hope you and your lady enjoy it, Lucas. Let me know if you need anything else."

"Will do, Johnny."

As he and Liz sipped the champagne, Hallam watched her and was glad to see that she seemed to be having a good time. There was a happy glow in her eyes that had nothing to do with the liquor. This probably reminded her of the old days in some of the opulent saloons she had seen, but evidently all the memories were good ones.

He was having a fine time, too, such a fine time that he almost hated to go to work.

He downed the last of the champagne in his glass and said, "Not bad for sody water."

"It's lovely, Lucas. This whole evening has been lovely . . . once we got past the door."

Hallam shrugged. "You can run into proddy folks just about anywhere, I reckon." He turned the champagne glass in his hands, its narrow stem looking even more fragile surrounded by his blunt fingers. "Listen, Liz, you reckon you could sit here a few minutes and listen to the music? I need to go talk to a feller about a dog."

She frowned for an instant, as if afraid that Hallam was up to something that would spoil the evening, but then with a sigh, she nodded. "All right, Lucas," she said. "But don't be gone long."

"Don't you worry. I won't be."

Hallam got up and made his way toward the staircase at the back of the room, skirting the still-busy dance floor. He joined the stream of people up the stairs, and when he reached the second-floor landing, he saw that they were splitting into groups and going into the different rooms that opened off the long central hall. He had heard the gambling den described and knew that Burke had knocked out several walls on this floor converting what had been bedrooms into separate rooms for poker, roulette, blackjack, and all the other games of chance.

What Hallam wanted was at the other end of the hall.

The stairs leading to the third floor, the floor where Jocko Burke had his office and his private quarters.

No one seemed to be paying any attention to him as he went down the hall toward the stairs. His eyes scanned the staircase for a guard, but there didn't seem to be one. There had to be some way of keeping the club's guests from wandering up to the third floor, though. Maybe the guard was at the top of the stairs.

There was only one way to find out. Hallam grasped the banister of carved, highly polished hardwood and started up.

Sure enough, at the top of the stairs was a thick rope made of red velvet, stretched from side to side. That would be enough to keep most people from continuing. There was still no sign of a human guard, though.

Hallam lifted a long leg and stepped over the barrier.

The hall at the top of the stairs went both directions, reached the corners of the house, and turned. Hallam couldn't see around either corner, but there were no doors here where he was. He headed left on impulse.

When he reached the corner, he stopped, edging his head forward so that he could peer around. The hall seemed to be deserted, so he started forward, moving almost soundlessly on the thick rug that ran down the middle of the hall. The corridor was lit by chandeliers of heavy crystal, and the glow from the lamps struck highlights off the gold-flecked wallpaper. There was a door up ahead on the left, a heavy wooden panel decorated with ornate carving. Hallam stopped in front of it, leaned his ear toward it trying to hear any voice that might be coming from inside the room beyond.

Behind him, Nate Farraday said angrily, "I should have known I couldn't trust a goddamn shamus."

Hallam resisted the impulse to whirl around. Instead, he straightened up slowly and turned his head to look over his shoulder. Farraday stood in the hall about ten feet away, flanked by two big men of the same sort as the guards on the front door. There was a scowl on Farraday's face.

"There a bathroom up here, Nate?" Hallam asked.

Farraday's features twisted angrily. "Get him!" he barked at the two men with him.

They lunged forward, but by reacting the way he had, Hallam had given himself a chance to get set. He leaned to one side and let a punch slip by his head, then lashed out at the second man. His fist cracked into the man's jaw, sending him staggering back toward Farraday.

The first man hooked a punch that Hallam couldn't avoid. It smacked into his side with plenty of power behind it, rocking Hallam. He spread his legs and caught his balance before he went down, then blocked the next blow and drove one of his own into the man's stomach. Smelling of bootleg gin, the man's breath gusted in Hallam's face.

Hallam put a hand against his chest and shoved him hard against the wall. The second man had caught himself by then and was charging again. Hallam tried to set himself once more, but before he could, the man bulled into him, wrapping long arms around him and staggering him. Hallam felt his balance going.

They crashed to the floor, two big men whose heavy landing made quite a thud. Hallam had already had one good fight today—the little fracas downstairs didn't hardly count, as far as he was concerned—and he wasn't sure he was ready for another one. They hadn't given him much of a choice in the matter, though.

He hooked his fingers under the man's chin and jerked his head to the side, at the same time smashing an elbow into his body. That got Hallam loose from the bear hug. He rolled away, came up on hands and knees in time to catch a quick punch on the jaw. He fell again, but this time was able to pull one leg up and kick the fellow in the chest.

There had been no sounds in the hall during the fight except the grunts and harsh breathing of the men and the thud of fists against flesh. Now Hallam heard the rapid patter of running footsteps and looked up just in time to see three more of the tuxedoed bruisers hurrying to join the battle. He muttered, "Damn!", and tried to surge to his feet, but by then they were on him.

The door at which Hallam had been trying to listen suddenly slammed open, and an angry voice demanded, "What the hell's going on here?" A short, slender man stepped into the hall, a furious glare on his face. His dark eyes darted to the pile of struggling men on the floor a few feet away, then flicked back to the worried visage of Nate Farraday.

"It's nothing, Mr. Burke," Farraday said quickly. "I've got it all under control. Just a smart guy who tried to snoop around—"

"Get off him and let me see," Jocko Burke ordered sharply. The men on the floor untangled themselves and hauled Hallam to his feet, a couple of them hanging on tightly to him.

Hallam shook his head to clear some of the cobwebs and stared at the little man who was studying him. He recognized Jocko Burke.

Burke wasn't hard to spot. He was just under five and a half feet tall, and though he had gained a little weight since his days as a jockey, he couldn't go more than a hundred and forty pounds even now. His dark hair was parted in the middle and slicked down, and he wore a thin moustache that looked more like a pencil line. Rumor had it that his fortune had gotten its start when he took payoffs to change the outcome of races in which he had ridden, and he looked capable of that and much worse. There was something vicious about his eyes that said he would stop at nothing to get what he wanted.

He certainly wouldn't be above ordering some sabotage on a movie set if it would accomplish his ends.

Hallam made a mental note to find out if anyone in the movie company was a heavy gambler. Gambling debts would be one way that Burke could get a hold on an inside man.

He decided he'd look into that if he lived long enough, because right now Burke was saying, "I don't know what this is all about, but you'd better have a damn good reason for being up here, mister. Otherwise you're going to be feeding the fishes."

"Was lookin' for a bathroom," Hallam rumbled. It wasn't much of a story, but he might as well stick with it. Farraday couldn't disprove it.

Burke's thin upper lip lifted in a sneer. "A rube like you looks more like the outhouse type. Anyway, there are bathrooms downstairs, and you know it."

"He's a detective, Mr. Burke," Farraday said, "a private snoop named Hallam. I warned him downstairs not to try anything funny. He said he was just here to show his girl a good time." Farraday stepped up to Hallam and without warning punched him in the face.

The men holding Hallam's arms tightened their grips, and another thug slipped a blackjack out of his pocket just in case. Hallam just shook his head, though, shrugging off the blow. He grinned at Farraday, and as a small drop of blood welled from the corner of his mouth, he said, "Reckon I'll remember that, Nate."

"You don't scare me, cowboy." Farraday glanced at Burke. "What about it? Do we get rid of him?"

"I still want to know what he's doing here." Burke moved closer to Hallam. "What about it, Hallam? It'll go easier on you if you come clean."

"Told you I was lookin' for a bathroom," Hallam said stubbornly. Inside, he was seething with anger, but he was determined to stay calm.

Hallam looked past Burke, toward the door. The room beyond was obviously Burke's office, because Hallam could see a big mahogany desk littered with papers. He could see something else too. There was a large armchair on this side of the desk, and someone was sitting in it. Hallam could see the man's shoulder and arm, clad in an expensive suit. As he watched, the man in the chair reached forward to tip the ash from the big cigar he was smoking into a heavy glass ashtray. He seemed to have no interest in the ruckus out in the hall.

Burke slipped an ornate gold watch from his pocket and flipped it open. He glanced at it, then said, "All right, I don't have time for this shit. I've got plenty of enemies who could have hired this bozo to spy on me. I don't suppose it matters who. Get him out of here."

"Kill him?" Farraday asked flatly.

Burke shook his head. "No, just give him a . . . message to take back to his boss. You said his girlfriend was here?"

Hallam felt a sudden jolt of fear, fear for Liz. If they planned on hurting her, they'd have to kill him first.

And he'd damn sure take some of them with him.

"Find out from the gate man which car this guy came in, and when you're through dump him in it. Then have the lady escorted out as well."

"Sure thing, Mr. Burke." Farraday jerked his head at the goons holding Hallam. "Let's get this over with."

Hallam let them pull him away down the hall. As long as they weren't going to hurt Liz, he could take whatever they wanted to dish out to him.

But they'd pay a price for it.

He twisted his head and saw Burke going back into the office. As Burke started to close the door, Hallam heard him say, "Sorry about the interruption."

The man in the chair stood up and turned around, saying, "That's quite all right. Our friend won't be arriving for another few minutes."

Hallam heard that much and saw the man's face before the door closed. He stored the face away in his memory—round, soft features, thinning dark hair, and a neatly trimmed, graying beard. He would remember the voice as well, with its rich, slightly British tone.

He had never seen the man before, had no idea who he was, but there was no telling what might turn out to be important.

Right now there were other things to worry about, though. He was hustled down the hall, past the stairs and around the corner on the other side of the big house. Another staircase, much narrower, led back down. Hallam let himself be forced down the steps, all the way down to the first floor. A door there opened into the kitchen, a large room filled with stoves and counters and good smells. Hallam might have enjoyed it if one of the men hadn't suddenly punched him in the kidney.

They let him go and he took a couple of involuntary steps forward. He caught himself and turned, ignoring the pain in his back. He tried to throw a punch at the nearest of Burke's thugs, but one of the other men still held the blackjack, and it cracked into Hallam's shoulder with paralyzing force. He bit back the yell of agony that came to his lips and hooked the fingers of his left hand in the ruffled shirt front of one of the others. He jerked the man toward him and smashed a knee into his groin. The man screamed thinly.

Hallam's right arm was useless, numb. He used his left,

smacking the fist into the face of another man, but then the blows were raining in on him. There were four of the men, not counting Farraday, who stood back with a pleased expression on his narrow face, or the man Hallam had kneed, who was curled up in a mewling ball on the tile floor of the kitchen.

Four was too many, especially when one of them had a blackjack.

There were several cooks in the kitchen. They exchanged glances and went on with their work. All of them had been working for Burke for a while. This wasn't the first beating they had seen.

Hallam went down. He felt the cool tile against his face. Something smelled downright delicious, he thought. Fists and feet slammed into him for a while, and then he didn't smell anything.

Lucas had been gone for a long time, and Liz was getting worried. She suspected he had brought her here because this place was tied in somehow with a case of his. She could forgive that, because she knew that he was actually trying to help her feel better at the same time. But if he had gone off and gotten himself into some sort of trouble . . .

She looked up and saw the man Lucas had been talking to earlier coming around the dance floor. What was his name? Farraday, that was it. Was he coming toward the table where she sat?

Liz felt a cold tingle of fear.

Farraday came up to the table, that suave smile on his face, and said, "Excuse me, ma'am, but I have a message for you from Mr. Hallam."

Liz forced her voice to stay calm and level. "Yes? What is it?"

"He'd like for you to meet him outside at his car."

"Is he all right?"

The smile never budged from Farraday's face as he said, "No, I don't believe he is. He seems to have been taken ill."

Liz didn't believe that for a second. Something had happened to him, and this grinning jackanapes had probably had something to do with it. As Liz came to her feet, she fought down the urge to kick him where it would do the most good.

She had to get to Lucas. That was the most important thing. He might need her help.

There would be time enough later to let Mr. Lucas Hallam know what she thought of him getting her involved in something like this.

"All right," she said, picking up her heavy purse. "In the parking lot, right?"

"I'll walk you," Farraday said.

"That won't be necessary." Liz strode away from him, around the dance floor, toward the entrance.

As she left the mansion, she unsnapped her purse and slipped one hand inside it, her fingers closing around the derringer there. If anyone tried anything with her, they'd get one hell of a surprise. Close up, the little pistol could blow somebody's brains right out.

No one bothered her, though, as she walked quickly to the parking area. She spotted Hallam's flivver and angled toward it. As she approached, she could see someone sitting inside, behind the wheel, and from the bulk of the shadowy figure, she knew it had to be Hallam.

He heard the tapping of her heels on the pavement and looked up. The glow of illumination from the house was enough to show her his battered, bloody face, and she gasped.

Hallam got out of the car and took her in his arms, feeling the sharp ache of bruised muscles as he did so. "My God, Lucas!" she said. "Are you all right? What happened?"

"I'm fine, just bunged up a mite," he told her. "Some fellers and I had a little disagreement."

"Looks more like a war." She reached up and gently touched his cheek. "We'd better get you home."

"Sounds like a good idea," Hallam grunted. "I could use a

long soak in a hot bathtub." A grin creased his leathery face. "Care to join me, ma'am?"

"Your brains must have gotten jarred loose a little," Liz laughed. The banter helped cover the concern she was feeling but couldn't hide it completely.

"I'm all right, Liz," Hallam said, suddenly serious. "I've had worse beatin's in my time."

"Was it worth it, Lucas? Did you find what you were looking for?" Anger tinged her words now.

Hallam thought about the man he had seen in Burke's office. "I don't know," he answered with a shake of his head.

Liz started to say something else, but light suddenly washed over them as another car came up the driveway. It rolled past them, a long Rolls-Royce Silver Ghost with a liveried chauffeur at the wheel. As Hallam and Liz watched, it came to a stop near the flagstone path that led to the verandah. The chauffeur hopped out and opened the rear door. A tall man got out of the limousine and walked to the verandah with the help of a heavy walking stick. He wore a gray suit and a hat of soft gray felt, and though Hallam couldn't tell much about his face from this angle, he could see that the man had a white beard.

"Who the sam hill's *that*?" he muttered, more to himself than to Liz. The man didn't look like the usual patrons of the Pimlico, and Hallam couldn't help but remember Burke's visitor mentioning that they were expecting someone else.

"I don't know and I don't care," Liz said. "Come on, Lucas. Let's go home."

Hallam had to agree with that part of her terse statement. There was nothing more he could do here tonight. He wasn't in any shape for another go-around with Burke's guards.

"Would you like me to drive?" Liz asked.

"Reckon I can handle that." Hallam put her in the car and then got behind the wheel, heading it back down the driveway to the street.

She was worried about him, all right, but she was mad, too, and Hallam supposed he couldn't blame her. The atmosphere inside the car was downright chilly as he drove back to the apartment building.

FIVE

There had been plenty of mornings in his life when Hallam woke up hurting. The next morning was no different. A cup of strong coffee helped the ache behind his eyes, and some stretching loosened up the sore muscles to a certain extent.

He used his straight razor to scrape the bristles off his face, trying not to look at himself in the mirror. His jaw was puffy and one eye was swollen, as well. The bruises weren't too bad, though.

Still, they were bad enough that Gladys Wilks would fuss over him. That was the last thing Hallam wanted. But Gladys ran the morgue over at the Hollywood *Citizen*, and Hallam wanted to do some digging in the old files.

It had taken him a long time to go to sleep the night before. Some of that was due to the pain he was feeling, but he had also been trying to figure out where he had seen the old man before. At the time, while watching the man leave his limousine and go into the Pimlico, Hallam hadn't thought he was familiar. But as he lay in bed and stared up at the plaster ceiling, he had realized that he had seen the man somewhere before.

He just couldn't put his finger on where.

Gladys would probably know, though. If the man's picture had ever appeared in the *Citizen*, Gladys would be able to find it.

Hallam drank another cup of coffee and tried to decide why he was worried about the man's identity. Chances were, he was just some old codger who liked to gamble. There was no way of knowing whether or not he was the other man Burke had been expecting. Even if he was, there was no reason to think that he had anything to do with the problems on *Death to the Kaiser!*

A hunch was a hunch, though, and Hallam knew better than to ignore his.

The air was a little cooler today. Summer was just about over and done with. Of course, it never got downright cold here in southern California, but Hallam wouldn't mind a little less heat and humidity. Between the coffee and the crisp air, he felt pretty much human again as he parked the flivver down the street from the *Citizen* building.

He nodded a greeting to the pretty receptionist in the lobby, then went down the old iron steps into the big, musty basement room where the morgue was located. There was a long table at the bottom of the stairs. That was Gladys's usual post, but Hallam saw that today the stool behind the table was empty. Maybe he would be lucky. If she wasn't here, that would make his research harder, but at least he wouldn't have to find an excuse not to have dinner on Sunday with Gladys and her daughter. She was a widow and not bad-looking, but Hallam didn't have the slightest bit of romantic interest in Gladys Wilks.

"Lucas!" Her voice came from the rows of tall filing cabinets. "How nice to see you! It's been a long time since you dropped by. It was during that business with Reverend Forbes, wasn't it?"

Hallam nodded. "Reckon it was. How are you, Gladys?"

"Why, I'm just fine." She came toward him, a broad smile on her face. The smile changed to a look of concern when she saw the bruises. "My goodness, Lucas, what happened to you?"

Hallam sheepishly rubbed his jaw. "Just a little ruckus with a few fellers. Nothin' for you to worry your pretty little head about."

The smile came back. Hallam was ashamed of himself for using flattery on her, but that worked better than anything else.

"You must be working on a case," Gladys said. "Can I help you?" She knew why he was here, all right.

"Yep, hope so. I'm lookin' for a gent I saw last night." Hallam quickly described the man as best he could, knowing that it wasn't much to go on. But the man was rich, that much was obvious from the Silver Ghost and the chauffeur.

Gladys laced her fingers together in front of her, steepling the index fingers and then pointing them toward Hallam. "You have a seat, Lucas," she said. "I'll bring you the society sections and the business pages for the last six months."

That seemed like the best bet to Hallam, too. He dug into the large stack of papers she brought to him, not reading any of the news stories, just glancing at the pictures.

He was down to the final few sections, thinking that it looked like he'd have to go back six more months, when he found what he was looking for. There was a photo in one of the business sections showing a new oil-drilling rig being set up. Standing in front of the rig was its owner, Orville Cooke. According to the caption, the wealthy Los Angeles oil tycoon Orville Cooke . . . Though Hallam hadn't gotten a good look at the man's face the night before, Cooke had the white beard and was even wearing the same gray felt hat.

Hallam carried the newspaper over to Gladys and laid it on the table in front of her. "Orville Cooke," he said. "Reckon you can find me some more information on him?"

"Certainly. Mr. Cooke is quite a famous man, you know."

Hallam had heard of him, all right, but he knew him only as

one of the men who had been lucky enough to find oil in Los Angeles and get in on the start of the boom. Over the next hour, he learned quite a bit more, as Gladys brought him clipping after clipping.

Orville Cooke had been a simple merchant with a dry-goods store in downtown Los Angeles until the oil boom. Then, suddenly, he had more money than he knew what to do with. He had a wife and five children, but he had divorced the wife and alienated the children. There was a big house in the Hollywood Hills which had been built to his order, and he still lived there alone. Despite the fact that he had not reacted well to his sudden wealth, he was respected, primarily because of his charity work. He had donated a great deal of money to a local orphanage and could always be counted on for a sizable contribution to any relief agency that asked for his help. It was as if he regretted driving his own family away from him and was trying to make up for it by doing good works for others, Hallam thought. He was also a noted art collector, having acquired paintings, sculptures, and various *objets d'art* from all over the world.

What the hell had a man like that been doing at the Pimlico?

Hallam reviewed all the stories that Gladys brought him for any sign of a connection between Cooke and Jocko Burke. There was none, as far as he could determine. There were no hints of scandal other than the fact that Cooke was divorced, and even that didn't seem to have been due to another woman.

Hallam sat back and rubbed his eyes, which were tired from looking at the dense blocks of type. Gladys hovered over him and asked, "Did you find what you were looking for, Lucas?"

"Don't reckon I know just exactly what I *was* lookin' for," Hallam replied, shaking his head. "Or maybe it's there and I just don't see it."

"Well, I'm sure you'll figure it out. You always do."

Hallam wished he felt as confident. He had what should have been a simple case here, but his instincts kept dragging him off on tangents. He should have been concentrating on

B. W. Garrettson, instead of trying to establish a connection between two men who probably weren't even involved with the case.

He stood up and stretched, again feeling the pull of sore muscles. He had bounced back reasonably well from the beating that Burke's men had given him, he thought, but there was no getting around the fact that he wasn't as young as he used to be. His recuperative powers weren't as strong as in the old days.

His face became more grim as he thought about what had happened at the Pimlico. Regardless of whether Burke had anything to do with the sabotage, Hallam had a score to settle with him now.

"Thanks, Gladys," he said. "Reckon I'd better get back to work now."

"A man can't work all the time, Lucas. Sunday, for example. A man shouldn't work on the Sabbath."

Hallam knew what was coming and cast around for some way to head it off. "That's so," he said. "This Sunday I'm goin' to take a little trip, in fact."

"Oh. Well, enjoy yourself." Gladys hesitated, then went on, "Going alone, are you?"

Hallam shrugged. "Don't really know yet. Haven't had a chance to ask the lady." That was true enough. He hadn't seen Liz this morning. He had intended to stop by her apartment before leaving, but for some reason had kept on walking.

Now, he saw the way Gladys's face fell. He grimaced, realizing he had said something that he shouldn't have. After she had spent a couple of hours helping him, he had gone and told her that he was going away on a trip with another woman.

There didn't seem to be any point in trying to repair the damage. He'd probably just make it worse if he did. He said, "Thanks again, Gladys. I really got to be goin'."

"Of course. Good-bye, Lucas."

He went up the iron steps, his boots seeming to clang even louder than usual. As he came out of the building into the sunshine once more, he squinted against the glare and frowned. A man just never knew how a woman was going to react to things. Sometimes, it seemed like you got in trouble no matter what you said or did. Liz, after all, hadn't been any too happy with him the night before.

A man didn't have that trouble with a horse, he thought. A good horse would do anything you asked it to do and never complain.

"Reckon it's high time I learned women ain't horses," he muttered to himself as he drove away.

He headed toward the studio where *Death to the Kaiser!* was being made. Hallam's telephone call to Carl McGinley before leaving his apartment had told him that the company was going to be shooting interiors today. McGinley would be there, and there were a few more questions Hallam wanted to ask the producer.

As he passed the intersection of Hollywood Boulevard and Cahuenga Avenue, he glanced over at a plain gray frame building less than a block away on Cahuenga. The Waterhole was a far cry from being as fancy as the Pimlico, but it was a speakeasy, too, and all the real cowboys in Hollywood spent a great deal of time there. It was still fairly early in the day, but there would be a poker game going on in the back room. There was *always* a poker game going on in the back room. It hadn't come to a halt in the time Hallam had been in Hollywood, and that was going on ten years.

He'd stop by later, he decided, and have a drink and some palaver with his friends. Right now he had work to do.

McGinley had left word with the guard at the studio gate that Hallam was to be admitted any time, so it was no trouble getting into the compound. Unlike some of the smaller studios which had their offices in old farmhouses and their shooting stages in deserted barns, this one was headquartered in stucco office buildings constructed for that purpose. The big buildings housing the stages had been freshly built, and beyond them was a good-sized back lot where various sets could be constructed, from a Western street to a European castle. Hallam parked the flivver near a long white building where the main offices were located.

A secretary who was stunning enough to have been one of the studio's stars ushered Hallam into Carl McGinley's office. The producer was sitting behind a paper-littered desk, leaning back in his chair and studying a bound script. He glanced up and waved Hallam into a plush armchair, said, "I'll be through with this in just a minute, Lucas."

Hallam sat down, gave one more appreciative glance at the secretary as she closed the door behind her, then waited for McGinley to finish reading. A few moments later, the producer sighed and closed the script, then threw it negligently onto the desk. "Playwrights!" he said in disgust. "When will they learn that Hollywood ain't Broadway? Movies have to *move,* not sit around talking! That script's nothing but dialogue, can you imagine?"

Hallam allowed that he couldn't. "Don't reckon that'd sit too well with Tom or Buck or Bill Hart, neither."

"That's right." McGinley shook his head. "Sorry I ranted and raved at you, Lucas. It's sure as hell not your fault that this guy couldn't write a decent film if his life depended on it, no matter how many awards he's won back East." The producer leaned forward. "You're here about the case?"

"Well, I ain't quite sure. I wanted to ask you a question."

"Shoot."

"You know a feller name of Orville Cooke?"

McGinley frowned. "Orville Cooke? Isn't he some kind of oil tycoon or something?"

"That's right. You know him?"

"Why the hell should I?" McGinley seemed sincerely puzzled. "What does he have to do with Garrettson and the Klan?"

"Don't know that he has anything to do with 'em. He wouldn't happen to have any kind of financial interest in this studio, would he?"

McGinley shook his head. "Not that I know of," he

declared. "And I'd know, I promise you. What's this all about, Lucas?"

"Thought maybe he might've been a silent partner. How about at one of the other studios?"

McGinley shrugged. "I suppose it's possible, but I've never heard anything about that. And I still don't see what it has to do with the case."

Hallam thought about the trail that had led him from Lorraine von Ottenhausen to Jocko Burke to Orville Cooke, and he decided that he didn't want to try to explain it. McGinley was a fairly practical businessman; Hallam didn't think he would understand about hunches.

"Nothin' for you to worry about," he said. "Just something I stumbled across while I was pokin' around. Looks like Garrettson is still our best bet. Did you get me that list of everybody connected with the picture, so I can check them out for Klan activities?"

McGinley dug a couple of sheets of paper out of the chaos on his desk and passed them across to Hallam. "I think that covers everybody," he said. "That seems to be the best way to go, though I'm still having a hard time believing that somebody on our payroll is really working for Garrettson."

Hallam scanned the list of names and addresses. "Maybe it won't take too long to find out." He stood up, folded the papers and put them inside his coat. "Any trouble so far today?"

"Nothing, thank God. Danby is shooting some of the interiors, the aerodrome stuff, and I hope it's going well. I was just thinking about going over there when I finished that script. Want to come along?"

"Sounds good. Wouldn't mind seein' how it's goin' myself."

As the two men left the building, Hallam said, "That's a mighty nice-lookin' filly you got workin' as your secretary."

McGinley grinned. "Don't you go thinking anything you shouldn't, Lucas. Gloria happens to be very good at her job, and she has absolutely no interest in becoming an actress. I'm a happily married man, you know that."

Hallam laughed and said, "Reckon that was just the detective in me comin' out. You get to thinkin' that ever'body's guilty of something."

"And most of the time you'd be right."

The light over the big door into the building was off, so it was safe to go inside. Swan wasn't shooting a scene at the moment but rather was setting one up, Hallam saw as he and McGinley went into the vast, shadowy interior. McGinley slid the door shut behind them.

"All right, Rodger," Swan was saying to his star, "this is the scene where you've just received the news that your best friend has gone down behind enemy lines. You decide that you're going to fly across the lines yourself and try to find him, to make sure that he's dead if his plane crashed or to try to rescue him if he managed to land. Vesta arrives just as you're leaving and tries to talk you out of it. Do you understand all of that?" There was a patient tone in Swan's voice, as if he were explaining to a child.

"Of course I understand," Rodger Kane said somewhat testily. "It's not that complicated a scene, Danby. Do you think I'm some kind of idiot?"

"Certainly not, dear boy. I just wanted to make sure you have a grasp on your motivation."

Hallam and McGinley were standing well back from the set that was dressed to look like the squad room of an Allied aerodrome, out of the way of the actors and crew who were gathered around Danby Swan. McGinley leaned over to Hallam and said in a whisper, "Danby thinks all actors are idiots. In Rodger's case he may be right."

Hallam just grunted. He was used to the gossip and innuendo and downright viciousness that was so common in Hollywood, even in otherwise friendly folks like Carl McGinley. But he tried to keep his mouth shut and not get caught up in it himself. Where he came from, a man only spoke when he had something to say.

Swan looked around. "Vesta?" he called. "Dammit, where's our leading lady?"

A script girl spoke up. "I think I saw her going into her dressing room a few minutes ago."

"All right. Go see if you can find her."

The girl hurried away from the set, going over to a long hallway with doors on both sides. Those doors led into the actors' dressing rooms, and the girl went to one that was marked with a large star.

Hallam and McGinley watched as the script girl knocked on the door, waited a few moments, knocked again. Hallam could sense the sudden tension in the building. Beside him, McGinley had fallen silent and was watching with a taut, anxious look on his face.

The script girl knocked again and called, "Miss Quist? You're needed on the set, Miss Quist." When there was still no response, she reached down and tried the knob. The door swung open. The girl stuck her head inside, then stepped back, looked at Swan, and shook her head.

Swan threw both hands in the air. "My God, what now?" he exclaimed, his voice full of exasperation. He stalked over to the dressing rooms, pushed past the script girl, and went into Vesta Quist's sanctum. He came back out a few seconds later and called, "All right, everyone, take a break! We seem to have a missing star."

Throwing a look over his shoulder, McGinley hurried forward. "Come on, Lucas. Looks like trouble."

The thought had already crossed Hallam's mind that if wrecking a plane would slow down production, kidnapping the female lead would bring it to a screeching halt.

He was right on McGinley's heels as the producer came up to Danby Swan. Swan glanced at him and said dourly, "I can tell you've already heard the bad news, Carl."

"Where could she have gone?" McGinley asked. "A person doesn't just disappear into thin air."

Hallam wasn't so sure about that. He said, "There a phone 'around here we can use to call the gate?"

"That's a good idea," Swan said. He went over to a corner where an interoffice phone was mounted on the wall. It took only a moment to get the gate guard on the line. "Has Miss Quist left the studio in the last few minutes, Warren?"

It was clear from Swan's expression what the answer was.

He hung up the phone and came back to Hallam and McGinley. "The guard says he hasn't seen her. No one has left in the last few minutes, in fact."

"Is he a good man, not the type to make mistakes?"

"He's very reliable, Lucas," McGinley said. "It looks like Vesta is still here in the studio somewhere, unless she climbed over the fence. And I can't see Vesta doing that."

Hallam didn't know Vesta Quist, but he had seen her on screen and he was inclined to agree with McGinley. The thought of her climbing a fence didn't jibe well with her fragile, haughty beauty.

"Reckon we better spread out and look for her," he said. "Happen we can get a few more men, we should be able to cover the studio pretty quick."

"You're right," Swan said. He called over the AD and the cameraman and a couple of grips. "We're going to look for Miss Quist, men," he told them. "She should still be somewhere around here, so split up and cover as much ground as quickly as you can."

They nodded in understanding as McGinley said, "Lucas and I will take the main office building, Danby."

Hallam would have preferred searching the back lot, but he didn't say anything. McGinley obviously didn't want to start out on this search alone.

Maybe he was afraid of what they might find.

The search party divided, and Hallam and McGinley headed

back toward the offices. As they hurried across the parking lot, Hallam said, "Don't you reckon we'd've spotted the gal a while ago if she was headin' for the office building?"

"Not if she was hiding out somewhere else and waiting until we were out of the way." McGinley shook his head. "Anyway, that's not what I'm worried about, Lucas, and you know it. I'm afraid that Vesta didn't leave the set of her own accord."

"You think somebody carried her off?"

"That's what I'm afraid of. And if we can't find her, I'll have no choice but to call in the police. God, I hope she's all right. We're getting to the point now where we can't afford any more delays."

Hallam thought McGinley could have spared a little worry about the actress's welfare, rather than the effect her disappearance would have on the production, but he didn't say anything. He knew Carl McGinley well enough to know that he just wasn't thinking straight at the moment. There had been so much trouble that McGinley was just mixed up on what was important.

McGinley led the way directly to his office and asked the attractive secretary, "Have you seen Vesta Quist, Gloria?"

"Not this morning, Mr. McGinley," Gloria answered. "What's the matter?"

"Oh, nothing, she's just gone missing," McGinley muttered under his breath. "I guess we start knocking on doors, Lucas."

"You can handle that, Carl," Hallam said. He didn't think for one minute that Vesta Quist was in this building. If she had been kidnapped, whoever snatched her wouldn't bring her here.

No, the best way out for a kidnapper would be through the back lot. There was a fence at the rear of the compound, but it would be simple enough to cut it. Hallam's instincts told him to get out there so that he could pick up the trail before it got too cold.

"Maybe you best call the gate, get a list of all the folks on the lot today," he went on, well aware that he was giving orders to his client instead of the other way around. But dammit, this was his job. He didn't tell McGinley how to make movies.

"All right," the producer said after a moment's hesitation. "Where will you be, Lucas?"

"Thought I'd cover the back lot, if one of the others ain't already done it."

McGinley nodded. Hallam went out the front door of the office building and turned around the corner. His long-legged stride carried him past the other buildings. There was a little slope behind them, leading down into the shallow valley where the back lot was located. A small creek ran through the area, and beside the creek was the dusty street where Westerns were sometimes filmed. Some of the sets were in place now, indicating that a picture had just wrapped up or was about to begin in the next day or so. Most of the buildings were just false fronts with nothing behind them, but there were a few actual buildings along the street. The Red Devil Saloon was one of them, and Hallam thought he'd check there first.

As he strode down the hill and into the middle of the street, he was glad he had strapped on his shoulder holster before leaving the apartment this morning. The old Colt was sometimes awkward and it was a little hard to conceal under a jacket, but right now the weight of it was reassuring. If Vesta Quist had indeed been kidnapped, he could be walking into a whole passel of trouble.

He angled toward the Red Devil and stepped up onto the plank sidewalk. It creaked under his weight, announcing his presence to anyone inside, and Hallam spotted a sudden flicker of movement in the shadows of the building. He went through the batwings in a rush, his hand darting under his coat and flashing back out with the Colt. He thumbcocked it as he brought it up, lining the barrel on the two people he had seen near the bar.

"Hold it right there!" Hallam barked.

Count Wolfram von Ottenhausen lazily lifted his hands. "I surrender," he said dryly.

Beside him, Vesta Quist glared angrily at Hallam and demanded, "Who the hell are you?"

She wore a simple tan suit that was all the more elegant for its simplicity, and a small green hat with a tiny feather in its band was perched on her carefully waved brunette hair. As she waited for Hallam's answer, the toe of one expensively shod foot tapped impatiently on the wooden floor.

"Name's Lucas Hallam, ma'am," he told her. "You'd be Miss Quist?"

"Of course I'm Miss Quist. Now stop waving that cannon around and tell me what's going on."

Before Hallam could say anything, von Ottenhausen commented, "From the looks of things, I'd say that you've been missed up on the set, Vesta."

"That's right, ma'am," Hallam said. "Carl McGinley thinks you've been kidnapped. He was talkin' about callin' the police when I came down here."

"Well, of all the damned stupidity—" Vesta Quist broke off and shook her head.

"As you can see, Mr. Hallam, the lady is in no danger," Von Ottenhausen said. "Why don't you go back and tell the others?"

Vesta Quist seemed all right, Hallam had to admit. But in that split second when he had first seen them in the saloon, he was almost sure they had been in each other's arms. There was a faint smudge of lipstick on the count's mouth, too.

"Don't know how all-fired safe any beautiful lady is with you, Count," Hallam said, trying not to grin. "'Pears that Miss Quist ain't been kidnapped, though." He slid the Colt back into its holster. "Reckon both of you had best come back up the hill with me."

"What we do is our business," Vesta snapped. "And I don't take orders from any cowboy."

Von Ottenhausen put a hand on her shoulder. "Perhaps Mr. Hallam is right, my dear. He found us here, so others could, too. And we don't want to embarrass you. That would be bad for your career."

She pouted prettily for a moment, then said, "I suppose you're right, Wolf."

Hallam stepped back and held the batwings open for them. As they emerged onto the sidewalk, von Ottenhausen looked thoughtful and said, "Perhaps you wouldn't mind taking Miss Quist back by yourself, Mr. Hallam?"

"But where will you be?" Vesta asked him, looking surprised.

"I am not sure it would be a good idea for everyone to know that Mr. Hallam found us together." Von Ottenhausen smiled ironically. "You know how tongues can wag in this town, darling." He looked at Hallam. "What about it, sir? Would you be willing to keep quiet about this little tryst that you so rudely interrupted?" The count's easy smile took any sting out of his words.

"Well, I ain't so sure about that," Hallam said slowly.

"Come, come, sir. I am appealing to your sense of honor. You wouldn't wish to compromise a lady's reputation, would you?"

Hallam wasn't sure that Vesta Quist had that much of a reputation left to compromise, but he finally nodded. "All right. You can make yourself scarce, mister. I'll take care of the lady."

"Thanks," Vesta said sarcastically. "One man can't wait to run out on me and the other acts like being around me is some kind of chore. You two do wonders for a girl's ego."

"Come on, ma'am," Hallam said. Trading barbs with an angry actress was the last thing he wanted to do right now.

Vesta sighed and fell into step beside him. Hallam kept his stride down so that she would be able to keep up. Von Ottenhausen disappeared around one of the other buildings, obviously intending to head back up the hill by another route.

After walking for a few minutes in silence, Vesta suddenly said, "You probably think I'm some kind of tramp, don't you?"

"No, ma'am," Hallam told her. "Can't say as I've given the matter much thought."

She didn't know whether to be angry about that response or not. "Do you work for the studio?" she asked.

"Right now I do. I'm a private detective. Tryin' to find out who's been causin' so much trouble for this picture."

"Well, it'll cause a lot more trouble if you don't keep your mouth shut about what you saw back there," she said. "All we need is for Danby to get jealous and get in some kind of snit." Vesta sighed again. "Lord, he can be so tiresome."

Hallam didn't say anything, but he was thinking. Now that she mentioned it, he recalled that she and Danby Swan had been a pretty hot item in the gossip columns not that long ago.

And added to everything else that had happened, that could prove to be downright interestin'.

SIX

Carl McGinley had returned to the set by the time Hallam and Vesta Quist got there. The producer was talking heatedly to Danby Swan as Hallam and Vesta walked into the building. McGinley broke off in mid-sentence and both men turned sharply as the big door slid open.

"Vesta!" Swan cried out. "My dear, where have you been?"

Vesta didn't meet his eyes as she said, "I went for a walk. Really, Danby, I don't understand why everyone is making such a fuss."

"A walk?" McGinley exclaimed. "We thought you had been kidnapped by Garrettson and some of his Klansmen!"

Vesta glanced at Hallam. "That's what this, ah, gentleman seemed to think as well. It's all so ridiculous. I was perfectly fine."

"Where did you find her, Lucas?" McGinley asked.

"Down on the back lot," Hallam replied, well aware that Vesta Quist was watching him closely while trying to appear that she was ignoring him. She was anxious to know if he would keep his word and not say anything about her rendezvous with Wolf von Ottenhausen. He went on, "Like the lady says, 'pears she was just takin' a walk."

A look of relief flashed through Vesta's eyes.

"Well, of all the fine times to go for a stroll!" McGinley groused. "You had us all very worried, young lady."

Swan moved in and put an arm around Vesta's shoulders. "I'm sure she didn't mean any harm, now did you, Vesta?"

She shook her head. "Of course not. I'm sorry, Carl. I . . . I suppose I was just nervous, what with all the trouble that's been going on . . ."

Swan believed her story, Hallam saw, and McGinley had no choice but to accept it, too. The producer walked away muttering to himself. Swan faced Vesta and put his hands on her shoulders. "Really, we were all quite concerned," he told her. "Next time you feel the need to get away for a few minutes, tell someone first, all right?"

Vesta shrugged out of his grip. "Really, Danby, you needn't scold me like I was a child," she snapped.

Swan's face reddened, but he kept his anger under control. As Hallam watched from a few feet away, he thought that under the circumstances, he might've taken the young lady over his knee.

At any rate, this crisis seemed to be over. The men who had been sent out to search were coming back in to report that they hadn't been able to find the missing actress, only to discover that she was already back in the fold.

Hallam hurried after McGinley as the producer headed for the door. As he caught up, McGinley glanced at him and said, "It never ends, does it, Lucas? There's just no limit to the things that can wrong when you set out to make a movie."

"Reckon not." Hallam grinned. "But that's part of what makes it fun, ain't it?"

McGinley paused, looked at him like he was crazy, and then walked on with a shake of his head.

"I'm going back to my office," he said over his shoulder. "I need to do some paperwork. Although that'll probably blow up in my face, too."

"Answer a couple of questions for me first, Carl."

McGinley stopped. "All right. Shoot."

"I seem to recollect that Vesta Quist and ol' Swan in there used to be sparkin' one another. Is that right?"

"If that's your way of saying they had a hot and heavy romance going, that's right, okay. As far as I know that's all over, though."

"Which of 'em decided to end it?"

"I believe it was Vesta. I know Danby was pretty broken up about the whole thing for a while."

Hallam rubbed his jaw in thought. "Wouldn't figure he'd want her workin' in his picture, then."

"I had the final say in the casting. Besides, that was a couple of months ago. The guy should be over it by now." McGinley shrugged. "Sometimes I think he's still carrying a little torch for her, but it's no big deal. Danby Swan's a pro. He can work with just about any actor in the business, regardless of whatever personal stuff is going on."

Hallam nodded. "Figured when he stuck up for the lady that he was a little fond of her."

"What's that got to do with anything?"

Hallam sensed from the tone of McGinley's voice that the producer was getting a little tired of these little side trails. Over the years, though, Hallam had learned not to ignore tracks just because they weren't right where you expected them to be.

"Probably not a damn thing," he replied. He changed the subject by saying, "I noticed them pilots ain't around today."

"No flying scenes on the shooting schedule. There's no other reason for them to be here. The count is the only one with an actual part in the picture, though we've used the flyboys as extras here and there."

"Happen to know where I could find 'em?" Hallam asked. "I

want to ask a few more questions about the sabotage on that airplane."

McGinley pursed his lips and hesitated a moment before answering. Finally, he said, "I'm not sure if they want it noised around or not, but they've got a hangout down on Highland, a speakeasy they use like you cowboys use the Waterhole. It's called Lafayette's, because of the Lafayette Escadrille, you know."

Hallam had heard of the group of American flyers who had gone to France to get into the war in the air before the United States officially joined the conflict, but he hadn't heard of the speakeasy called Lafayette's.

"Reckon they'd mind if I went over there and talked to them?" he asked.

"Don't see why they would. You're not a cop, and you don't want to close the place down." McGinley gave Hallam directions to the speakeasy, then said his farewells and continued on toward the office building, shaking his head and talking to himself. This whole affair was getting him down, all right.

Hallam left the studio and drove over to Highland, finding Lafayette's with no trouble. The speakeasy was in what had been a private residence, a good-sized two-story brick building behind a green lawn dotted with palms. The grass was a little tall, and the building itself wore an air of age and neglect. The planks of the wooden porch sagged slightly under Hallam's weight as he climbed onto it.

His knock rattled a screen door with a couple of tears in it. There was no response. Hallam looked at the driveway where several cars were parked. He felt sure someone was inside. Again, he knocked on the door.

After a few moments, the wooden inner door opened a couple of inches. "Yeah?" a voice asked.

"This place called Lafayette's?" Hallam asked.

"Sorry, bud, I don't know what you're talking about." The man inside started to close the door.

"I'm lookin' for a feller called Simon Drake," Hallam said

quickly. "He'll vouch for me." That was an assumption on Hallam's part, but he felt fairly sure that Drake would back him up.

The man hesitated, said, "Wait a minute." He went away without closing the door.

Hallam supposed they had to be careful. Chief August Vollmer's police force didn't go out of their way to close down speakeasies, but occasionally they had to pull a raid to look good in the papers.

The door opened wider. "Mr. Hallam!" an enthusiastic voice said. "Come on in." Hank Schiller stepped back and grinned.

Hallam went in past the young aviator and found himself in an entrance hall that led into a shadowy parlor. Heavy curtains were over the windows. A long bar had been hauled in and placed against the back wall of the room. Long wooden tables and benches were scattered around the floor. The walls were covered with drawings and photographs of airplanes. The drawings usually depicted the aircraft in battle, while the photographs were for the most part of pilots standing in front of their parked planes. The men wore flying suits and helmets and several had goggles looped loosely around their necks. Many had pistols holstered on their hips.

Wartime souvenirs, Hallam knew. He had seen similar photographs in forts all over the West, with horses taking the place of the planes and cavalry uniforms the rule instead of flying suits. Here in Lafayette's there were no crossed sabers on the wall behind the bar, but there was a bullet-chewed propeller that spoke volumes with its battle scars.

Besides Hank Schiller and a bartender in a dirty white shirt, there were eight men in the room, sitting at a couple of the tables. Hallam recognized Simon Drake, Mackey Russell, and Pete Goldman. Art Tobin wasn't there, and Hallam didn't know any of the other men.

"Come on over and have a drink, Mr. Hallam," Hank said.

"Reckon I won't be intrudin'?"

"Not at all, sir," Drake told him. "Please join us."

Hallam sat down at the table. The wooden bench was hard, but no harder than a lot of places he had sat. Hank called over to the bartender for another glass of whiskey. The liquor was pretty raw stuff, Hallam discovered, but again, no worse than he had sampled many times before.

"You must be quite a detective to find this place," Drake said. "We try to keep its existence a secret."

"Hell, Simon, you know there's no secrets in the movie business," Mackey Russell said with a short laugh. "Hallam probably just asked somebody over at the studio where we spend our time."

Hallam grinned. "Matter of fact, that's right. Hope you fellers don't mind that I came over to talk to you."

Goldman frowned and leaned forward. "Is something wrong? Has something else happened at the studio?"

Hallam shook his head and said, "There was a little ruckus this mornin' when the leadin' lady wandered off, but it didn't amount to nothing. She was just takin' a walk down on the back lot."

"With that German, I'll bet," Hank said.

Hallam shot a glance at him, looked at the others. They seemed to know what Hank was talking about. After a moment, he said, "I reckon it ain't a secret, then, about Miss Quist and von Ottenhausen carryin' on."

"It's no secret to us," Drake said. "But it's also none of our business." He sent a stern look in Hank's direction. "You know that the film industry runs on gossip, Mr. Hallam. I don't think we need to add to it."

Hallam downed the rest of his whiskey and set the empty glass on the table. "My business sometimes depends on gossip, too," he said. "I ain't out to ruffle any feathers, but I'd like to know anything you can tell me about what's goin' on behind the scenes."

"It's simple," Russell said. "The count's got the hots for

Vesta Quist and the feeling is mutual. They've been sneaking off together almost since the picture started."

"And everybody knows about this?"

"Everybody but Swan. He's still in love with her, if you ask me, so he can't see a damn thing."

"I think he knows," Goldman added. "I just think he realizes there's nothing he can do about it." The pilot snorted contemptuously. "If you ask me, Swan's better off without her. She may be pretty, but she's a real bitch. Let von Ottenhausen have her."

Hallam had gotten that same feeling about Vesta Quist. But there was no denying that she was a very attractive woman, and men often did foolish things when it came to attractive women.

Changing the subject, he asked, "You find out anything more about that airplane that nearly crashed yesterday?"

Hank shook his head. "There wasn't anything else to find out. The engine was fine except for that damaged oil line. So somebody was definitely trying to kill me."

"Nah, they weren't trying to kill *you*," Mackey Russell said. He grinned. "They were after the count."

Hallam frowned. "The count? What do you mean by that?"

Simon Drake answered. "Von Ottenhausen was supposed to be piloting that plane yesterday, Mr. Hallam. None of us thought of that until after you had left. Hank wasn't even supposed to be in that scene."

"Why not?"

Hank spoke up. "They thought I couldn't handle some of the stunts that we were supposed to do. Of course we never got to them, what with the other trouble." He grinned brashly at the other pilots. "Seems to me like bringing that bird in dead-stick was riskier than the stunts we were going to do."

"We still shouldn't have let you go up in the Spad," Drake said. "One of us should have taken it when von Ottenhausen couldn't."

"Hold on there a minute," Hallam said. "How come von Ottenhausen didn't do the flyin' he was supposed to?"

"His sister came up a few minutes before the shooting and said she had to talk to him, that it was urgent family business. Von Ottenhausen tried to tell her it would have to wait, but she was raising such a fuss that I told him to go on and see what she wanted. Hank offered to take his place." Drake frowned at the young pilot. "I let myself be convinced by his enthusiasm."

"Hell, I can do anything in a plane that the Boche can," Hank declared.

"That's pretty harsh language from somebody named Schiller, kid," Goldman pointed out.

Hank just grinned. "Shoot, I'm a Texan, not a German."

"Remember that the next time you get a craving for sausages and sauerkraut."

That set off a round of verbal jabs between Hank, Goldman, and Russell. As they bantered, the bartender cranked up a Victrola and the strains of "It's a Long Way to Tipperary" filled the speakeasy. The flyers at the other table sang along with the music, and Hallam thought fleetingly that this must be something like how it had been in France. Song and drink and the knowledge that tomorrow you might not come back from the front. . . .

Most of his thoughts were taken up with what he had just learned, though. The fact that Wolf von Ottenhausen had been scheduled to fly the plane that had nearly crashed put things in a different light.

He leaned over to Simon Drake, who was watching quietly and not joining in the banter of his comrades. "You ever worked with Swan before?" Hallam asked.

Drake shook his head. "This is the first aviation film he's made. Why?"

"I was just wonderin' if he knew anything about flyin'."

"I happen to know that he's a pilot himself," Drake said. "That's one reason he was assigned to this picture. He wasn't in the war, though, if that's what you're asking. I don't think he even took up flying until after the war was over."

Hallam nodded thoughtfully.

So Danby Swan knew something about flying, enough to know that a slashed oil line would eventually cause an engine to fail. And Swan was probably still in love with Vesta Quist, who was now carrying on with the man who had been scheduled to fly the sabotaged Spad.

This case was getting as kinked up as an old lasso, Hallam thought.

"You happen to notice whether Swan was around that plane any before the shootin' started?" he asked Drake.

The pilot shook his head. "There's always a great deal of confusion before a shoot, you know that. I don't remember Swan being around the plane, but that doesn't mean he wasn't." Drake frowned at Hallam. "Surely you don't think that *Swan* might have been responsible for the sabotage?"

"It's somethin' to ponder."

Drake shook his head. "He'd hardly try to ruin his own picture. It means a great deal to him."

"As much as Vesta Quist?"

Drake's eyes widened as he realized what Hallam was talking about. The other pilots had fallen silent and heard enough of the conversation to know what Hallam meant. Hank shook his head. "I don't believe it," he said fervently. "If that was what happened, then Mr. Swan let me go up in that plane knowing that it was likely to crash. He wouldn't do that."

"How could he have stopped you without admittin' he gimmicked the thing?"

They had no answer for that, but Hallam could tell that none of them really believed that Danby Swan was a would-be killer. He wasn't sure he believed that himself, but he wasn't going to rule out the possibility. The theory fit the facts. Now all he had to do was come up with some proof.

"Why don't you tell us about the Wild West, Mr. Hallam?" Hank Schiller suddenly asked, breaking what threatened to turn into an awkward silence.

"Yeah," Mackey Russell agreed. "Was it really like it is in those Tom Mix pictures?"

Hallam had to suppress a grin. He had worked with Tom Mix several times and had even helped the flamboyant actor out of a jam once, but like all the real cowboys in town, he knew that Mix was mostly flash and hot air. The stories he told about his colorful background were pretty much fiction, and his films were equally fanciful. The man had a great deal of personal bravery and did many of his own stunts, but as far as being an authentic cowboy . . .

"Well, I don't reckon old Tom would lie about the West," Hallam said. He had learned long before that folks liked made-up stories better than the truth, and he didn't see any point in taking their notions away from them.

It was a relief to lose himself in yarn-spinning for a while. As he related tales of making Western pictures and anecdotes about actual life in the West, he was able to put the case out of his thoughts. The pilots called for more whiskey, and Hallam kept talking.

With the curtains drawn, there was no way of telling how much time had passed, but Hallam felt sure the afternoon was well along as he started to wind up a story about the time he had been bear-hunting in Montana.

"So there was that big ol' bear a-chargin' after me," he told the circle of eager listeners. The other pilots had moved over to the table where he sat, and he had everybody in the place hanging on to his every word. "My rifle was busted and I was plumb out of shells for my Colt. Not that they would've done any good against that bear. He was the biggest damn varmint you ever did see, seven feet if he was an inch, and teeth half a foot long. He was slobberin' as he chased me, just a-hankerin' to get his belly on the outside of ol' Lucas."

"What did you do?" Hank asked, totally caught up in the story.

"Well, I still had my bowie knife, so I headed for a tree I saw not far off."

"Wait a minute," Pete Goldman protested. "I may be a city boy, but even I know that bears can climb trees."

Hallam held up a big, callused hand. "Damn right they can climb trees, but you ain't let me finish yet."

"Go ahead, Mr. Hallam," Hank said eagerly.

"I ran as fast as I could to that there tree and commenced to climbin' it. I got right up there in the top of it, where the trunk weren't so thick, and then I hauled out my ol' bowie. That bear was climbin' already, so I didn't have much time."

"What did you do?" Hank was almost breathless by now.

"Well, sir, I reached right down there and lopped through the trunk of that tree, yellin' *Timbeeeer!* as I done so." Hallam reached out and picked up the mug of beer on the table in front of him, having switched from whiskey an hour earlier. He drained the rest of the beer and licked his lips in satisfaction. "And that was that," he said, thumping the mug down. "The tree fell, and that ol' bear didn't have no way of climbin' up to get me then. So I just waited until he got disgusted and give up and went away."

Simon Drake chuckled. Several of the men shook their heads and got up to go to the bar. Hank just stared openmouthed at Hallam, though, until a slight frown began to crease his forehead.

"Wait a minute," he finally said. "Let me get this straight. You were in the top of the tree, and then you cut through the trunk with your knife—"

"In the parlance of the Old West, I believe Mr. Hallam just ran a windy on you, my boy," Drake told him. "I wouldn't bother trying to figure it out if I were you."

Hallam grinned.

Drake's expression became more serious. "I met Frank Luke several times during the war. He was from Arizona, I believe. We thought of him as a cowboy, at any rate. He was a damn good man. There was none better at shooting down enemy balloons."

"Don't reckon I ever knew him," Hallam said, his own face more solemn now. He figured he knew what was coming. "What happened to him?"

"He shot down three German balloons one evening." Drake smiled thinly. "He was supposed to be grounded at the time, but Luke was never one for following orders. He was wounded and his Spad damaged, and he had to set down behind enemy lines. The way I heard the story, he shot it out with the German troops with his forty-five. Eventually, they killed him, of course."

The table was quiet now, the ebullient mood gone. Hallam had known men like the one Drake was describing. Most of them were Westerners, men who would go down fighting if they could. The way he saw it, there wasn't a whole hell of a lot of difference between facing down German troops in a French field and trading shots with an Apache war party in the Arizona mountains.

All it took was a hell-for-leather fighting man.

"You remind me somewhat of Frank Luke, Mr. Hallam," Drake went on. "I hope you don't someday get yourself killed like he did."

Hallam grinned. "No, sir. I'm plannin' to die in bed with my socks on."

"Oh, no!" Hank exclaimed. "You're a gunfighter, Mr. Hallam, just like in the movies. You need to go out with guns blazing."

"Them days are gone, son," Hallam told him. "But go get me another beer, and I might just reminisce some more about them. Providin', of course, that you ain't bored by the ramblin's of an old man."

Hank went and got the beer.

SEVEN

There was still some time left in the afternoon when Hallam left Lafayette's, so he started in on some of the legwork that had to be done. Regardless of how interesting some of the things were he had stumbled across, the leading suspect in the attempted ruination of *Death to the Kaiser!* still had to be B. W. Garrettson.

Hallam took the list that Carl McGinley had provided and began checking out the names, starting with the members of the crew. It was more likely that one of them would be a secret member of the Klan and Garrettson's inside man. It would be much harder for an actor to be involved in something like that and still keep it a secret.

For the next couple of hours, Hallam drove from address to address on his list, pretending to have a delivery for each person he was interested in. The story worked best when no one was home and he could talk to the neighbors; as he had told Simon Drake, sometimes his business depended on gossip, and there was no better source than a nosy neighbor. Several of the places he went, the man's wife would be home, and then Hallam had to pretend that he had been given the wrong address for the phony delivery. He still managed to work a few questions in at each place, though.

As evening began to set in, he had to admit that he hadn't found out a damned thing.

One more stop, he decided, and then he would call it a day and head home. He was anxious to find out how Liz's first full day in the city had gone.

He parked the flivver at the curb in front of a rooming house at the next address on his list. The place was just on the bottom edge of respectable. There were a few bare spots on the roof where shingles had fallen off, and the paint on the walls of the old frame house was peeling. Hallam got out of his car and crossed a narrow lawn, paused at the bottom of several steps leading up to a covered porch.

A man and a woman were sitting in cane-backed rockers on the porch. Both of them looked to be in their mid-seventies. They were rocking aimlessly and paid little attention to Hallam until he said, "Excuse me, folks. Wonder if you could help me?"

"We ain't buyin' nothing, mister," the old woman replied without looking at him. "This place don't make enough money for frivolity."

Hallam wondered if he looked like he was selling frivolity. Somehow he didn't think so. "You run the place, do you?" he asked.

"That's right. We're all full up right now, if you're looking for a room."

That was a neat change of direction, Hallam thought, from salesman to potential tenant. He said, "Nope, just lookin' for a feller who's supposed to live here. Larry Brownlow? He here?"

The woman shook her head, glancing at Hallam for the first time. "What you want with Larry?" she asked.

"Got a package I'm supposed to give to him. Don't suppose you'd know where I could find him?"

"I imagine he's over at that movie studio he works at." The woman's mouth twisted bitterly. "He's around them stars all day. Don't know why he never brings any of 'em home with him so that the rest of us could meet them."

According to the list that McGinley had given him, Larry Brownlow was an assistant prop man. Hallam didn't think it would do any good to explain to the woman that Larry wouldn't be likely to be hobnobbing with any stars.

"That does seem a shame," he said. "Larry a good tenant, is he?"

"Pays his rent and keeps to hisself. That makes a dang good tenant, if you ask me. What business is it of yours, anyway?"

"None at all," Hallam admitted innocently. "I was just makin' conversation."

"Larry don't make no trouble, him nor his friends. That's all we care about."

"Friends?"

The old woman shook a clawlike finger at Hallam. "I don't care what nobody says, them boys are just tryin' to help this country." Her voice became more vicious. "What the hell do we need with a bunch of niggers and Jews and foreigners, anyway?"

"That's just what I always say, ma'am," Hallam replied, trying to make his voice sound sincere. Years of doing this sort of thing had given him the ability to keep his true feelings from showing. From what the old lady was saying, he might have just gotten lucky.

"Didn't mean to talk out of turn," she went on. "Why'nt you just leave Larry's package with us? I'll see he gets it."

"Wish I could, ma'am, but I've got to have him sign for it. I'll take it over to the studio, or catch him here some other time. He here most evenings?"

"'Cept when he has a meeting with his friends. He don't run

around with them loose Hollywood women." The old voice became wistful. "Sure wish he'd bring some of them stars over here."

"You know when his next meetin' is, so I'll know when not to come?" Hallam knew he might be pushing things with this question, but it was worth a try.

"Tomorrow night," the old woman said. "You come back any other night, and he'll be here, I promise you."

"Thank you, ma'am, I'll do that." Hallam turned and walked back to the flivver. He could hear the creak of the rocking chairs on the porch behind him. The old man had never spoken to him, hadn't even lifted his head and looked at him, just stared straight ahead at nothing.

Maybe Hank Schiller had been right. Maybe it would be better to go out with guns blazing . . .

There were lights on in Liz's apartment when Hallam pulled up in front of the building. She had said that she might take a walk around the neighborhood today, but that was all she had planned as far as Hallam knew. She opened the door almost before he had a chance to knock on it.

"Hello, Lucas," she said, a smile on her face. "Please come on in."

Hallam stepped into the apartment and looked around. She had obviously spent part of the day getting things arranged more to her liking. There were pictures on the walls and a soft rug on the floor. Hallam smelled something good, too, and realized it was a mixture of food cooking and whatever that toilet water was that Liz used.

"You look right nice," he told her, holding his hat in his hands and turning it around rather nervously.

"Thank you, Lucas. Why don't you sit down?"

Well, it looked like she had forgiven him for the excursion to the Pimlico the night before. Hallam was glad of that. As he sank down onto the sofa, he felt twinges from his sore muscles. Most of the day he had been so busy that he had been able to ignore the aches and pains of the beating he had received. Now he relaxed and they came back.

Best thing in the world for them, he knew, would be the touch of a good-looking, sympathetic woman.

Liz sat down on the sofa beside him, not touching but close enough that he could feel the warmth from her body. She said, "I thought you might stop by earlier, Lucas."

"Started to this mornin'," Hallam said. "I was runnin' a little late, though, and had to get on with my work."

"The same case you were working on last night?"

He nodded. "Yep. Seems like there's plenty of angles to it. Reckon most of 'em won't turn out to mean anything, but you've got to check all of them out."

Liz lifted a hand and gently touched his bruised face. "How are you feeling?"

"Oh, I'm fine, Liz, no call to worry about me. This weren't nothin'."

"It looked bad enough to me."

"Well, I am a mite sore . . ."

"Let me see your neck."

Hallam turned partway around on the sofa and felt her move up closer behind him. Her fingers took hold of the back of his neck and began to massage. Hallam grinned, knowing that she couldn't see his face. She was over being mad at him, all right.

"Lucas?" she said after a moment.

"Yep?"

"Do you know where I could get a job?"

Hallam lifted his head and frowned. "A job? Why do you want a job?" He happened to know that she had plenty of money. Where she had gotten it, he wasn't exactly sure, though he suspected that most of it had come from the days when Chuckwalla had been a boom town and she had operated the best saloon in a hundred miles.

"I want a job because I don't want to sit in this apartment all day long. You know I've always been one to do for myself."

Hallam knew that, all right. He was surprised that her independence hadn't gotten her in a lot of trouble, in fact. Living alone out in the wilderness like she had was just downright dangerous.

But he could see her point. When he had started trying to persuade her to move into town, he hadn't really thought this far. Of course she'd want something to do. He just wasn't sure about her going out and getting a *job*.

"I'll have to think on that," he said. "Might be able to find you something around one of the studios. What can you do?"

Liz laughed shortly. "Run a saloon. Maybe I should open up a speakeasy."

Hallam wasn't sure if she was joking or not. He hoped so. Speakeasies could get rough; they were no place for a lady like her.

He said as much, turning to face her again. She shrugged. "Well, other than watering down booze, about the only thing I know how to do is play a piano," she said.

"Well, we'll see what we can come up with," Hallam promised. "I'll start askin' around tomorrow."

"I'd appreciate it, Lucas." She leaned closer to him. Her voice got lower and huskier as she said, "You know, there are a few other things I'm good at."

"You reckon so?"

"Sure." She whispered in his ear as his arms came up and went around her, drawing her even closer to him.

Hallam felt his face getting red and warm.

"I thought you was cookin' dinner for us," he said.

"It can wait."

Hallam took a deep breath. "I'm an old man, Liz."

"The hell you are."

"What am I goin' to do with a sweet, good-lookin' woman like you?"

"What's the matter? Can't think of anything?"

He grinned. Lucas Hallam had never been a man to back down from a challenge. Damned if he was going to start now!

Hallam had an idea when he woke up the next morning. He felt much better, he found as he got out of bed, and he was sure that much of his recovery was due to Liz. The meal she had made for him had been excellent, once they got around to it, and an evening spent relaxing instead of chasing around Hollywood had done wonders for him. The least he could do now, he thought, was find a job for her that she would like.

Once again, he went past her door without stopping as he left the building. He'd see her later in the day, and maybe by then he'd have a surprise for her.

His first stop was the studio. Though it was still early, the parking lot was crowded. Shooting always got under way by eight o'clock in the morning, often earlier. Time was a precious commodity in the picture business. Days were long while a film was in production.

Carl McGinley was in his office. He looked up as the pretty secretary ushered Hallam in. He smiled, but the expression didn't hide the weariness in his eyes.

"You look a mite peaked, Carl," Hallam said as he sat down. "You been gettin' enough sleep?"

"Lack of sleep is an occupational hazard in the movie business, Lucas. You know that." McGinley stifled a yawn. "I had to go to a party at the Garden of Allah last night."

Hallam had heard about the parties at the lavish apartments on Sunset Boulevard. They went on until all hours, with guests wandering from room to room. When one tenant in the Garden of Allah threw a shindig, the whole place was included.

"Business or pleasure?" Hallam asked.

McGinley's grin became sheepish. "It was supposed to be business. I needed to talk to Louis B. Mayer, and while I was there I pitched a picture to Ramon Navarro." The producer grimaced. "I'm afraid he wasn't interested, though. So I wound up spending most of my time at the bar watching other people get kissed. It was a wild time, let me tell you."

Hallam knew that McGinley was probably exaggerating a bit. He had been to some of the infamous Hollywood parties, and except for a tendency to consume enormous amounts of bootleg hooch, the guests usually behaved themselves pretty well. There were always a few rendezvous and an occasional fistfight, but that was nothing compared to what he had seen in places like Hell's Half Acre in Fort Worth. When it came to hell-raisin', actors couldn't hold a patch to cowboys.

"Run into any problems on the set after I left yesterday?" he asked.

McGinley shook his head. "No, except for Vesta's little disappearance, things actually went pretty well yesterday. That makes me worry about what Garrettson has planned for today. Are you making any progress toward stopping him, Lucas?"

Hallam shrugged, not wanting to tell McGinley that he'd spent most of his time on other aspects of the case, aspects that might pan out to nothing. "Figured I'd go talk to him today, try to put the fear of God into him. I may have a line on who he's gettin' to help him from the inside."

McGinley leaned forward eagerly. "Who is it?"

"Don't want to say just yet," Hallam said, shaking his head. "I don't have any proof, and I ain't one to railroad a man."

"Of course not." McGinley was visibly disappointed that Hallam wasn't going to give him the name of the suspected inside man, but he knew better than to push the big detective. "I don't think Garrettson's going to listen to reason, though."

Hallam inclined his head in acknowledgment of the point. "Reckon you're probably right. Which same means we'll have to catch him doin' something illegal. Then you can light right in the middle of him with both feet."

"In other words, we have to wait until he tries something again and hope he doesn't succeed in killing someone this time."

"Unless I can get something definite to tie him in to things that have already happened. I ain't given up on that yet."

"Those pilots give you anything else you could use?"

Hallam grinned. "Naw, not really. But they got pretty good beer at that place of theirs."

"That kid was around here earlier looking for you."

"What kid? Hank Schiller?"

"That's the one." McGinley sat back in his chair. "Lucas, you've got a good case of hero worship on your hands. He's getting bored of flying aces. I think he wants to be a gunfighter now."

Hallam had seen that happen more than once, all right. A kid got grand notions in his head and wound up getting killed because of them. Hank had seemed more levelheaded than that to him, but you never could tell about a boy who was twenty years old.

"I'll keep that in mind," Hallam said. "You know where I can find this Garrettson?"

"He's a carpenter by trade. He's even done some work here at the studio from time to time. That was before he got so caught up in this Klan garbage, though. I can give you the address of his shop."

Hallam wrote down the address that McGinley gave him, tucked the stub of pencil he used back in his pocket, and stood up. "Reckon I'll go pay Mr. Garrettson a visit," he said.

"Be careful," McGinley cautioned. "You saw how crazy he is the other day."

"I'm in the habit of watchin' my back, Carl," Hallam told the producer in dry tones.

He left McGinley's office a few minutes later, exchanging smiles with the secretary as he went out. As he headed toward his flivver, a voice hailed him. He turned to see Hank Schiller coming toward him.

"Any luck on the case, Mr. Hallam?" Hank asked as he came up.

Hallam shrugged broad shoulders. "Maybe, maybe not. It's hard to tell about these things, son."

"I really enjoyed listening to your stories yesterday at Lafayette's. It sounded like you've lived a humdinger of a life."

"It weren't all that way, I promise you. There's been a heap of times when I was hungry and cold and downright miserable. Nope, times are better now."

"Maybe so, but you still have to miss the old days sometimes."

"Sometimes," Hallam admitted.

"I was wondering about something." Hank hesitated, as if not sure he should go on, but then he plunged ahead. "Could you teach me how to use a gun?"

"Like a fast draw, you mean?" Hallam had halfway expected the question.

Hank nodded eagerly. "I'd really like to learn."

"There's no place in today's world for a gunfighter, Hank. It ain't the Wild West no more."

"I know that. But you could teach me, couldn't you?"

Hallam considered. The boy had good reflexes, otherwise he couldn't have been a pilot. If he had the necessary dedication, Hank could probably learn how to use a gun like an old-fashioned shootist. But what the hell good would it do him?

"I reckon not, son," Hallam said slowly.

Hank's face tightened. "Why not?"

"You best stick to flyin' them airplanes. That's a hell of a lot bigger thrill than gunfightin'."

"How would you know? Have you ever been up in a plane?"

Hallam shook his head. "Them contraptions are too new-fangled for me, boy. Took me five years to get used to an automobile."

Hank got a calculating look in his eyes. "You mean you're afraid to fly in one."

Hallam frowned and told himself not to get mad. Hank was just a kid. He wanted something, and Hallam had told him he couldn't have it. Now he was trying to get back at the older man.

"I ain't afraid," Hallam told him. "Just don't see the need in it."

"Well, I'll bet you a gunfighting lesson that you won't go up in a plane with me."

Hallam knew he ought to get in his car and drive away from here, just let the boy think what he wanted to. He had work to do, for one thing.

But he knew a dare when he heard one, and he'd never been one to let a man throw a dare in his face and get away with it.

"You're on, boy," he said abruptly. "You just let me know when."

Hank's grin was cocky. "How about right now?"

Hallam had been afraid he was going to say that. He sighed. "If you're so dead set on this foolishness, let's get on with it."

A half hour later, he was wondering just why he had to be so dad-blamed cussed at times. If he hadn't been so stubborn, he wouldn't be sitting in a pile of wire and canvas about to fly up into the sky.

He was sitting in the rear cockpit of a D.H.4 reconnaissance bomber, one of the planes that was being used in the filming of *Death to the Kaiser!* Hank stood next to the big craft and held up a flying helmet and goggles to him.

"You'll need these, Mr. Hallam," he said. "It can get cold and windy up there."

Hallam wondered if it was too late to back out and realized grimly that it was. He had to go through with this now, or look like an old fool in front of Hank.

"Reckon this ain't the first time my damn pride's got the best of me," he muttered to himself as Hank climbed agilely into the front cockpit. At least none of the other pilots were around to see this debacle. Hank had told him that they were probably at Lafayette's, since no more location shooting was scheduled for a couple of days. Even at this hour, there would be pilots there hoping to pick up a day's work on some production. Hank had been at the studio to see if Danby Swan wanted him for any extra bits. Running into Hallam there had been pure luck.

Bad luck, Hallam thought. But there was nothing he could do about it now.

A mechanic in grease-stained overalls was wiping his hands on a rag and standing near the D.H.4, looking dubiously up at Hank and Hallam. "You sure this flight's authorized, kid?" he called out to Hank. He had already asked that question at least three times, but despite his doubts he showed no signs of trying to stop them.

"I'm sure," Hank said confidently. "Call the studio if you like. Ask for Mr. Swan himself. I'm sure he won't mind being bothered."

The mechanic waved a hand and stepped over to the propeller. "Ah, never mind. Let me know when you're ready."

Hank settled down in the cockpit, looked over the few instruments on the panel, then called, "Ignition off!"

The mechanic reached up and grasped one blade of the propeller. He swung it down as hard as he could, spinning the propeller and priming the engine. "Contact!" he shouted.

Hank answered with a confirming "Contact!", then hit the ignition switch. The engine turned over a couple of times, then caught with a throaty, building roar. The propeller became little more than a spinning blur.

"Ready, Mr. Hallam?" Hank shouted over the thunder of the engine.

Hallam's stomach was threatening to come right up his throat, but he swallowed hard and replied, "Rarin' to go, son!"

Hank opened the throttle, and the plane began to roll down the hard-packed ground of the runway.

Hallam saw the buildings of the little airfield in West Hollywood roll by at a dizzying speed. He forced down his nausea again, and then suddenly the ground seemed to fall out from under the craft. He caught a glimpse of trees looming up in front of them, and then the trees were gone, too.

There was nothing in front of them but open sky.

Nothing underneath them but air.

"Goddamn," Hallam breathed. He became aware that he was gripping the sides of the cockpit so hard that his fingers were going numb.

Wind buffeted his face, and Hank had been right. It was cold.

The plane climbed steadily, and though the last thing Hallam wanted to do was look down, he couldn't help himself. Far below, he saw Hollywood unrolling like a funny-colored carpet. He could even see downtown Los Angeles, several miles away. Lord, he suddenly realized, he could even see over the hills with their HOLLYWOODLAND sign to the San Fernando Valley beyond.

"Well, what do you think?"

Hallam squinted at Hank, who was craning around to look over his shoulder. "Watch where you're goin'!" he called out.

"There's nothing to run into up here, don't worry. How do you like it?"

"Mighty fine!" Hallam answered, his voice booming out over the wind. "I been on Sunday strolls more excitin' than this, boy!"

"Oh?" Hank grinned.

And Hallam knew he should have kept his damned big mouth shut.

Hank threw the bomber into a roll, and Hallam had to close his eyes and hang on as the earth below tilted crazily. He realized after a few seconds that his lips were moving, but no sound was coming out and he didn't know if he was praying or cussing. A little bit of both, he suspected.

Hank straightened up the plane. "How about that?" he asked.

"You're impressin' the hell out of me, kid. But I reckon I won that bet."

"Reckon you did. Anything you'd like to see while we're up here?"

"Just the ground, boy." Hallam couldn't keep from telling the truth. "Just the ground."

He'd heard tell that immigrants to this country sometimes kissed the ground when their ships landed. He supposed he was an immigrant of sorts, because he felt like doing a little sparking himself when the D.H.4 touched down and rolled to a stop. He hauled himself out of the cockpit and dropped to the ground, wincing at a twinge of pain in his bad knee as the weight hit it.

Hank vaulted out lightly, his face stretched in a wide grin. "What did you think?" he asked.

Hallam wrenched the helmet and goggles from his head and thrust them into Hank's hand. "I think there's no fool like an old fool, and the next time I go that high in the sky I'm goin' to be headin' for Heaven!"

Hank laughed. "Just give flying a chance, Mr. Hallam. I'll bet you'd get to like it."

"I won this bet with you, son. You ain't suckerin' me into another one."

The young pilot shrugged. "You won, all right, fair and square. I sure would have liked to learn how to handle a six-gun, though."

"Well, tell you what. Maybe when this case is wrapped up, if we can find the time I'll show you a thing or two. Just for fun, mind you. Like I said, there ain't no more place for gunfighters."

Hank's face lit up in a smile. "That'd be great, Mr. Hallam."

"Lucas."

Hank nodded. "Lucas."

Hallam clapped a big hand on his shoulder. "Right now, though, I'd best get back to work. Providin' my legs still work, that is."

"Don't worry. You'll get over that in no time."

Despite Hank's assurances, Hallam still felt a little wobbly in the legs as he went to his flivver. It was parked on the asphalt next to the airfield office, beside Hank's little roadster. He looked back and saw Hank watching him. Hank lifted a hand and waved. Hallam returned the gesture and then climbed into his car.

It had been a hell of a morning, hadn't turned out anything like what he had expected. He still had work to do and errands to run.

But for a moment, he had had a glimpse into a whole new world. He wouldn't want to go back, he knew, but there was something just in the experiencing of it.

Gone to see the elephant. That was what the old-timers said.

He drove out Sunset to Hudson, turning past the big building that housed the Hollywood Athletic Club. Garrettson's shop was on a side street just off Hudson. Hallam parked at the curb and paused a moment before getting out of the flivver. A small stone cottage sat close to the street, and behind it and to one side was a big frame building that evidently doubled as a garage and Garrettson's workshop.

The double doors of the shop were open, and Hallam could hear hammering coming from inside the structure. He got out of the flivver and went up a cracked sidewalk to the narrow front porch of the cottage. There was no screen door on the entrance, just a wooden one. He bounced his knuckles off it.

The door opened a moment later, and a young woman peered out at him curiously. "Yes?" she asked. "Can I help you?"

Hallam took off his hat. "Yes'm. You'd be Mrs. Garrettson?"

"That's right." The woman was thin, with washed-out blond hair and a face that might have been pretty if it had had any life in it. "What can I do for you, mister?"

"Would your husband be home, ma'am?"

"He's out in his workshop. Can't you hear him?"

As a matter of fact, Hallam had figured that Garrettson was

in the shop, but he had wanted to see who would come to the door of the cottage. He didn't hear any children in the house, didn't see any toys scattered on the floor when he looked past her into the living room. Just the woman, alone in a quiet house, it looked like.

"Just wanted to make sure that was him, ma'am," Hallam told her. "Be all right for me to go on back and talk to him about some work?"

"You planning to hire him?" There was an unmistakable touch of eagerness in the woman's question.

"Sure might."

"I hope so. B.W.'s a good worker, he really is."

And they could use the money, Hallam thought. The woman's shapeless dress had seen plenty of wear, and the furniture he could see was pretty threadbare.

He nodded, said, "Thank you, ma'am," and went around the side of the cottage, putting his hat back on as he did so.

Garrettson was still hammering, but he stopped as Hallam stepped into the doorway and threw his shadow into the big room. He looked up curiously from the cabinets he was building.

"Howdy, Garrettson," Hallam said.

The Klan leader's face turned a deep, angry red. "You son of a bitch!" he grated. "What the hell do you want?"

"Just thought I'd make sure you wasn't cookin' up no more trouble for them folks at the movie studio," Hallam said.

"Those traitors, you mean." Garrettson took a step toward Hallam, the hammer still in his clenched fist. "You people make me sick, the way you stick up for foreigners."

"I ain't overly fond of Wolf von Ottenhausen or his sister, but that don't mean I aim to shut down the picture just because he's in it. Ain't got the right to do that."

"Well, I've got a right to defend my country against anybody who wants to ruin it." Garrettson lifted the hammer and came a step closer. "Now you just get the hell out of here, mister!"

"B.W.! What are you doing?"

Hallam hadn't heard Mrs. Garrettson come out of the house, and evidently Garrettson hadn't noticed her, either. He froze where he was, the hammer still raised threateningly. Hallam glanced over his shoulder and saw her standing about ten feet behind him.

"You get back in the house, Junie," Garrettson grated at her. "This ain't none of your business."

"But this man said he wanted to hire you."

"He's a goddamn liar. Now do like I tell you."

The woman gave Hallam a sullen, disappointed look, then turned and walked slowly back to the cottage.

"I didn't like you to start with, mister," Garrettson said when the back door had closed behind her. "Now that I know you been lying to my wife, I think I'll just teach you a lesson."

"Back off, Garrettson," Hallam said softly. "You ain't got Larry Brownlow here to help you with your dirty work now."

Garrettson paused for an instant, his eyes narrowing, and it was enough of a reaction to let Hallam know that his shot had gone home. But then the Klansman shook his head and started forward again. "I don't know what the hell you're talking about, and I don't give a damn. You had your chance to leave."

He lunged forward, swinging the hammer.

Hallam ducked to the side, moving faster than Garrettson must have expected. He didn't move quite fast enough, though. The head of the hammer thudded into his right shoulder. Hallam grunted as pain raced down his arm.

He reached over with his left hand and clamped long fingers on Garrettson's wrist. Any thoughts of taking it easy on the man had vanished now. Hallam twisted savagely, bringing a howl from Garrettson as the hammer dropped from his hand. Hallam kicked out, his booted foot driving into Garrettson's right knee.

Garrettson staggered but didn't go down. He hooked a punch into Hallam's belly. Hallam jabbed at his face. Any wobbliness left over from the plane ride with Hank had vanished now, washed out of Hallam's system by the urgency of this fight.

He knew that Garrettson would beat him to death, given half a chance.

Hallam surged forward, driving into Garrettson's body and knocking him backward. He followed with a left and then a right, both blows smashing into Garrettson's face. Hallam had the man off balance now and knew he had to keep him that way. He bore in, rocking Garrettson with a flurry of punches. The last one, a long, looping right, knocked the Klansman back through the open double doors of his shop.

Garrettson landed hard on his back. He raised himself into a sitting position, shook his head, and then suddenly reached for something to one side of the door. He came to his feet with a long-handled ax in his hands. The wildness in his eyes left no doubt he intended to chop Hallam into kindling.

He took one step, raising the ax as he did so, then stopped short, almost losing his balance again.

Hallam drew back the hammer of the big Colt he had pointing right between Garrettson's eyes. "Drop it!" he said coldly.

Garrettson swallowed. He had barely seen the flicker of movement as Hallam drew the gun from under his coat. His fingers opened and the ax fell to the ground.

Hallam let him stare down the barrel of the Colt for a long moment, then slowly let the hammer back down. Instinct had made him draw the gun when Garrettson came up with the ax, and he knew that if the man hadn't dropped the weapon, he would have pulled the trigger.

"You're on my property," Garrettson said tightly. "I'm going to call the cops and report you."

"You do that."

"You haven't heard the last of me, mister." Hatred burned in Garrettson's narrow eyes. "You and that bunch of traitors are going to pay for what you've done."

"Figured you'd see it that way. You just remember I'll be waitin' for you, though."

An ugly grin stretched Garrettson's mouth. "I wouldn't have it any other way."

Hallam kept the Colt in his hand until he was back in his flivver and driving away from Garrettson's. As he holstered the old weapon, he grimaced and hoped he hadn't done more harm than good by his visit. He had confirmed his suspicion that Larry Brownlow was working with Garrettson, but he had also let Garrettson know that he was on to him.

Garrettson was a stubborn man, full of hate. Regardless of what Hallam knew or didn't know, Garrettson would try something else to stop *Death to the Kaiser!* He would have to.

And Hallam would be waiting, just like he had promised.

EIGHT

As he drove away from Garrettson's house and turned back onto Sunset Boulevard, Hallam's stomach told him it was getting to be time to eat. He stopped at a Pig 'n' Whistle, then headed for Grauman's Egyptian Theater.

The Egyptian wasn't as famous as its sister theater, Grauman's Chinese, but it had been the first of the ornate, extravagantly decorated movie palaces. Its stage was also used from time to time for live performances. The huge pipe organ next to the stage provided thunderous accompaniment for the pictures that played on the big screen.

And Hallam happened to know that the manager of the Egyptian was looking for an organist to replace one who had recently left.

Liz could play the piano, she had said. Seemed to Hallam that an organ wasn't too much different.

The manager was working in his office, as Hallam had

known he would be, even though the theater wouldn't be open for hours yet. His face lit up in a smile when Hallam told him he knew someone who might be able to solve his problem.

"Bring her around," he said eagerly. "The girl I've got playing the organ now just isn't working out. She keeps straying away from the program I've got lined up for her. She started playing Wagner the other day during a Buster Keaton feature." The man laughed. "Actually, it was pretty funny, at that. But still . . ."

Hallam nodded. "I'll sure bring my friend over."

"Has she had any dramatic experience?"

Hallam thought about the years Liz had spent running a saloon. "Reckon she's had some."

"Well, whatever. Thanks for stopping by, Lucas."

Hallam stood up and shook hands with the man, then left with a grin on his face. Liz was going to be surprised.

He had one more stop to make before he went back to the apartment house and told her about the new job, though.

The old woman at Larry Brownlow's place had told him that the Klan had a meeting scheduled for tonight. There was a good chance that Brownlow would be there and that Garrettson would have some new instructions for him.

Hallam intended to be there, too.

The Hollywood Police Department had been part of the Los Angeles force for several years now, but the old Hollywood station on Cahuenga was still in use. Ben Dunnemore worked out of that station quite a bit, and Hallam hoped he could find Dunnemore there now.

He parked in front of the small, vine-covered cottage that had originally housed the station. There was a newer building next door which had been built for the police department, and the local fire station was there as well.

The desk sergeant told Hallam that Lieutenant Dunnemore was back in the detectives' room and jerked a thumb over his shoulder to indicate that Hallam could go on in. Dunnemore was sitting at one of the desks, papers spread out in front of him. He was the only person in the room.

"'Lo, Lucas," he grunted, glancing up from his work. "What brings you down here?"

Hallam reversed one of the straight-backed chairs next to the desk and straddled it. "Just come by to see your cheerful face, Ben."

Dunnemore grunted again. He was a thick-bodied man of middle years, with rumpled hair and a shaggy moustache. His hair was mostly gray now, and his face was lined. He had been a cop for over twenty years, and it showed.

"Sure," he said. "What do you really want?"

"Know anything about the Klan?"

"The Ku Klux Klan?" Dunnemore shook his head. "Just what I've read in the paper, like anybody else. I've never had any official dealings with them. They've been pretty quiet since that Inglewood business."

Hallam remembered the case Dunnemore was referring to, but some of the details were fuzzy in his mind. "I don't recollect everything that happened there, Ben," he said.

"Some of the Klansmen raided a house out in Inglewood where a Mexican family lived, said they were making and selling bootleg wine. The local cops heard about it and went out to see what was happening and wound up getting into a shooting scrape with the guys in the hoods. A couple of the Klansmen were killed, and it turned out one of them was a constable. Raised quite a stink."

Hallam nodded. "I remember now. Seems to me the district attorney got into the act somewhere along the way."

"Yeah, Woolwine had his men raid the Klan office. They got their hands on a bunch of membership lists and found out that there were a lot of cops and elected officials under those hoods. It was a pretty messy situation, and the Klan still hasn't quite recovered from it. I have heard that they're stirring around more these days, though."

"You wouldn't know where they hold their meetin's, would you?"

Dunnemore frowned at Hallam for a long moment, then said, "Are you working on a case again, Lucas?"

Hallam shrugged.

Dunnemore put his hands flat on the desk and said, "I wish you'd stick to making movies."

"Now, there's no call to get upset, Ben," Hallam said. "Nobody's gotten killed."

"Yet."

Hallam supposed that the sabotage on the plane Hank Schiller had been flying could be considered attempted murder. As such, it was within Dunnemore's jurisdiction. But McGinley and Swan hadn't reported it, and Hallam didn't think he wanted to, either.

"I reckon that means you don't know where I could find one of their get-togethers."

Dunnemore sighed. "I've heard they have some place up in the hills where they hold rallies and burn crosses and nonsense like that. You thinking about paying a visit to the local klavern?"

"That what they call it?" Hallam shook his head. "I'm just curious, Ben. I'll let you know if it goes beyond that."

"You'd damn well better."

Dunnemore was in a bad mood, and judging from the amount of paperwork spread out on his desk, Hallam could see why. Ben Dunnemore was an old war-horse; he didn't like being tied down with details just like Hallam himself.

Hallam didn't think it would hurt to ask a few more questions, though. He said, "What's Jocko Burke up to these days?"

"Running his club, as far as I know." Like all the cops in the city, Dunnemore was aware of the existence of most speakeasies. None of them tried to do anything about the illegal clubs unless they were under direct orders, though.

"He still mixed up in gambling and fencing and all them other hobbies?"

"I wouldn't know about that. Like I said about the Klan, I haven't had any official dealings with him."

"Reckon you wouldn't be interested in anything I might turn up on him, then."

Dunnemore's eyes glinted. "I didn't say that."

Hallam knew that Dunnemore would be more than happy to get his hands on some evidence that would justify hauling Burke in. Ben was an honest cop, working in a system that left his hands tied a lot of the time. He'd take any chance to actually accomplish some good and throw a real crook behind bars.

"I'll keep that in mind," Hallam promised. "Happen I stumble across anything interestin', I'll let you know."

"You do that."

"How about a feller named Orville Cooke?"

The furrows on Dunnemore's forehead became deeper. "The oil tycoon? Now you're really getting me confused, Lucas. Why would I know anything about him?"

"No rumors about any shady deals?"

Dunnemore laughed shortly. "You're talking about a pillar of the community. I know sometimes that don't mean much, but this time it does. As far as I know Cooke's completely clean, Lucas."

Hallam knew damn well that nobody was *completely* clean, but he didn't argue the point with Dunnemore. He stood up and said, "Well, I appreciate your time, Ben. Don't want to keep you from what you're doin', though."

Dunnemore grinned sourly. "You're welcome. And Lucas . . . if you're working on something, you stay in touch, you hear?"

"I hear, Ben."

Hallam headed back to his apartment, leaving Ben Dunnemore to wade through his papers. As he parked beside the narrow flower beds that lined the yard next to the road, he looked toward the building and saw Liz standing on the second-floor landing, just outside her apartment. She waved at him.

Hallam felt his heartbeat speed up slightly. Liz looked good, standing there in the sunshine with the breeze tugging at her red hair. From this distance, she looked like a girl again, her body trim and lithe. He was a damned lucky man, Hallam thought.

He hoped she would like the news he was bringing.

"Hello, Lucas," she said as he came up the steps. "I suppose you've been out working all day, as usual."

"A detective's got to do a lot of trompin' around." He grinned. "They call it legwork."

"Well, at least you're home now, in time to show me a few of the sights in this town."

Hallam leaned on the metal railing beside her. "Afraid not, Liz. We got places to go, all right, but not on no sight-seein' tour."

She frowned at him in puzzlement. "Where, then?"

"I got you a job," Hallam said proudly.

Liz arched carefully plucked eyebrows. "A job? What kind of job?"

"You said you wanted something to do. I stopped by Grauman's Egyptian Theater and talked to the manager about you playin' the organ for them. Ought to be real convenient for you; the bus runs right by here."

Liz stared at him for a long moment, then said, "Lucas, I've never played an organ in my life."

"You play the piano, don't you? That's what you said."

"But the organ is a completely different instrument!"

Hallam shrugged. "Looks about the same."

Liz held up her hands, palms out. "All right, Lucas. I don't want to argue about this. I appreciate what you've done, and I'll go talk to the man. But I don't know if I can do it."

"Hell, I've got confidence in you, Liz."

She smiled thinly. "Thanks, Lucas. I'm sure that'll be a big help."

"I'll run you over there now," he said. "That way you can show the feller what you can do. Who knows, maybe he'll put you right to work."

"For heaven's sake, Lucas, don't rush a girl so! At least let me go inside and change clothes."

"Why? You look right nice."

"To you maybe. And I do appreciate the compliment, I promise you. But just give me a few minutes, all right?"

Hallam shrugged. "Sure."

He didn't mind waiting a little while for Liz to get ready. It wouldn't take long to run by the Egyptian and let her demonstrate her skill. He'd still have plenty of time to get back to Larry Brownlow's rooming house before nightfall.

It would have to be good and dark before the Klan meeting could get under way, Hallam had decided.

Otherwise the burning cross wouldn't show up near as well.

"I don't see why he hired me," Liz was saying an hour later. "Are you sure you're not collecting on a favor, Lucas?"

Hallam shook his head. "I promise you, Liz, all I did was ask him to listen to you play. The feller don't owe me a damn thing."

They were sitting in Musso's Grill, down the street from the Egyptian Theater, having an early supper in celebration of Liz's new job.

"I was lost on the thing. I didn't know what I was doing."

"Sounded mighty good to me," Hallam told her. "Don't worry about it, Liz. You're goin' to do just fine."

Liz sighed. "I hope so, Lucas."

The food was good, as usual. For Hallam's money, John Musso served one of the best steaks in California. Musso himself stopped by their table to say hello. Hallam introduced him to Liz, and Musso said, "Welcome to Hollywood, Miss Fletcher. I hope you enjoy your stay here."

"Liz ain't just visitin', Johnny," Hallam said. "She's here to stay."

"That's right," Liz said, but Hallam noticed that she didn't sound too convinced of it.

Musso moved on to greet some of his other customers. Hallam spotted Clara Bow and Gloria Swanson and the Gish sisters. Doug Fairbanks and Mary Pickford were at the next table. Chaplin came in with a young girl on his arm and headed for a spot in the corner. This little grill was a popular eatery for movie folks, Hallam knew. Even early in the evening like this, seeing stars was no problem.

And Liz didn't recognize a damned one of them, he realized. Living in Chuckwalla for all those years, she hadn't even seen a movie until a couple of months earlier, when he had brought her into town for a premiere.

When they had finished their dinner and were strolling back to Hallam's car, Liz asked, "What now? Do you have some more plans for the evening?"

"Well . . . reckon I do. But they ain't the kind I wish they were."

Liz had her arm linked with his. She didn't break stride, but she glanced up at him and said, "You're going back to work, aren't you?"

"Got to, Liz. This case's comin' to a head. With any luck, it'll be all wrapped up in another day or two. Then I'll have plenty of time to spend with you."

"Yes, but I'll be working in the evenings at the theater starting tomorrow night."

"We'll have the days."

"Until another case comes along, or Bill Hart wants you to work in a picture with him."

Hallam didn't say anything in reply. It seemed like things had been a lot touchier between him and Liz since she had come to Hollywood. Before, when he only saw her when he could make it out to Chuckwalla, they had both enjoyed his visits. Enjoyed them a hell of a lot, in fact.

Right now there wasn't much he could do about the situation. He had an obligation to Carl McGinley and Danby

Swan to put a stop to whoever was trying to wreck their picture. That looked like B. W. Garrettson and the Klan. There were still a couple of other possibilities to check out, too, if the Klan angle didn't pay off. For one thing, all of his instincts told him that Jocko Burke was mixed up in this some way.

When the case was over, he'd straighten out this business with Liz. There'd be plenty of time then.

"I think I'd like to go home, Lucas," she said in a quiet voice.

"Reckon that'd be a good idea," Hallam said.

The sun had ducked below the horizon and shadows were creeping across everything when Hallam parked the flivver down the block from Larry Brownlow's rooming house. He leaned back in the seat as he cut the engine. There was no way of knowing how long he'd have to wait for Brownlow, but he had a feeling it wouldn't be long.

Hallam knew he had to put the problems with Liz out of his mind and concentrate on the job at hand. That wasn't so easy to do, though. It was starting to look like he was in love with her, and he knew for damn sure that he didn't like seeing her unhappy.

The sound of a door slamming cut through his thoughts. He looked up quickly and saw a young man crossing the porch of the rooming house. He went down the steps to the yard and headed for a Model A parked at the curb.

Hallam recognized him, all right. He had thought before that he vaguely remembered meeting Larry Brownlow on an earlier picture. The riding extras and the stuntmen and the prop boys all got along pretty well. They were the lower classes when it came to movie-making, but they all knew damn well there wouldn't be any pictures without them.

Brownlow was a young man of medium height with rusty hair and a thin face. He was competent at his job, if Hallam remembered right, and got along well with his fellow workers. Hallam wouldn't have picked him as a Klan member and a possible saboteur, but he had learned long ago that you couldn't always pick out the bad ones by looking.

Brownlow cranked the Model A into life and then got in, pulling away from the curb. Hallam gave him a little lead, then fell in behind him.

If he'd had his druthers, Hallam would rather track a man across the wilderness on horseback than tail a car in the big city. Once a car had passed along a road, it didn't leave any signs behind it. You had to stay within sight of your quarry, and if you could see him, that meant *he* could see *you*.

And if Brownlow *was* part of the plan to ruin *Death to the Kaiser!*, there was a good chance he'd be nervous and watching his backtrail.

Hallam stayed as far behind as he could and still keep an eye on Brownlow's car. Their route led north, as Hallam had suspected it would, toward the hills. Brownlow drove up Laurel Canyon to Lookout Mountain Road, going ever higher. The engine of Hallam's flivver began to labor slightly, and he knew that Brownlow's Model A was probably doing the same. At one time, there had been a trolley running up to the top of Lookout Mountain, and a luxury hotel there had attracted quite a bit of business for a while. But the inn had burned down and the trolley had been scrapped, and now the area was fairly deserted.

A good place for a secret meeting, Hallam mused.

His speculation proved to be right. Brownlow drove to the ruins of the old inn and parked his car there. There were a couple of dozen vehicles already parked there, and Hallam had spotted more headlights behind him on the road. This looked like it was going to be a well-attended rally.

And the best thing for him to do, he realized, might be to join right in.

He parked a little way from Brownlow's car. Other autos were pulling in behind him, and there was a steady stream of people walking past the burned-out inn to a large, sloping meadow behind it. Some of them were wearing the white robes and hoods, but others were just in street clothes.

The moon had come out by now, casting plenty of light to guide Hallam as he fell in step with several other men. So far he hadn't seen any women, and he didn't think he was going to. There were women in the Klan, from what he had heard, but he had a feeling these rallies were all-male affairs.

He hadn't spotted B. W. Garrettson, either. Brownlow was about twenty yards ahead of Hallam on the trail, and Hallam was keeping an eye on him. If his suspicions were correct, Garrettson would probably contact Brownlow sometime during the evening.

A large shape bulked up out of the darkness at the other end of the meadow, and as Hallam drew closer, he recognized it as a rough stage with chairs on it. The crowd of men was grouped in front of it, and to one side was a tall cross. Hallam smelled the sharp odor of kerosene as he approached the wooden cross.

A smaller group of men came out of the trees to one side of the meadow, several of them carrying blazing torches. All of them wore white robes and hoods. The ones carrying torches spread out around the clearing while the others climbed steps onto the platform. The light from the torches was garishly bright and cast deep shadows. A red glow covered the whole meadow.

Hallam stood among the Klansmen, well aware that he was taller than most around him, hoping that he didn't stand out too much. One of the men next to him glanced over and said, "Ayak?"

Hallam frowned. "Bad ear," he said, tapping his right ear. He wondered what in the blue blazes the man was talking about.

"Ayak?" the man said in a louder voice. He had a large metal button pinned to his coat proclaiming AKIA. "Are you a Klansman?"

There was nothing Hallam could do but venture a guess.

Looking at the button the man was wearing, he said proudly, "A Klansman I am."

The man smiled and nodded, and Hallam knew that his wild shot had hit the mark. He just hoped to hell that the man didn't use one of the secret handshakes on him. There was no way he could bluff through that.

"I don't think I've seen you here before," the man said. Everyone seemed to be chatting before the actual meeting got underway. It reminded Hallam of a church service that hadn't quite gotten started yet.

"Just moved here from Colorado," Hallam said. That was probably far enough away to be safe.

"I hear that Grand Dragon Locke is doing great work there."

"Yes, sir," Hallam agreed. He'd never heard of this Locke fellow, but with a title like Grand Dragon, he had to be important.

"Do you know any of the leaders here?"

"Not yet. Figured I'd meet 'em tonight."

The Klansman nodded. "I'll introduce you to Kleagle Garrettson."

"That'd be mighty nice of you."

So Garrettson was a kleagle, whatever that was. The title suited him, Hallam thought wryly.

The rally got underway with a long, rambling prayer from one of the men on the platform. He threw back his hood before he began praying. Hallam supposed that was so God could see who was talking to Him.

Following the prayer, another of the hooded men got up and spoke, and what started out as a general welcome to the meeting soon turned into a passionate speech about the evils of colored people, Jews, Catholics, and foreigners, and the need to protect white America against their insidious influences. Hallam quit listening after the first few minutes and just kept his eye on Larry Brownlow, who was watching and listening with an enraptured look on his face.

The boy had been sucked in, all right, and Hallam didn't doubt that he'd do anything his kleagle asked him to. A prop man had access to just about all of a movie studio, and folks tended not to notice him as long as he got his job done. Brownlow could have been responsible for all the trouble, even the sabotage on Hank's plane. Hallam wanted to talk to Hank again and find out if he remembered Brownlow being around the Spad before it took off.

A familiar voice caught Hallam's attention. He looked up at the platform and saw that another man had come forward to give a speech of his own. His hood was thrown back, too, and the flushed features of B. W. Garrettson stared out triumphantly at the scores of men who had come to the rally.

"Fellow Klansmen!" he shouted. "We are here to put an end to the degradation of white men! We are here to cast out the corruption and putrid stench of foreign lands! We are here to give a sign to all the polluters of our God-given freedoms as white Americans!"

The words didn't sound like something Garrettson would normally say, and Hallam suspected that someone else had written the speech for him. He delivered it with fire in his eyes and sincerity in his shouted tones, though. Hallam had seen plenty of hellfire-and-brimstone preachers who operated the same way.

Garrettson flung an arm out toward the cross. "Here is our sign!" he trumpeted. "The symbol of our power that comes straight from God!"

One of the Klansmen carrying a torch stepped forward and tossed it at the base of the cross, stepping back quickly as the kerosene blazed up. The fire climbed the cross, spreading out both arms and leaping on up to the top. The inferno made the light suffusing the clearing more hellish than ever.

And in that bright red light, B. W. Garrettson surveyed the crowd, *his* crowd. His eyes fell on one particular man . . .

Hallam saw his lips moving and knew that Garrettson had

said his name. The kleagle of Hollywood suddenly pointed a finger that was shaking with anger at him, and his voice ripped out above the crackling of the flames.

"*Get that man!*"

NINE

The man next to Hallam frowned and then looked from Garrettson to Hallam. "What the hell . . . ?" he muttered. A similar ripple of confusion went through the whole crowd. Hallam started to turn away, but the man reached out and grabbed his arm. "Hold on a minute!"

"Sorry, friend," Hallam said.

He hit the man in the jaw.

The Klansman staggered, his hand coming off Hallam's arm. Hallam lunged away from him, pressing past other men toward the back of the crowd. A few reached out and tried to stop him, but he was moving faster now, bulling past them almost before they knew what had happened.

"Kill him!" Garrettson shrieked.

Hallam ducked a punch and drove an elbow into the attacker's side, knocking the man out of the way. Others were taking up the chant now, yelling for him to be stopped.

This was going to get ugly in a hurry.

Hallam didn't want to have to shoot his way out of here. He

had no sympathy for the Klansmen, but he didn't want to kill any of them, either.

Still, he had heard stories about the floggings and the torture that the Klan handed out to those it considered its enemies. Damned if he'd stand for that.

He burst out of the knot of angry men with blows raining on his back. Sort of like running the gauntlet, he thought fleetingly, and these Klansmen might turn out to be just as dangerous as any Indians. He headed for the parked cars, circling around the old inn and losing precious seconds.

His knee was already aching, a steady throb that turned into a jolt of pain every time his weight came down on that leg. Most of the men behind him were younger and in better shape. He had to slow them down.

Hallam jerked to a halt, spinning around and yanking the Colt out of its holster. He had never been one to fan a revolver. It was hard on the gun and damned near impossible to hit anything when you did it. But sometimes it could have its uses.

The five cartridges in the cylinder exploded in one long, rolling roar of thunder as Hallam used the base of his left hand to slam the hammer back again and again. The slugs went wild, all of them plowing into the ground well in front of his pursuers, but the blast of the gunshots and the flickering flame from the Colt's muzzle made the men scatter.

Hallam ducked around a corner of the inn. The wall here was still partially standing, and it gave him a little cover. He heard shots behind him but didn't wait to see how close they were coming. As he ran, he dug more shells out of his pocket and started reloading the Colt. He glanced over his shoulder, saw robes flapping in the night as the Klansmen rounded the corner.

The flivver was only a few yards away now. Hallam threw another wild shot behind him, then piled into the car, his foot thumping against the starter. It ground away maddeningly for a few seconds, then the motor caught with a spluttering roar. Hallam slammed it into gear and took off.

As he spun the wheel and fed gas to the motor, he heard the thud of a bullet into the flivver's body. Hoping that the next one wouldn't find the gas tank, he sent the car into a tight turn that made it graze one of the other vehicles. Then he was heading away from the old inn, bucketing down the rough surface of Lookout Mountain Road. Rugged or not, he didn't slow down until he reached Laurel Canyon Road and turned onto it.

As he headed back down the canyon, craning his neck every now and then to check for lights behind him, he could see the whole glittering panoply that was Hollywood. As always, it looked like the entire town was throwing a party. If the lights of the city were visible up here, that meant that the burning cross could be seen from down below. He was sure that had been the Klan's intention.

They were sending a message, Garrettson had said. A message that Hollywood couldn't keep ignoring forever.

And as far as he could see, Hallam decided, he hadn't accomplished a damned thing tonight.

Well, he *had* confirmed that Larry Brownlow was a dedicated member of the Klan, but he had been pretty sure of that already. He was still in the position of having to wait until Garrettson and Brownlow made another attempt to ruin the picture so that he could catch them in the act.

If he could nab Brownlow, the boy would collapse and implicate Garrettson. Hallam was sure of that.

He followed Laurel Canyon back down from the hills. By the time he got to Hollywood Boulevard, he had come to the conclusion that no one was chasing him. Maybe Garrettson had decided that tonight would throw a scare into him.

If that was the case, then Garrettson didn't know the first damn thing about Lucas Hallam.

He was limping pretty badly as he climbed the stairs to his apartment. The lights were still on in Liz's place, since it wasn't even ten o'clock yet, but Hallam didn't stop. Even if she wasn't too happy with him these days, he knew she'd feel sorry for him and fuss over him, and he didn't want that. The knee would be better by morning, and if he didn't have to go running hell-for-leather away from a bunch of crazy folks again for a few days, it'd be as good as it ever was.

As he unlocked the door of his third-floor apartment and stepped inside, the telephone began to ring.

Hallam left the lights off and went over to the entrance to the kitchen. The phone was on the wall there, just inside the door. He reached around and lifted the receiver to his ear, leaned his head closer to the mouthpiece.

"Hallam," he said.

"Hello, Lucas, it's me," a worried voice said quickly.

It took Hallam a second to realize who was on the other end, then he said, "Howdy, Hank. What can I do for you?"

"Are you busy right now, Lucas?"

Hallam thought about his aching knee and the way it would feel to sink down into a tub of hot water, and he said, "I did have some plans. You got trouble, boy?"

"I don't know. I've been thinking about everything that's happened, and I've come up with something pretty strange. Can you come out to the studio?"

Hallam tried not to sigh. "What the hell are you doin' out there at this time of night?"

"Like I said, thinking. I'd really appreciate it if you could come out here, Lucas."

"Reckon I can." Excitement began to take the place of Hallam's weariness. "This is somethin' about the case, right?"

"Well . . . I'm not sure. I don't think I can explain it over the phone."

"All right. Reckon if the guard'll let you in, he'll let me in, too."

"I didn't come in through the gate. I came through the back lot."

That was the kind of thing a young hothead like Hank would do, all right, Hallam thought. "Where'll I find you?"

"I'll be in Building A, where the aerodrome sets are."

"I'll be there as quick as I can," Hallam promised. He hung the phone's earpiece back on the hook.

The boy had sounded serious and plenty worried and confused. For all of his youth and brashness, Hallam thought that Hank Schiller had a good head on his shoulders. Whatever the young pilot had discovered, it might well be worth checking out.

That hot water would just have to wait.

Hallam knew where to find the small gravel road that led around behind the studio back lot. He followed it until he found Hank's roadster parked next to the wire fence. Hallam wasn't too fond of the idea of clambering over the fence, but that seemed to be the only way in.

When he looked closer, though, he found that a section of fence was loose and only required bending back slightly to create an opening. It looked like Hank and maybe some others made a habit of sneaking into the back lot.

Hallam frowned. McGinley ought to know about this. If he could think of a way to tell the producer without getting Hank into trouble, he would.

There was still plenty of moonlight, and as Hallam moved through the streets between empty shells of buildings, he was struck by the eeriness of the place. He had been on other back lots when they were dark and deserted, and they had never failed to remind him of some of the ghost towns he had seen scattered through the West. There was an important difference, though—the ghost towns had once been alive and were now dead. The only real inhabitants these movie back lots had known were shadows and fantasies.

Here it was hard to believe that the hustle and bustle of Hollywood Boulevard was only three blocks away. The picture business lived in its own insulated world, all right.

Hallam followed the path up to the studio complex itself. There were a few lights on in the office building. Somebody working late in an editing room, maybe, or else just the cleaning lady making her rounds. There were small lights burning over the doors into the other buildings, as well.

Hallam headed for Building A. As he passed the little alleyway between A and B, a small side door down the alley opened and a figure darted out. Whoever it was, they were coming from Building A.

"Hank? That you, boy?" Hallam called.

The figure stopped in its tracks, and Hallam saw an arm lift in an all too familiar motion.

He threw himself to the side as a gun blasted.

Instinct had the Colt in his hand before he hit the asphalt. The shadowy figure was running away, but as Hallam scrambled to his feet, the stranger paused and flung another shot at him. Hallam heard the bullet whine close by his head.

Hallam didn't like shooting at somebody when he didn't know who it was, but damned if he was going to be a helpless target. He brought the Colt up and squeezed off a shot.

The figure ducked around the far corner of the building, and from the way it was moving, Hallam knew he had missed. He loped down the alleyway, the Colt ready in his big hand. He knew he might be running into an ambush, but whoever the stranger was, he had been up to no good. Hallam didn't want him getting away just yet.

He hauled up before he got to the corner and edged around it, staying low. He heard the sound of running footsteps getting fainter. Hallam threw himself into a run again, grunting with the effort.

As he went around another corner, he saw the running man silhouetted against one of the lights in the office building. Hallam couldn't tell anything about him at this distance. Skidding to a stop, Hallam raised the big pistol for a final shot, knowing it was one he could make.

His knee buckled just as he squeezed the trigger.

"Dammit!" Hallam howled as he caught himself before he

could fall. He knew that his shot had gone way high and wild. He peered toward the front gate, having seen his quarry dart in that direction as the Colt blasted, but he couldn't spot the man anymore. Hallam headed that way himself.

He heard the whine of the motorized gate sliding open and uttered a heartfelt curse. Hurrying past the guardhouse, he paused in the open gate and looked up and down the street.

Nothing.

A grimace jerked at Hallam's mouth. The man could have ducked in a hole somewhere, or he could have had a car waiting outside the gate. Hallam hadn't heard a motor, but that didn't mean anything. The street was on an incline here; a car could have easily coasted a few blocks before being started.

Where was the guard?

Hallam swung around as that question occurred to him. He went to the guardhouse, the Colt still gripped tightly in his hand. The door into the little building was ajar. Hallam reached out and shoved it all the way open with the barrel of his gun.

Light spilled out. Hallam stepped into the doorway and looked down at the sprawled figure of the blue-uniformed guard. His cap was crumpled in a corner, telling Hallam that it had been knocked off the man's head. Hallam knelt beside him and studied the ugly gash in his scalp.

The guard must have heard the shooting and stepped out just in time to get in the way of the fleeing man. The man had slugged him, knocking him back into the building, and then paused long enough to operate the controls that opened the gate.

Well, there might be some good to come out of this after all, Hallam thought. The guard might have seen the intruder well enough to recognize him.

Could it have been Larry Brownlow, or Garrettson himself? It was possible, Hallam supposed. He had had time to drive home from the Klan rally and then come out here. There would have been time for either Garrettson or Brownlow to get here, too.

He glanced up at the hills, his eyes scanning their dark ridges for any sign of the burning cross. It must have burned itself out by now, though, because there were no flames to be seen.

The guard let out a moan. Hallam put a finger against his neck and found a strong pulse. He didn't think the injured man would be waking up any time soon, though.

"Reckon you'll be all right, old son," Hallam muttered. He straightened and picked up the telephone on the small desk in the corner. A quick call to the police brought a promise of an ambulance on the way. "You stay put, mister, you hear?" warned the cop who had taken the call.

Hallam hung up. Staying put was something he didn't intend to do. Ever since he had seen that mysterious figure skulking around, a cold fear had been growing inside him.

He had to find Hank.

Hallam replaced the two shells he had fired with new rounds as he strode toward Building A. His knee still hurt, but he didn't pay any attention to it. The big door made a lot of racket when he opened it, enough to alert anyone inside. He called Hank's name anyway.

There was no response.

The coldness inside him growing, Hallam walked through the huge building, heading toward a light on one of the sets. He could see well enough to make his way around the equipment that cluttered the place, weaving through a labyrinth of lights and cameras and cables and scenery flats.

He saw the aerodrome set with its plain wooden walls covered with military maps. It looked a lot like the speakeasy Lafayette's. There were long wooden tables and straight-backed chairs. An empty wine bottle sat on one of the tables.

Hallam saw a booted foot on the floor.

He knew what he was going to find, but it was still a shock when he stepped around the table and saw Hank Schiller lying in a lifeless heap. There was a thin coating of sawdust on the plank floor, and from the marks in it, Hallam could tell that Hank's fingers had scrabbled aimlessly against the wood as he died.

The boy was on his right side. He had been shot once in the chest. There wasn't much blood.

Hallam went down on his haunches beside the body and looked bleakly at what was left of Hank Schiller. For a moment, instead of a corpse, Hallam saw the young daredevil of the skies again, the wind whipping his scarf, an excited grin playing over his face as he put his plane through one reckless maneuver after another.

He had wanted to be a gunfighter, too. Who knew what other dreams he had had?

Whatever they were, they wouldn't come true now. Hallam forced his mind back to the task at hand. He looked closely at the marks in the sawdust, just on the chance that Hank had lived long enough and been coherent enough to leave some kind of message. There was nothing there, though. From the looks of the wound, the slug had taken him in the heart. He wouldn't have been conscious long enough to do anything.

Hank had said on the phone that he had found out something strange. The identity of the person causing all the trouble on the picture? That was Garrettson and Brownlow, wasn't it? Suddenly, Hallam wasn't sure of that. Hank's murder was one more twist in a case that just refused to stay simple.

But Hallam was sure of one thing. Somebody had snuffed out this boy's life, ending all his hopes and joys and promise with one damn bullet. Hallam was going to find that somebody.

And then he'd do a little ending of his own.

There was a step behind him. A shaky voice ordered, "Hold it, mister! Drop that gun!"

Hallam put the Colt on the floor beside him and slowly stood up, lifting his hands into the air as he turned. He didn't want to spook some trigger-happy cop into shooting him.

The blue-suited patrol officer didn't look much older than Hank, and he was scared. The barrel of the big pistol that he gripped in both hands was quivering.

"Take it easy, son," Hallam told him quietly. "It's all over."

For now, he thought . . .

TEN

Hallam remembered a time when he had ridden thirty miles in a sandstorm with a bullet in his arm.

He hadn't felt much worse then than he did the morning after finding Hank Schiller's body.

Most of the night had been spent talking to cops. First he had told his story to the young patrolman who had answered the call, then repeated it every time someone new showed up. Finally, Ben Dunnemore came slouching in, and Hallam had to tell it one more time.

By that time, it had been pretty well established that Hallam hadn't shot Hank Schiller, that there had been someone else at the studio. The guard had recovered consciousness before being taken to the hospital to get his head sewed up, and he had told the cops about being clubbed by somebody running up to the gate.

Unfortunately, it had all happened so fast that he hadn't

gotten a good look at the man. He was able to say positively that it hadn't been Hallam, however.

"He had something on his head," Hallam heard the guard telling one of the detectives. "Some kind of mask or disguise. But it was dark, you know. I just saw his shape running at me, and then boom."

Yeah, boom, Hallam thought. Probably the last sound that Hank Schiller had heard.

When Dunnemore arrived, he talked briefly to his detectives, then jerked a thumb at Hallam. "Come on, Lucas," he said. "We've got to talk."

They went to a secluded corner of the building while the photographers and fingerprint men worked on the actual murder scene. Dunnemore took the makin's from his jacket pocket and started rolling a cigarette. "Why don't you tell me about it, Lucas?" he asked mildly.

Hallam ran through the story again, starting with the sabotage on the airplane and its near crash. He held back any mention of Jocko Burke and didn't detail his suspicions about Danby Swan, but other than that, he came clean.

Those omissions would be more than enough to make Ben mad when he found out about them, but he couldn't get too upset if Hallam gave him the killer. And that was exactly what Hallam intended to do.

This was personal, and where Hallam came from, there were some things a man tended to himself. Dunnemore wouldn't see it that way, but Hallam couldn't do anything about that.

Dunnemore made notes on a pad while Hallam talked, then nodded as the big private detective wrapped up his story. "All right," Dunnemore said. "I've got the statement from the guard at the gate. It looks to me like you're in the clear on the killing itself, Lucas. But there's still the matter of you trespassing on studio property."

"I don't reckon the studio'll want to press charges, Ben. I'm workin' for them, after all." Several raised voices from the entrance of the building drew their attention, and Hallam glanced in that direction. "Reckon you can ask Carl McGinley about that," he went on. "There he is now."

McGinley came striding into the building past the cops at the door, and Dunnemore went to meet him. The producer looked worried and angry at the same time, and he was so upset that his pudgy body was quivering.

He spotted Hallam and exclaimed, "Lucas! What is this? Somebody said something about Hank—"

"It's true, Carl," Hallam said. "He's dead."

McGinley shook his head. "I can't believe it. It doesn't make any sense."

"Most of the time murder makes sense if you know where to look for the reason," Dunnemore said. "I'm Lieutenant Dunnemore from Homicide, Mr. McGinley. Hallam here has been telling me about your troubles on this picture. You should have reported them to the police."

McGinley grimaced. "You know how the movie business is, Lieutenant. We like to wash our own dirty laundry if we can. I don't understand why anybody would want to kill Hank, though."

Hallam glanced at Dunnemore, who nodded his permission. Quickly, Hallam told McGinley about the telephone call that had summoned him to the studio. "I figure Hank found out something about what was happenin' on this picture, maybe even found some hard evidence. But whoever he had the goods on found out about it, too, and panicked. They got here before I did."

"But I thought that Garrettson—"

"Could have been him. Or it might've been a feller you've got workin' here called Larry Brownlow."

McGinley frowned. "Brownlow? The prop boy?"

"He's a member of the Klan." Hallam told him about the rally he had disrupted earlier in the evening. McGinley began to nod.

"Brownlow could have set up some of the sabotage, all

right," he admitted. "Hell, he could have done all of it. Who pays attention around a movie set? Everybody's worried about their own particular job."

"I'm going to have Brownlow and this Garrettson picked up," Dunnemore said. "You've got addresses on both of them?"

Hallam nodded. "Either one of them would have had time to get here and kill Hank, Ben."

"Not if they've got alibis. We'll just have to wait and see."

That was going to be interesting, all right. Hallam had a feeling that both of the Klansmen would have alibis. Whether or not the alibis would be genuine was another question.

Something occurred to Hallam. "How'd you know something was goin' on here, Carl?" he asked McGinley. "Did the cops call you?"

"I was wondering about that, too," Dunnemore said. "We hadn't gotten around to calling yet."

"Danby Swan called me and told me," McGinley replied. "Isn't he here? He said he was driving by and saw all the commotion, so he stopped at a drugstore to let me know about it. He said he was coming back here to check it out."

Hallam and Dunnemore glanced at each other. "Haven't seen him," Hallam said.

"I'll check." Dunnemore went over to one of the other officers and conferred with him for a minute, then came back to Hallam and McGinley and said, "He could have been here. One of the men on the gate reported that somebody tried to get in earlier. The guy said he worked for the studio. Our man wouldn't let him in, though, since the investigation was still in progress."

"I had to practically fight to get in myself," McGinley said. "The cop at the gate wouldn't let me inside until I insisted he use the gatehouse phone and call in here. One of your detectives told him to pass me on through."

A frown creased Hallam's craggy brow. The fact that Danby Swan had been in the area earlier wasn't necessarily incriminating, but it was sure as hell interesting. Hallam hadn't forgotten about the tryst between Wolf von Ottenhausen and Vesta Quist that he had interrupted, or the fact that Swan and the leading lady had had their own romance.

And the count *had* been scheduled to pilot that sabotaged Spad . . .

"I'll talk to Swan," Dunnemore said. "In the meantime, you remember that this case is in our hands now, Lucas. I don't want to be tripping over you everywhere I go."

"Now, Ben, you know me better than that. I don't go stickin' my nose where it ain't wanted."

The Homicide lieutenant laughed dryly. "Then how did it get busted like that?"

"Hell, that happened when I was just a younker back in Texas. This feller in a saloon thought I was takin' a shine to his gal. Actually, she was anybody's gal who had some dinero, but that ain't the point . . ."

Dunnemore shook his head and went to check notes with the other officers.

In a low voice, McGinley asked, "Are you going to keep investigating, Lucas?"

Hallam didn't say anything for a long moment, then: "I liked that boy, Carl. What do you think?"

"I think I feel sorry for whoever killed Hank."

Well, Hallam didn't feel sorry for the killer. As he climbed the steps to his apartment at four in the morning, the anger he felt was stronger than his weariness, stronger even than the pain in his knee. He was going to hold on to that anger. It would keep him probing and prodding until he got some answers.

And then there would be a reckoning.

He didn't sleep much. Several slugs from a bottle of bootleg whiskey helped the aching knee, but they didn't do anything to slow down the wheels racing in Hallam's head. He lay in his bed and stared up at the blank ceiling, trying to make some sense of the case, trying not to think too much about the way Hank had looked lying on the floor of the set.

Somewhere along toward morning, though, he dozed, the long hours finally taking their toll. When he woke up again, sunlight was streaming in the window of his bedroom and his mouth tasted like a possum had slept in it.

Hallam walked stiffly to the little kitchen and shoved the bottle of whiskey aside. He had left it sitting on the counter the night before in case he might need it this morning, but a little hair of the dog was the last thing he wanted.

Coffee. Strong and lots of it.

That and the much delayed soak in a tub of hot water helped. By the time he left the apartment, it was nearly eleven o'clock and he felt almost human again.

He stopped by the police station, but Ben Dunnemore wasn't there and Hallam didn't want to talk to anyone else in the department right now. Ben would play straight with him and tell him if they had come up with anything. Anybody else would think he was just a meddling shamus and tell him to stay out of the case.

The guard at the studio had heard all about what had happened the night before, a highly exaggerated version probably. He tried to pump Hallam for a few moments, then gave it up. "Go on in," he said. "Mr. McGinley's probably expecting you."

"Reckon he is," Hallam agreed.

He was right. McGinley's beautiful secretary was on the phone, but she didn't ask Hallam to wait. Instead, she just waved him on through to the producer's private office.

McGinley was talking on the telephone, too, when Hallam went in and closed the door behind him. He looked up and nodded a greeting to Hallam, then said, "I know it's got you upset, Sid. It's got us all upset. Murder's never a good thing to have happen on a picture. But there's nothing we can do now but go ahead. There's no point in suspending production." McGinley listened a moment, then went on, "I'm glad to hear that, Sid. We won't let you down. Good-bye, sir."

He cradled the mouthpiece and looked at the instrument for

a long moment as if he wanted to take a club and smash it into a million pieces.

"One of the executives?" Hallam finally asked.

McGinley nodded. "They're worried about their investment. I suppose I can't blame them. This is a mess, just an absolute mess."

"The boy's dead, Carl," Hallam said softly.

McGinley winced. "You're right, of course. Problems with the boys in the front office aren't nearly as important as finding Hank's killer. We all liked the kid." He leaned back in his chair. "How are you feeling this morning, Lucas? From what you were saying last night, you'd had a pretty rough time of it."

"I've seen better days, but I ain't ready to throw in my cards just yet," Hallam said. "Anything new around here this mornin'?"

McGinley shook his head. "Everybody's upset, naturally. And the fact that there are cops hanging around just keeps reminding all of us what happened. But there haven't been any problems. Danby has everybody working. They're shooting some of the Parisian nightclub stuff over in B. You hear about Brownlow?"

Hallam shook his head and asked, "Did they find him?"

"Arrested him last night, according to that cop friend of yours. He called a little while ago."

"What happened? Did he confess to workin' for Garrettson?"

"He didn't confess to *anything*. The lieutenant said he was one scared kid when the subject of murder came up, but he didn't lose control. He has an alibi for last night, Lucas. Says he went right home after that Klan rally, and his landlady confirms that he was there."

"Reckon her testimony is solid?"

"Dunnemore seemed to think so."

That eliminated Larry Brownlow as a suspect in the murder, if the old woman at the rooming house was telling the truth, but he still could have been the inside man in Garrettson's campaign against *Death to the Kaiser!*

"Dunnemore holdin' him?"

"Yeah. They hadn't been able to locate Garrettson yet, and I think they want the Brownlow kid to sweat some more."

Hallam nodded. Not a bad idea.

"What do you plan on doing, Lucas? Are you going to try to find Garrettson?"

Hallam hesitated, then said, "I ain't sure Garrettson is our man, Carl. He maybe did some of them other things, but somebody else could've killed Hank. Reckon the cops can find Garrettson quicker than I can, so I figured I'd look into some of the other angles."

McGinley frowned. "I don't understand. Why else would someone want to kill Hank Schiller?"

"Don't know," Hallam admitted with a shrug of his broad shoulders. "But I aim to keep pokin' at this thing until maybe I come up with something. You ever poke around a bunch of rocks, Carl?"

"Not since I was a kid, I suppose. What's that got to do with anything?"

"You poke around long enough, you're liable to scare up a scorpion."

"Then what?"

"You stomp the hell out of the little bastard. He ain't good for nothing."

McGinley laughed humorlessly. "And that's what you intend to do to the killer."

"Like I said, I'm goin' to poke around, see what comes out from under the rocks." Hallam stood up.

"Well, good luck."

The telephone rang again as Hallam left the office.

He paused at the secretary's desk. "Been pretty hectic all mornin', has it?"

She smiled up at him tiredly, beautifully. "I'll say. You

wouldn't want to answer the phone for a while so that I can take a break, would you?"

Hallam grinned back at her. "Don't use them modern gadgets any more than I have to, ma'am."

He walked over to Building B, where the filming of *Death to the Kaiser!* was going on today. On the way, he passed several actors and crew members whom he knew, and most of them had heard what had happened and wanted to know the inside story. Hallam put them off and hoped he wasn't too sharp with any of them. The aviation picture was hardly the only film the studio had in production, and these people hadn't known Hank Schiller. They could be forgiven a little morbid curiosity.

Hallam hadn't known Hank long himself. He had only spent part of two afternoons and a morning with the boy. That had been long enough to start to like him, though. Besides, Hank had been a fellow Texan. That counted for something, too.

McGinley had said there were cops around the studio this morning, but so far Hallam hadn't seen any of them. Probably they were in Building A, he decided. No one challenged him as he went into B.

Swan was setting up a shot on a big set that was supposed to be the inside of a hot nightspot in Paris. Hallam spotted Rodger Kane in a fancy uniform and Vesta Quist in a low-cut, sparkly evening gown. There were a lot of extras sitting at the tables surrounding the dance floor, some of the men in uniform, some in tuxedos. The women were all lovely and all wearing fake jewels. Hallam saw Lorraine von Ottenhausen at one of the tables near where Kane and Vesta were sitting.

"Then you turn and look and see your rival sitting there, Vesta," Danby Swan was saying. "You have to struggle to hold your anger in, but at the same time you're determined to fight for your man."

"Of course, Danby darling," Vesta said. "I never give up on a man when I want him."

Swan's mouth tightened, but he made no response other

. than to say, "All right, I think everyone understands what's going on in this scene. Let's run through it once, and then we'll shoot it."

Hallam found a spot well out of the way and watched as the cast ran through the scene. A dance band was playing on a small stage at the back of the set. Actually, Hallam saw, they were pretending to play. A stagehand cranked up a Victrola and played a scratchy record of dance music during the rehearsal. Cheaper to pay extras than actual musicians, Hallam knew.

The script had Kane and Vesta drinking champagne and laughing gayly, then getting up to dance. Before they could reach the floor, though, the character played by Lorraine intervened, trying to get Kane to dance with her. As Hallam watched, he thought that if the confrontation had been between some of the saloon girls he had known, there would have been some eye-gouging and hair-pulling going on.

That made him think of Liz. He frowned. Today was the first day of her new job, and he hadn't even stopped to wish her luck. He hadn't thought of it. He had been anxious to get to the studio and start his digging.

"A bit of typecasting, don't you think?" a low voice asked from beside Hallam.

He looked over and saw Simon Drake. The pilot's already lean face was even more drawn this morning. Hallam had seen the way all the veteran pilots had taken Hank under their wings. The news of Hank's death must have hit Drake hard.

"Don't reckon I know what you mean," Hallam said.

Drake nodded toward the set. "Casting Lorraine von Ottenhausen as a German spy in Paris. All the rumors during the war said she actually was one."

Hallam remembered McGinley and Swan mentioning that fact. He said, "You ever run into her there?"

Drake shook his head, a thin smile on his lips. "I'm afraid that Lorraine and I moved in different circles of society. Before the war I was a schoolteacher in Connecticut, Mr. Hallam. When I was in Paris I went to the museums, rather than the nightclubs. But I heard a great deal of talk about Miss von Ottenhausen."

"You believe any of it?"

"I never saw any reason not to. She was a close associate of a man named Alain Freneau, and Freneau ran the German intelligence apparatus in France. At least he did until he was killed under mysterious circumstances."

"Mysterious circumstances, eh?" Hallam asked, years of habit making him curious about any unusual death.

Drake shook his head. "You must understand, Mr. Hallam," he said. "Many people died under mysterious circumstances in Paris during the war, especially people connected with some kind of secret service. I've heard Paris described as a veritable hotbed of spies, and believe me, it was. It would have been unusual if Freneau *hadn't* been murdered sooner or later." Drake paused a moment, then added, "I was glad I was at the front. Give me a good machine and an honorable enemy to face."

Hallam could understand that. "Better'n a smoky room and a knife in the back, I reckon."

Danby Swan called out, "Cut! That was very good. Now let's do it for the cameras, shall we?"

The actors moved back to their starting places while Swan conferred with his cameraman. Hallam knew they would do the master shot first, then get the close-ups and the cutaways. The cameraman called out to one of the grips to move a light standard slightly.

Hallam turned back to Drake. "What are you doin' here today? There ain't goin' to be any flyin' scenes, are there?"

The trenches in Drake's lean cheeks became deeper. "I'm here to invite some of the crew to Lafayette's tonight. Hank got along well with most of them. He'd want them to be there."

"A wake?" Hallam guessed.

Drake nodded. "I realize that's an Irish custom, rather than a German one, but most pilots have adopted that attitude to a certain extent. You have to be rather devil-may-care to trust your life to a plane."

Drake didn't strike Hallam as being devil-may-care at all, but he understood what the man was saying. He had seen the same attitude among cowboys. There were some jobs where being a little crazy helped.

"I believe Hank would have wanted you to be there, too, Mr. Hallam," Drake went on. "He told us about taking you up in the D.H.4 yesterday. He said you were a natural flyer."

Hallam couldn't help but grin. The boy had been kind to him. "He wanted me to show him how to be a fast gun," he said. "Reckon he liked most anything if it was excitin' enough."

"Yes," Drake agreed. "That was Hank. You'll come, then?"

"I'll be there," Hallam promised.

Drake nodded and moved over to talk to the stagehand who was playing the record on the old Victrola. The scene was under way again, this time with the cameras turning, but Drake was able to slide around the periphery of the set and talk to several members of the crew. Inviting them to Hank's wake had to be a painful duty for the man, but he wasn't going to shirk it.

Hallam lifted a hand in farewell as Drake slipped out of the building as soon as the shot was over. Danby Swan must have noticed the big door opening and closing, because he glanced over to see what was going on. His eyes met Hallam's, and his gaze narrowed. A few minutes later, after talking to the cameraman again, Swan came over to where Hallam was standing.

"Good morning, Mr. Hallam," the director said. "Could I help you?"

"Wouldn't mind havin' a word with you, when you get the chance," Hallam told him. "Don't want to interfere with your shootin', though."

"We're going to set the lighting up for some close-ups. My cameraman can do that, and it'll take a few minutes. I can talk to you right now, if you like."

"Reckon that'd be fine. You heard what happened last night?"

"I saw all the police cars here, in fact. I was the one who called Carl and told him that something was wrong."

So Swan wasn't going to deny that he was in the area. That meant he wasn't going to try to come up with an alibi. Of course, if he hadn't had anything to do with Hank's murder, the possibility of needing an alibi might not have occurred to him.

Or he could be trying to make Hallam, and the police, think just that.

"Mind tellin' me where you were goin' at that time of night?"

"It wasn't even midnight yet, Mr. Hallam. That's hardly as late as you make it sound, especially in Hollywood. There's something in the atmosphere here, you know, that seems to make a person require less sleep."

"The cops didn't ask you why you were drivin' by the studio?"

Swan's face tightened, and his eyes became unfriendly. "As a matter of fact, they did ask me, and it seems like you're going to persist in doing the same thing. Very well. I was on my way home from a party at the Montmartre. If you'll check the route, you'll see that there's nothing out of the ordinary about my driving by the studio."

Hallam figured that Ben Dunnemore would get around to doing just that. For the moment, he'd accept that part of Swan's story. "You happen to recollect what time you left that party?"

"Not precisely," Swan said in a frosty voice. "Am I to understand that you consider me a suspect in young Schiller's death, Hallam?"

"The cops have a pick-up order out on Garrettson," Hallam replied.

"That doesn't answer my question. What do *you* think?"

"I ain't made up my mind about anything yet."

Swan was obviously having a hard time keeping his temper under control. "Why the devil would I kill Hank Schiller?"

Hallam returned the director's glare, his own temper getting a little edgy. "Maybe he found out who sabotaged that airplane."

"He was nearly killed in that plane. Why would I try to ruin my own picture, for God's sake?"

"Wolf von Ottenhausen was supposed to be flyin' that crate. Could be he was the target." Hallam hesitated, then said, "I heard tell that von Ottenhausen and Miss Quist have been gettin' kind of close these days."

Swan flushed angrily, and for a moment Hallam thought the director was going to take a swing at him. He tensed to block the blow, but then Swan turned abruptly away from him.

"I'm going to see Carl," Swan snapped over his shoulder. "I'm going to put a stop to this senseless harassment."

He called out to the startled cast and crew to take a break, then strode furiously off the set.

Hallam ambled after him.

By the time Hallam reached the office building and started down the hall toward Carl McGinley's office, he could hear Swan shouting at the producer. As Hallam came into the outer office, the young secretary, on her feet and obviously flustered, said, "What did you *do* to Mr. Swan?"

"Ruffled his feathers, I expect." Hallam grinned.

"Well, you'd better get in there and unruffle them."

Hallam stepped into the inner office and closed the door behind him. Swan was standing over McGinley's desk, leaning on it with his palms flat on its surface. McGinley was staring up at him with a startled look on his broad face. As Hallam came in, Swan broke off and swung around to glare at him.

"Lucas!" McGinley exclaimed. "Did you accuse Danby of killing Hank Schiller?"

"Don't reckon I did," Hallam said calmly. "Happen he wants to confess, though . . ."

"You goddamn cowboy!" Swan spat. "You're through, Hallam. You're fired! I don't want to see you on this lot ever again!"

"That the way you want it, Carl?"

McGinley stood up and held out his hands, trying to soothe both of them. "I think we should all just calm down," he said. "We don't need any talk about firing anybody."

"I won't have him on the lot!" Swan insisted. "If you won't fire him, I will."

"The studio's payin' me, Swan," Hallam said. "Not you, and not Carl here. If there's any firin' to be done, I reckon the board of directors would have to do it."

"We hired you, not the board. And by God we can fire you."

McGinley sighed. "Danby . . . shut up."

Swan's mouth dropped open in shock. Hallam started to say something, but McGinley silenced him with a pointing finger. "You, too, Lucas," the producer continued. For a short, overweight man, he suddenly seemed totally sure of himself and his control over the situation. Producing pictures in Hollywood for a while could give a man that ability . . . if it didn't drive him crazy first.

Hallam knew that, and he suppressed a grin.

"Lucas, I think you'd better leave for now," McGinley went on. "Danby, you need to get back to the set. Time is money, you know, and we've got a picture to make."

"A picture I may well walk off of," Swan threatened when he got over his shock.

"No you won't. You're too good a director, too much of a pro. You'll get the job done."

For a long moment, Swan switched his angry stare from McGinley to Hallam and back again, then he said, "You haven't heard the last of this, Hallam." He turned on his heel and stalked out of the office, slamming the door behind him.

McGinley sank down in his chair with a heavy sigh. "Did you *have* to do that, Lucas?" he asked.

"Just asked the man a few questions," Hallam said.

"And made it sound like you think he killed Hank." McGinley frowned. "You don't, do you?"

"I ain't made up my mind," Hallam told him.

"Hell, you might as well suspect me!" McGinley looked up at Hallam's expressionless face for a moment, then started shaking his head and saying, "Oh, no. Oh, no."

"Right now I reckon I suspect everybody, Carl," Hallam said. "Figure I'll just keep pushin' and proddin' until some answers pop out." Hallam shrugged. "Maybe the cops'll arrest Garrettson and he'll confess."

"But if by some chance he's not guilty . . . ?"

"I'll find the one who is," Hallam said.

ELEVEN

Hallam spent the rest of the morning and the biggest part of the afternoon doing legwork that was necessary but futile. He found out from Carl McGinley where Swan lived and checked the route between Swan's home and the Montmartre Cafe. The director had been telling the truth about that much. If he had really been returning home from a party at the nightclub, it wouldn't have been unusual for him to drive by the front gate of the studio. And Eddie Brandstetter, the owner of the opulent Hollywood Boulevard nightspot, confirmed that Swan had indeed been at the party. Brandstetter didn't remember what time Swan had left, though.

So even though what Swan had told him was the truth as far as it went, Hallam knew that the director didn't have an alibi that would stand up in court.

Hallam had made a lot of friends in Hollywood, and as Simon Drake had pointed out, this was a town that practically ran on gossip. Plenty of people knew about the romance between Swan and Vesta Quist and were willing to talk about it, and by late afternoon, Hallam had a picture of a jealous man who had been thrown over by a woman whom he loved passionately. And since that time, half a year earlier, there had been no other women in Swan's life, at least none that anyone knew of.

Danby Swan was carrying a torch, no doubt about that.

Was that enough to drive him to murder?

Hallam headed back to his apartment around four-thirty. Liz would probably still be at her place. He hoped so; he wanted to wish her luck in her new job.

But when Hallam knocked on her door, there was no answer. He called her name, but there was still no response.

His mouth quirked in a grimace, and he said softly to himself, "Damn." He wished now that he had thought to stop and see her this morning before leaving.

Well, he thought, he could at least stop by the Egyptian Theater on his way to Lafayette's tonight. He might not get to talk to her, but maybe she'd see him and know that he was thinking about her.

The Egyptian was showing a DeMille picture. Hallam hadn't seen it and didn't want to. Like most of the cowboys working in Hollywood, he had no use for the pretentious director. He had to admit that DeMille's pictures were good box office, though. The Egyptian was packing in the customers.

The girl at the box office knew Hallam and waved to the usher at the door to let him go on through. Hallam went to the office and knocked on its door. A second later, the manager called for him to come in.

The man looked up from his desk with a smile. "Hello, Lucas," he said. "Say, Miss Fletcher is working out great so far. You hear her?"

Hallam could indeed hear the rich, melodious organ music

coming from inside the vast auditorium. It was muted out here but still distinct enough for him to know that inside it would be powerful and sweeping.

"Sounds like she's really poundin' that thing."

"I couldn't believe she'd never played an organ until yesterday. She came over today and practiced all afternoon, but she sounded fine to me from the start." The man's grin widened. "That's some lady you've got there, Lucas. If I wasn't a happily married man, I might go after her myself."

"Reckon she's special, all right." Hallam nodded. "Any chance of me gettin' to talk to her?"

The theater manager glanced at his watch. "The first feature will be over in about an hour. She'll have a few minutes then before the second showing starts. You could talk to her then."

Hallam pulled his turnip from his watch pocket and flipped it open. He shook his head. "Got to be movin' on," he said. "Reckon I'll just see her at home after work. Think I could step into the auditorium, get a look at her?"

"Sure. Help yourself. Just buy a ticket if you decide to stay and watch the picture."

Hallam grinned and shook his head.

Another usher opened the auditorium door for him. Hallam slipped into the vast, darkened room and stood for a moment at the back, beside one of the pillars that supported the big balcony. The pillar was covered with intricate scrollwork depicting Egyptian scenes. Hallam saw a sphinx and a pyramid and a pharaoh. The motif extended into the courtyard outside the theater, where there were plaster replicas of the same things.

Liz sat at the huge organ to the right of the screen. Hallam couldn't see her very well, but he caught the flash of her red hair. He didn't look at the film's images flickering on the big screen, but he did find himself getting caught up in the intensity of the music. She was good, damned good, and Hallam was glad he had found this job for her. He wanted her to be happy here, so that she wouldn't miss Chuckwalla too much.

He ducked out of the theater a few minutes later, striding

back down the street to his flivver. He was glad he had stopped, though he wished he had gotten a chance to speak to Liz, to find out what she thought about the job so far.

Time enough for that later, though.

Right now, he had a wake to attend.

Art Tobin opened the door a couple of inches, saw Hallam standing on the porch, and said, "Oh, it's you. Come on in." He stepped back and opened the door all the way.

Hallam walked into Lafayette's, his hat in his hands. Music filled the old house, and he recognized the bittersweet melody of a love song that had been popular back during the war.

Tobin had a drink in his hand. He gestured with it. "Come on, all the boys are in here."

He led Hallam into the big room that was appointed like the pilots' quarters of an aerodrome. There were perhaps forty men in the room, and Hallam recognized only a handful of them. He saw a few men from the movie studio, the ones Simon Drake had invited earlier in the day. Drake, along with Mackey Russell and Pete Goldman, was sitting at one of the long tables. Tobin headed in that direction.

Drake glanced up and saw Hallam. "Good evening," he said. "Evenin'." Hallam nodded.

"What're you drinking, Mr. Hallam?" Russell asked. "We've got whiskey and beer and whiskey."

"Reckon I'll have whiskey and save the beer for later."

"Sit down," Tobin said. "I'll bring you a drink."

He went over to the bar as Hallam sank down on the bench next to Pete Goldman. Goldman was staring morosely into his own glass of amber liquid.

Most of the men in the room were on their feet, milling around and drinking and talking. Hallam heard an occasional burst of laughter, but on the whole the event seemed rather subdued for a wake. The fact that Hank had been so young—and that he had been murdered—had to have something to do with that.

Tobin set a shot glass in front of Hallam and thumped a bottle of bootleg whiskey down in the center of the table. "There," he said. "That'll save us from having to go back to the bar as often."

Russell snagged the booze, refilled his glass, passed the bottle on to Drake. Drake shook his head and shoved it across to Goldman. From the looks of his glass, which was almost full, Drake wasn't drinking much.

The pilot was looking intently across the table at Hallam. After a moment, over the hubbub of talk and music, he leaned forward and said, "I heard what happened at the studio this morning, Mr. Hallam. Do you really think Danby Swan could have had anything to do with Hank's murder?"

Hallam glanced around at Tobin, Russell, and Goldman. They were watching him with grim interest. After a moment, Hallam said slowly, "Don't know if the cops consider him a suspect or not. Reckon I do."

"You're still investigating the case, then?" Russell asked. "I heard that Swan fired you."

"Swan tried to," Hallam admitted. "Carl McGinley talked him out of it. Don't reckon it would've mattered, anyway. I ain't backin' off this case."

"You were hired to find out who has been trying to ruin the filming of *Death to the Kaiser!*, as I understand it," Drake said. "Do you think Hank's murder is connected to that?"

Hallam shrugged his shoulders. "Could be. It's possible Garrettson was at the studio last night and Hank caught him there. But somebody else could've had a reason for killin' him that don't have a thing to do with the sabotage. That's what I'm lookin' into. Garrettson's gone to ground, but the cops'll root him out. Then maybe we'll know for sure."

Drake looked around at his companions. "We've been talking about all of this, Mr. Hallam, and we've come to a decision. If the studio does fire you, we want to hire you to investigate Hank's murder. His killer can't be allowed to go unpunished."

"Damned right." Hallam nodded. "Don't you worry about hirin' me. Like I said, it don't matter what the studio does. I'm on this case to the end."

He picked up his glass of whiskey, threw the fiery liquor down his throat.

He reached for the bottle and poured another shot into the glass. Several other men were drifting over to the table and sitting down. Hallam passed the bottle on to them.

Gradually, the liquor began to work on the gloomy atmosphere of the speakeasy. A few men began singing along with the records being played. The gramophone sitting on the bar was an old-fashioned one that might well have come from a French farmhouse that had been turned into a barracks. The songs it played were a mixture of love ballads and patriotic music, and the drinking men were carried away by the feelings evoked by the melodies.

Hallam sang along. He didn't know the words to many of the songs, but that had never stopped him before. He remembered going to brush arbor revival meetings as a boy. He hadn't known the words of the hymns, either, but he had joined in lustily on them.

The words hadn't mattered then, and they didn't now, either. Feelings were what counted.

The bootleg hooch flowed freely, and Hallam downed his share of it. He had never been one to get drunk easily, and he wasn't drunk now. But he was feeling a glow brought on by more than his feelings for Hank Schiller.

The evening wore on. Men drifted away. Most of the men who had come to this wake hadn't known Hank well. They were pilots, though, and that meant there had been an unspoken bond between him and them. They had come to honor his memory. That done, there was nothing else they could add.

Before the wake broke up, though, Simon Drake stood up and called for attention. Slowly, the conversations subsided, and someone stopped the music. When everyone in the room was looking at him, Drake raised his voice and said, "Before we go, I think some of us would like to say a few words about Hank Schiller."

The men nodded, waiting.

"Hank had not been one of us for a long time," Drake began. "He came to Hollywood a little less than a year ago. He was a good pilot, though, and he had no trouble getting work, despite his youth. I'd like to think that working with my friends and I made him a better pilot, but I don't want to take that much credit for something that may not be true . . . He had the touch to start with. When he was aloft, he and his plane were like one being." Drake blinked rapidly. "I shall miss him very much."

He sat down, his head sagging.

Pete Goldman stood up next, swaying slightly, his drink in his hand. "The kid was crazy," he said emphatically. "Don't let anybody tell you different. There wasn't a stunt he wouldn't try, no matter how wild it was. Directors loved him for that. But he wasn't foolhardy. He was smart. He could find a way to do things that the rest of us didn't think could be done. He hadn't been flying for years and years, like us, so he didn't know he was breaking the rules. He may have taught us as much as we taught him."

When Goldman was done, Mackey Russell slowly got to his feet. Hallam remembered how the stocky pilot had watched so intently as Hank landed the disabled plane. Now Russell said, "Pete told it right. Hank didn't give a damn for rules. He came to us all the time to ask us questions . . . I guess we were all like big brothers to him. He'd ask me how to do something, and I'd tell him, 'Hell, kid, that can't be done.' He'd want to know why not. If I told him that it never had been done, he'd say that was no reason not to try. He was so confident he'd get on your nerves sometimes, but you had to like him." Russell's voice broke slightly as he went on, "I guess he finally ran into something he should have backed off from."

He sat down heavily.

After a moment, Art Tobin stood up. "What Mackey said is true. Hank should have backed off from whatever got him killed. But since he didn't, it's up to us to settle the score for him." Tobin put his hand on Hallam's shoulder. "Some of you know this man. His name's Lucas Hallam, and he's a detective. He's going to find out who killed Hank. And then the score will be evened up. You have our word on that."

Hallam didn't know if he was supposed to say something or not. He hadn't known Hank well enough to make a speech about him . . . just well enough to want to find his killer. But from the way they were all looking at him, he knew something was expected from him.

Slowly, he climbed to his feet. "Reckon that's right," he said. "I aim to find the skunk who pulled the trigger on Hank. But right now it seems to me like we ought to maybe drink a toast to the boy. It ain't my place to make it, though." He looked at Drake.

Drake nodded and stood up. Raising his glass, he said in a loud, clear voice, "To Hank Schiller. Smooth flying, son."

He tossed back the drink.

Everyone in the room echoed the toast and then drank.

Most of the men left shortly after that, and the others didn't linger much longer. The wake was over, Hank had been said farewell to, and now it was time to get on with life. Soon, there was no one left in Lafayette's but Hallam and the four pilots who had worked so closely with Hank.

Hallam pushed his empty whiskey glass away and got up to go to the bar. He drew a mug of beer and leaned on the hardwood. "Noticed that von Ottenhausen wasn't here tonight," he commented.

"He wasn't invited," Russell said sharply. "Things are bad enough without having that Heinie around when you don't have to."

"Hank and von Ottenhausen weren't close at all," Drake said, his tone calmer than Russell's. "We didn't feel that he would be comfortable here, anyway."

"Because he was a German pilot and maybe shot down some of your friends?" Hallam asked.

"That's a good enough reason, don't you think?" Tobin replied. "He was with the Flying Circus the day they tore us to shreds. I can't forget that, and neither can anyone else who was there."

Hallam carried his beer back over to the table. "But Hank and von Ottenhausen got along all right during the filmin', didn't they?"

Drake said, "We all got along with von Ottenhausen. That's part of our job, after all. That doesn't mean we have to like him." Drake peered thoughtfully at Hallam. "Are you thinking that perhaps von Ottenhausen had something to do with Hank's death?"

"Like I said, I'm still suspectin' most everybody."

Drake smiled thinly. "Just on the basis of personalities, I'd say you'd do better to suspect Lorraine von Ottenhausen."

"Damned right," Goldman said. "That bitch would shoot anybody who got in her way. She killed her boyfriend in Paris, didn't she?"

"We don't know that. All we know is that someone killed Freneau."

"Knifed him. That's the way a woman would do it."

Hallam wasn't sure about that. He had always considered poison more of a woman's weapon. But this talk about Lorraine maybe being a murderess had him interested. "What happened to this Freneau feller?" he asked. "When was he killed?"

"Just a few days after that *Jadgstaffel* ambushed us," Drake said. "There was a great deal of speculation that Lorraine might have killed him, but no one could ever suggest an adequate reason for her to have done so. They were lovers, after all."

Russell laughed shortly. "Maybe that was reason enough. They had a fight over all the men Lorraine was sleeping with."

"That was Freneau's idea," Drake pointed out. "He was the one running the spy ring. He gave Lorraine her jobs."

"Maybe so, but I still think she killed him."

Goldman and Tobin nodded in agreement with Russell.

Drake turned back to Hallam. "I don't believe we answered your question, Mr. Hallam. Alain Freneau was stabbed in the back in his apartment in Paris. The place was ransacked, and the police said he was the victim of a robber. That seems likely to me. As you've heard, though, there was a great deal of gossip about Lorraine von Ottenhausen. She left Paris not long after that."

"How come you know so much about it?" Hallam asked.

"We were given a few days' leave following the dogfight that wiped out our squadron," Drake explained. "There was no place else to go but Paris. The newspapers there were full of the story, and naturally we read them."

"I was glad to see Freneau dead," Russell said savagely. "If it wasn't for him and Norton, a lot of my friends might still be alive!"

Hallam frowned. "Who's this Norton feller?"

Drake sighed and said, "Jack Norton. He was a pilot in our squadron. He went down that day in the ambush. He attacked three German planes at the same time. It was a very foolhardy maneuver, but we discovered later that he may not have wanted to come back from that mission."

"Why's that?"

"Because it seems very likely that Jack Norton is the one who sold us out and gave our plans to the Germans, passing them on via Alain Freneau. And Lorraine had a part in that, too." Drake's mouth tightened. "Jack thought he was in love with her."

Hallam was starting to understand now. "You think Freneau sicced Lorraine on your pal Norton and got him to give your squadron's flight plans to Freneau." It was a statement, not a question.

"You'd better believe it," Goldman said. "We found out later that Norton had been spending a hell of a lot of time with her in Paris. What else are we supposed to think?"

"Then how come he went along on that flight and got hisself killed?"

"Guilt," Drake replied flatly. "He finally realized what he had done and regretted it so badly that he went along to die with his friends. He made sure of it, in fact, by being foolhardy. Jack was hardly the most coolheaded person to start with."

Hallam finished his beer and went to the bar for more. When he got back to the table, he gave in to his curiosity and said, "Reckon you could tell me about that day?"

"I don't see why not," Drake said. "I think you might understand."

The day had dawned clear and bright. There were few clouds in the sky. Good flying weather. But as the hours went by, more clouds rolled in, and as it had turned out, that was favorable for the Germans. The squadron had flown east from the aerodrome at Pont-á-Mousson, looking for Boche observation balloons that were supposed to be ruining troop movements along the front. During the early part of the flight, they had encountered one of the huge German Gotha bombers, accompanied by two fighter planes. Downing the Gotha and its escort had proved to be an easy chore, but the brief battle had given the enemy pilots hiding in the clouds ample opportunity to study the strength of the American squadron. The Fokkers had dropped from the heavens, their Mercedes engines screaming, and ambushed the outnumbered Yanks in their Spads and Nieuports. Though the battle had no doubt seemed like an eternity to the doomed Americans, it had really taken no longer than twenty minutes. At the end of that time, all of the American planes had gone down in flames except for the four piloted by Drake, Russell, Goldman, and Tobin. All of their craft had sustained damage, but they were able to cut and run. The Germans could have downed them as well, but this battle was obviously over. The four survivors had been allowed to limp back to their field.

"It was the worst moment of the war for us," Drake finished, his voice quivering slightly. "Everyone at the aerodrome heard us coming, and they could tell that something was wrong. My ship was smoking badly, and for a moment, as I looked down and saw all those people watching, I was tempted to let her crash. It would have seemed normal enough, considering the amount of damage the plane had taken, and then I wouldn't have had to live with the shame of living when so many of my comrades had died. But . . . I landed safely. Even dying seemed futile at that moment."

Mackey Russell shook his head. "Not me, boy. I wanted to live more than anything, so I could get back up there in a good crate and kill some more Germans. None of it was our fault, Simon. It was Norton and the goddamned Boches."

"That's right," Pete Goldman added, and Art Tobin nodded. "We were sold out," Goldman said, "and the best thing we could do was try to even the score. Still, I know what you mean, Simon. It might have been easier to go down with the rest of the squadron."

Hallam understood what the men were saying. Just as he had done on his first visit to Lafayette's, he had lost track of time and gotten caught up in the tales of war. At first, he had asked about Wolf von Ottenhausen thinking it was possible that the count might have had something to do with Hank's death, but he had put that aside as he listened to Drake's steady voice telling of that bloody day in the skies over France.

The pilots were all quiet now. Hallam finished the beer in his mug, and set it down on the table.

"Was in Texas once a lot of years back," he said. "I was a deputy sheriff at the time, workin' under a man I admired and learnin' a lot. One day a bunch of owlhoots rode into town and hit the bank, got away with a lot of money after killin' a couple of folks. Naturally, we got up a posse and went after 'em. After a couple of hours, we come up on a couple of the bandits who'd been wounded and fallen behind the rest of the gang. They tried to shoot it out with us, but they didn't stand a chance, two against a dozen. We didn't know the main bunch had forted up in some rocks just ahead of us. We were feelin' mighty good 'cause we'd just downed two of the gang. So we rode hard, tryin' to catch up to the others. We rode right into 'em."

The pilots were silent, as caught up in Hallam's story as he had been in theirs.

"There was more of 'em than there were of us, and they had us in a crossfire. Didn't take 'em long. They cut us to ribbons. I come out lucky, just got a pretty good bullet burn alongside my ribs. Three of us rode away from there like bats out of Hades, and the outlaws let us go. But we could hear 'em laughin' behind us. When we got back to town, folks were in the street waitin' for us. But we didn't have the robbers, and we didn't have the money, and we didn't have most of the men we started out with. I was just a younker, but my head was hangin'. Seemed I'd let all them folks down, and myself, too."

No one said anything for a long moment, then Simon Drake asked, "What happened after that? I suppose the robbers were never caught."

"Not then. We identified the two dead ones, though, and found out which gang they'd been runnin' with. There was no way of knowin' who all the boys were who were in on that job, but it was planned by a couple of brothers named Kadey." Hallam stood up and carried his mug to the bar to draw another beer.

"Did you ever find them?" Tobin asked.

"In San Antone about a year later," Hallam said over his shoulder. "I was a U.S. deputy marshal by then, so I went to arrest them."

"What happened?"

"Bexar County had to pay for the buryin'. They'd already spent all of their cut from that bank job, long since."

The pilots looked at each other and grinned, all except Simon Drake. He said severely, "Did you make that whole story up, Mr. Hallam? It sounds like a script for a Western film."

Hallam turned from the bar, sipped his beer. "So happens

it's the truth," he said, unoffended by the question. "Wish I'd had the chance to tell it to Hank. Glad you boys got to hear it."

"Yes," Drake said slowly. "So am I." He lifted his drink. "One more toast, just between us, gentlemen. To Hank . . . and to settling the score."

Hallam lifted his mug, drank. It was a good toast.

TWELVE

It was very late when Hallam left the speakeasy. The easy camaraderie he felt with the pilots was unlike anything he had experienced in Hollywood except at the Waterhole. He was a little surprised that he had encountered another group of men who understood some of the things he had been and done. He had thought that no one knew what it was like to be a cowboy—except another cowboy.

This was one time he was glad he had been wrong.

As he drove home, he remembered that he had intended to stop by Liz's place after the wake. Hallam grimaced. It was probably too late for that.

Sure enough, her lights were out, he saw as he paused on the landing outside her apartment. For a moment he thought about knocking anyway, since he hadn't talked to her all day, but then he shook his shaggy head and decided against it. He could wake her up, but she wouldn't like it. The morning would be soon enough to find out how her first day at the Egyptian had gone.

His head was a little light as he finished climbing the stairs to his apartment. He had taken on quite a bit of the bootlegged hooch during the evening, and while liquor had never muddled him much, eventually it affected him. He was glad to strip his clothes off and fall into bed. Sleep came quickly.

The sheets were sweated and tangled when he awoke the next morning, though he didn't recall being restless during the night. As sometimes happened, there was a clear thought in his head as he woke up, something that he had overlooked until now.

He had completely forgotten about Jocko Burke.

Listening to the flyers talking about Lorraine von Ottenhausen the night before was probably what had put the thought in his brain. In Paris she had been hooked up with Alain Freneau, the agent of the German secret service. Now, in Hollywood, she had some sort of liaison with Jocko Burke.

Was she up to something with Burke, as she had been in Paris with Freneau? Something besides a quick romance?

Even if she was, it might have no connection with Hank's murder. Probably didn't, in fact.

But Hallam didn't want to overlook the possibility. There could always be more than one scorpion under a rock.

And he'd enjoy stomping Jocko Burke.

He had his usual breakfast of strong coffee, then went downstairs to check on Liz. He rapped on her door, waited a moment, knocked again.

She opened the door with a smile on her face. "Good morning, Lucas," she said brightly. "I thought that might be you at my door. Come in."

Hallam followed her into the apartment. She seemed to be in a good mood, and he was glad of that. He wouldn't have blamed her if she had been mad at him for neglecting her on her first day of a new job.

"Can I get you some breakfast?" she asked. Hallam thought she looked lovely. Her hair was slightly disarrayed from sleep, and she wore a dark green dressing gown belted around her trim waist. Hallam started to tell her he didn't want anything, then suddenly changed his mind.

"Reckon I could use a little something," he said. "Whatever you're havin'."

"Eggs and bacon and biscuits, what else would an old desert gal like me be eating? Sit down."

Hallam sat at the small table in her kitchen while she fixed the food. She had coffee brewing, and as soon as it was ready she poured a cup for him. It was the way he liked it.

A strange feeling began to come over Hallam as he sat there, watching Liz bustle around the kitchen. This scene was downright domestic, he thought, an older couple at breakfast time, comfortable with themselves and each other. They might have been together for years, rather than months. Anyone looking at them right now probably would never take them for what they really were—a private eye and an ex-saloonkeeper.

The bad part about it, Hallam realized, was that he didn't know if he liked the feeling or not.

"How's your case going?" Liz asked from the stove.

Hallam looked up, frowning. He hadn't talked to her all day yesterday. If she hadn't read the newspaper, there was a good chance she didn't even know about Hank's murder. He said, "You get a chance to look at the paper yesterday?"

Liz shook her head without looking at him. "I didn't go out and buy one. I was too nervous about the job starting last night." She glanced around, a sudden look of concern on her face. "What is it, Lucas? Has something happened?"

"You remember that boy I told you about, Hank Schiller?"

"The young pilot? Sure, I remember."

"Somebody murdered him night before last," Hallam said heavily.

Liz paled. "Murdered . . . ? Oh, Lord, Lucas. That's awful."

Hallam nodded. It was awful, all right.

He told her what had been happening since he had left her after dinner two nights earlier. As the story unfolded, she became more and more worried, Hallam could tell. She knew logically that he could take care of himself, but with a killer around, any woman would worry about her man investigating the case.

And it looked like he was her man, Hallam thought.

Liz brought the food to the table as Hallam finished his story. It was overcooked a little, because she had been distracted by the news about Hank. Hallam fell to and ate it anyway, and he had to admit it wasn't bad.

"Listen," he said earnestly, "there ain't a thing you can do about this case, so why don't you just try to put it out of your head? Tell me how the organ-playin' went."

"It went fine." Liz smiled. "It's a lot easier than I thought it would be. The people at the theater are nice, too." Her smile became more forced, and Hallam could see something in her eyes as she went on, "I'm still not sure I feel at home here, though. I just don't know if it's going to work out."

She was missing Chuckwalla, that was all. Hallam said, "Sure it'll work out. You've been doin' fine so far. You've got a good job and a nice place to live, and an upstairs neighbor who thinks you're prettier'n a whole field of bluebonnets."

"Who would that be?" Liz asked. The twinkle came back in her eyes as she teased him, and Hallam was glad to see it.

When he left, he felt better about the situation. Liz would settle in in time, he was sure of it. And when she was used to living in the city, it would be time for him to do some long hard thinking.

He was going to have to decide whether to ask her to marry him.

First, though, he had a murder to solve.

He headed toward Cahuenga and the police station. On the way, he stopped at a newsstand and bought a paper and a copy of *Argosy*. Hank's murder, which had been on the front page the day before, had slipped all the way to the back of the first section. There were no new developments in the case, according to Lieutenant Dunnemore, but an arrest was still expected shortly.

Hallam folded the paper and threw it onto the seat on top of the gaudy-covered magazine. The news report had been true at the time the paper was printed, but something could have happened since then. He drove on over to the station.

Ben Dunnemore was in his office. His lined face looked even more tired than usual as he glanced up at Hallam. "Shut the door," he grunted.

Hallam reversed a chair and straddled it, as usual, then said, "Reckon you know why I'm here."

"To see if the hardworking servants of the people have done their job." Dunnemore's voice was bitter this morning. "You remember what I said about that KKK trouble up in Inglewood, how it was discovered that a lot of people in law enforcement were also Klan members?"

"I remember," Hallam said.

"Well, it seems like a lot of them still must be, though nobody will admit it these days. Garrettson is still hiding out, and we can't seem to get any help in locating him. The sheriff's office claims they're helping, but it seems to me they're only making things worse. If this keeps up, we may never find the guy, Lucas."

"Reckon you've got a man watchin' his house?"

Dunnemore gave him an impatient look. "Of course I do. Not around the clock, but pretty damned close to it. So far there hasn't been any sign of him."

"You'll turn him up," Hallam assured his friend. "If there's anybody who can find that old boy, it's you, Ben."

"I appreciate the vote of confidence, Lucas, but I ain't sure Garrettson's not hiding out with one of our elected officials. That could make things sticky, if not downright impossible."

"You talked any more to Danby Swan?"

A grin tugged at the corners of Dunnemore's mouth. "I talked to him a couple of times. The second time he was foaming at the mouth because of something you said to him. Seems like you think he's a murderer, or something like that."

"I never accused the man. Could be a guilty conscience workin' on him, though."

Dunnemore shook his head. "I don't think so. Swan strikes me as telling the truth. I don't understand why you think he might be mixed up in this, anyway."

Hallam explained about the romance between Swan and Vesta Quist, adding the facts that Vesta was now involved with Wolf von Ottenhausen and that the so-called Steel Wolf had been scheduled to fly the sabotaged Spad.

"I see what you're saying." Dunnemore nodded. "You think Swan was trying to kill von Ottenhausen. The kid found some proof of that, and Swan had to shut him up. It could hold water, but don't you think Garrettson's a lot more likely to have done it?"

"Can't argue with that." Hallam didn't say anything about Jocko Burke. Dunnemore had evidently forgotten that Hallam had been asking about the little mobster a few days earlier, and Hallam didn't want to remind him of it just yet.

"Well, I'll say one thing for you, Lucas. With the exception of getting Swan's back up, you've been staying out of this case remarkably well. You're going to continue that, aren't you?"

"Told you you wouldn't have to worry 'bout trippin' over me, Ben," Hallam said.

That was true enough. Hallam was taking a different road to the truth. Whether or not it would lead him there was another question entirely.

Hallam's visit to the studio the morning before was enough pressure on Swan for the time being. McGinley probably wouldn't mind if he came back on the lot, but Hallam was going to stick to another angle today.

If there was a connection between Jocko Burke and either

Hank's murder or the previous trouble during the filming of *Death to the Kaiser!*, Hallam was going to find out what it was.

Even a part-time detective like him had some sources of information on the street. Hallam spent the morning talking to all of them he could find. He knew quite a few folks who operated just out of the shady side of the law, and most of them knew Jocko Burke. As he wore down boot leather and made his bad knee begin to ache slightly again, he found that he wasn't getting anywhere, however.

Burke had a big stake in the city's gambling, a smaller piece of the local rum-running operation. Most of his profits came from selling bootleg hooch in his speakeasy, not from bringing the stuff in to start with. He was also one of the men you could go see if you had something valuable enough and too hot to move with one of the many smaller fences in town. That was a minor part of his setup, but from what Hallam heard, he made good money at it.

He was also a dangerous man to cross. More than one of his contacts warned him to steer clear of Jocko Burke. People who gave him trouble usually wound up dead, one way or another.

Hallam had heard those warnings before, about a lot of different men. He was still alive, though.

Most of the others weren't.

He did come across one bit of possibly useful information that he hadn't known before. A boxing promoter named Herbie Warrender let Hallam buy him a drink in a speak near Legion Stadium. Burke was rumored to have a piece of a fighter or two, and Warrender confirmed that fact.

"Yeah," he said, smacking his lips over the glass of gin Hallam had bought, "I been up to his place a time or two to talk about bouts. Don' get the idea that any of 'em was fixed, though. I put on clean bouts, Hallam, you know that."

"I know, Herbie," Hallam agreed. "Where was this you talked to Burke, at the Pimlico?"

Warrender shook his bald head. "Nah, he's got a bungalow at the Palm Court. That's where I seen him. I've heard he's got a big house in Bel Air, but I ain't never been there."

Hallam nodded thoughtfully. The Palm Court was a sprawling complex of bungalows and apartments, its courtyards full of palms—what else—and shrubbery. The tenants there valued their privacy, and there was more than one love nest among the waving fronds of the palms.

"You remember the number of the place?"

"Seems like it was bungalow four. Yeah, that was it, number four." Warrender frowned. "Why you askin' all these questions about Burke, Hallam? He ain't nobody you want to mess with."

"Reckon I know that, Herbie. You can just say I'm a curious feller sometimes."

"You mess with Burke and you're liable to be a dead feller." The promoter suddenly put his drink down and even in the dim light of the speakeasy, Hallam could see that he had gone pale. "You ain't gonna tell Burke you heard any of this from me, are you, Hallam?"

"Take it easy, Herbie," Hallam assured him. "Burke ain't goin' to know a thing about it. You got my word on it."

Warrender nodded nervously. "I hope you're right, Hallam." He finished off his drink and stood up. "I gotta be going. We didn't even talk today, okay?"

Hallam nodded, watched the little man scurry away. The gin had loosened Warrender's tongue, but now fear had burned away the alcohol. Burke seemed to inspire that reaction in people.

Hallam thought about the beating he had gotten from Nate Farraday and Burke's other flunkies.

He was going to enjoy tangling with Jocko Burke again.

The Pimlico operated around the clock. Hallam knew he couldn't waltz into the place and ask to see Burke, not after the ruckus there a few nights earlier. He wanted to find out if Burke was there, though, and Liz seemed to be the answer to that problem.

She made the telephone call and asked the questions that Hallam told her to ask, making her voice low and throaty and seductive. That didn't take much effort. Without giving her name, she found out that Burke wasn't at the club but was expected to be in late that afternoon. Liz thanked whoever she was talking to and hung up.

"That good enough for you, Lucas?" she asked when she had passed on the information.

"That was just fine," he answered. "I reckon a feller like Burke's got plenty of gal friends, or at least gals who want to be his friend. A call from one of 'em shouldn't warn him that anything's up."

"What is up? I mean, I helped you find out what you wanted to know. Don't you think you owe me an explanation?"

Hallam nodded. He told her about Lorraine von Ottenhausen and her connection with Burke. "I still don't know if Burke has anything to do with this case, but you can't overlook a feller like him. He's mixed up in too many other crooked deals not to suspect him of bein' involved in this one."

"What are you going to do about him now?"

"Follow him," Hallam said. "If he is tied up in this, he'll tip his hand sooner or later."

He couldn't pick up Burke's trail until later, though, and in the meantime he finally had a chance to show Liz some of the sights of Hollywood.

It was an enjoyable couple of hours. Hallam's flivver chugged up into the hills, giving them a spectacular view of the city and the canyons. Liz had seen the Hollywoodland sign, of course; now she saw what it was like looking down from that vantage point. Hallam wished they had packed a picnic.

There were other things to see, though. He showed her the Hollywood Bowl with its big band shell, then drove by the major movie studios. They had a quick meal at a hot dog stand, much to Liz's delight. All in all, Hallam thought she had a fine time, and the look of uneasiness in her eyes seemed to have disappeared.

All too soon, though, the sun began to slide down toward the horizon, and Hallam knew he ought to be getting to work again. He drove back to the apartment building and pulled to a stop at the curb.

Before he could say anything, Liz leaned closer to him and said, "You don't have to come in, Lucas. I know you're chomping at the bit to get back to your case. I hope it all works out and you find out who killed that boy."

"I'll find out," Hallam promised. "Either that, or Ben Dunnemore will. The score'll be settled, one way or another."

"I know it will." Liz lifted her face and kissed him quickly on the mouth. Hallam started to put his arms around her, but she had already pulled away and was opening the door on her side of the car. "Thank you for a lovely afternoon, Lucas," she said as she got out. "I don't think I'll ever forget it."

"Neither will I," he said to her through the open window. "So long, Liz. Maybe I'll see you tonight after work."

She nodded, then walked across the lawn to the building.

Hallam watched her for a moment, then put the flivver back in gear and pulled away from the curb.

He had discovered a long time before that a big part of manhunting was sitting and waiting. He found a place to park down the road from the entrance to the Pimlico and settled down to do just that. His joints might be getting a little stiff with age, but his eyes were still as sharp as a boy's. He knew he could probably spot Jocko Burke either entering or leaving the club.

Night fell, making Hallam's task a little more difficult, but there was an electric lamp on a pole just outside the gate. It cast enough light for him to see into the cars going through the gate. He had been sitting there just over an hour when a large limousine pulled out of the gate and turned in his direction. Hallam let himself slump slightly in the seat so as not to be so noticeable as the big car went by.

Jocko Burke was sitting in the back seat.

Hallam let them get well past him as he started the engine of his car. Then he swung the wheel around and moved out after the limousine.

As he followed the limo through the streets of Hollywood, Hallam reached under his jacket and slipped the Colt Cavalry .45 from its holster. He knew it was loaded, but he flipped open the cylinder and checked the shells anyway. That done, he replaced the gun and reached over to the glove compartment. Opening it, he took out his bowie knife in its leather sheath. The sheath was plain, no fringe or ornamentation, and the knife was the same way, simple wooden grips worn a little smooth with use. It was a functional weapon.

Up close, in Hallam's hand, it was *damn* functional.

He placed it on the seat beside him. When he got to wherever he was going, he would strap the sheath onto his belt.

It became obvious from the turns the limo made that Burke was heading for the Palm Court. That was no surprise to Hallam. If he hadn't been able to pick up Burke at the speakeasy, the bungalows would have been his next stop. Burke's bungalow was number four, Herbie Warrender had said. Hallam thought he might just pay a visit to it later.

The Palm Court took up a whole block, and there was a rear entrance off a side street. The limo turned in there. Hallam killed the lights and engine of his flivver and let it coast in to the curb before reaching the entrance. From here, he'd travel on foot.

Hallam stepped out of the car and softly closed the door. When he had the bowie's sheath on his belt, he walked toward the entrance, moving lightly on his feet, more quietly than a man of his size normally did.

An old Comanche had taught him how to walk. To a white man, walking was just a way of getting from one place to another. It was a lot more than that to an Indian. The old warrior had taught Hallam that.

He moved in silence through the trees and shrubbery.

He could see the taillights of the limousine and followed them to one of the bungalows. The place had a Spanish look to it, with stucco walls, tile roof, and a wide, arched doorway. The limousine stopped in front of a short flagstone walk that led to that doorway. The driver got out and went around to open the rear door.

Jocko Burke stepped out, then paused and reached back inside the vehicle to offer his hand to someone. Hallam was crouched behind a bush twenty yards away, and he wasn't surprised to see Lorraine von Ottenhausen follow Burke from the limousine. She had a fur stole draped over one shoulder, but her tight evening dress left the other shoulder bare. Her arm linked with Burke's, she strolled beside him to the open door of the bungalow.

A butler met them there, took Burke's coat and hat and Lorraine's stole. Hallam saw Burke say something to the man, but he wasn't close enough to catch the words. The butler nodded, then closed the door.

The driver was leaning on the fender of the big car, smoking a cigarette. Hallam waited a few minutes, trying to decide whether or not to catfoot around to the back of the bungalow. Then the heavy wooden door opened again, and the butler stepped out, wearing a hat and an overcoat now. He walked to the car and opened the front door on the passenger side. "The boss says for us to be back in two hours," he told the driver.

The man flipped his cigarette butt into the bushes and grinned. "Two hours, hunh? The boss must be plannin' on a long supper."

"It's no business of ours. We just follow orders and collect our money. You know that." There was a slight tone of reprimand in the butler's voice.

"Yeah, yeah, sure."

With a pair of thumps, the limo doors shut behind the two

servants, and the engine caught with a smooth roar. The driver turned on the car's lights and followed the little drive away from the bungalow.

Looked like Burke and Lorraine were all alone in there. Hallam knew that being a detective meant sometimes being a peeping tom, or else why would they call private eyes peepers? He didn't much like this part of the job, though.

Quietly, he moved toward the bungalow.

The shrubbery grew close against the walls of the building. Hallam hurried from the cover of the trees into the bushes and began working his way toward the glow of a lighted window. When he got there, he saw that curtains had been pulled over the opening, but they didn't quite come together in the middle. He straightened and looked through the narrow opening.

Inside was a living room so large that it must have taken up most of the building's floor space. On the other side of the room was a big fireplace, though it was screened off at the moment. The evening was much too warm for a fire. In front of the fireplace was a long, heavy sofa, and there were several overstuffed armchairs scattered around as well. An intricately woven Spanish tapestry hung on one wall. A chandelier of sparkling crystal hung from one of the thick ceiling beams.

Toward the back of the room was a table covered by a brilliant white cloth and set for two people to have dinner. A single candle burned in the center of it. On a cart nearby were several covered plates, the dinner prepared by the butler before his departure, no doubt. It looked like Burke and Lorraine would serve themselves. There was another cart on the other side of the table, this one holding a big bucket of ice in which a dark green bottle sat. It wouldn't be hard for the owner of a speakeasy to get his hands on some vintage champagne, Hallam thought.

Burke and Lorraine hadn't gotten to that part of the evening yet. They were standing in front of the fireplace, arms wrapped tightly around one another, lips pressed together. Lorraine was slightly taller than Burke, but that didn't seem to be bothering either one of them.

The way they were going at it, Hallam expected them to sink down onto that big sofa at any minute.

The sudden flash of headlights made him jerk his head around and crouch lower.

Another car was pulling up to the bungalow, a jaunty little roadster with one man in it. He stopped the car, got out, and walked up the path to the door. He wore tweeds and a dapper bowler hat, and there was a heavy walking stick in his hand. In the faint glow from the bungalow, Hallam saw the neatly trimmed beard on the man's round face.

Hallam had seen the man before, sitting in Jocko Burke's office in the Pimlico . . . just before Farraday and the others had hauled him away.

The man lifted the wrought-iron knocker on the door and rapped with it, but Burke had already heard the slam of the car door outside. He untangled himself from Lorraine's arms and said, "This business won't take long, my dear. Why don't you go freshen up?" It was a command, though, not a question.

"Of course, darling," Lorraine replied sweetly. She let her fingers trail over Burke's smoothly shaven cheek, then turned and went through a door beyond the little table. Her walk was deliberate and sensuous, and Burke had to tear his eyes away from her as he went to answer the knock at the door.

Hallam watched from the window as Burke admitted the bearded man. The little ex-jockey's attitude had changed in a matter of seconds. He was no longer a moonstruck lover. Now he was all business again.

"Hello, Lowell," he greeted the bearded man. "Is everything set up?"

"Yes, indeed," Lowell answered in the rich tones that Hallam remembered. "Our friend is in fact most eager to conclude the deal. There will be no trouble, I assure you."

Burke nodded and went to the cart where the bucket of

champagne rested. There was another, smaller bottle on the cart that Hallam hadn't noticed until now. Burke uncorked it, reached down to the cart's bottom shelf for glasses, and poured a couple of drinks. Whiskey, from the looks of it, Hallam thought. Burke gave one of the glasses to Lowell, then clinked his against it.

"To rich, greedy old men," Burke said with a smug grin.

"Long may they spend money," Lowell added.

Both men drank.

Rich, greedy old men . . . They were talking about Orville Cooke, Hallam realized.

What the hell was going on here?

"You'll have the merchandise soon?" Lowell asked, licking his lips after tossing off the whiskey.

"There's no problem there," Burke assured him. "I'll have some more very soon."

Some more what? Hallam's mind was racing. Maybe they were talking about morphine. Even though Hallam didn't personally know anyone who used the stuff, there were enough rumors floating around for him to be sure that there were dope rings in Hollywood.

Orville Cooke an addict? Could be, Hallam decided, but he knew that was sheer speculation on his part. The only thing he knew for certain from this eavesdropping was that Burke and this fellow Lowell—whoever he was—were selling something to a rich old man. Something obviously illegal . . .

But how could that have anything to do with Hank Schiller's murder?

Hallam had followed plenty of blind trails in his time. Maybe this one had led him to something completely unexpected.

Lowell was talking again. He looked at the place settings on the table and said, "It appears that I am interrupting something, my dear Jocko. Perhaps I should make a discreet exit now."

"Yeah, maybe you should. I'll be in touch."

"Very well."

Lowell left quickly, settling his hat back on his head and walking out to his car. He didn't have a limp that Hallam could see, so the walking stick had to be for show . . . or for use as a weapon if need be. Hallam watched the man drive off.

Inside the bungalow, Lorraine von Ottenhausen came back into the living room as Burke opened the door she had used earlier. "Is your business all taken care of, dearest?" she murmured.

"For a while," Burke answered, pulling her into his arms again.

Hallam grimaced. He didn't expect to see anything further here tonight except the two of them eating dinner and then . . . Well, he didn't expect to see anything that would have any bearing on the case. Besides, this evening had already given him plenty to think about. He slipped away from the wall and headed back toward the street.

He hadn't gone ten feet when he saw a figure come stalking unsteadily out of the darkness.

Hallam and the other man stopped short at the sight of each other. The man stared at him for a moment, then exclaimed, "Hallam! What the hell you doin' here?"

His voice was a little slurred, but Hallam recognized it anyway, the voice and the stocky figure. The newcomer was Mackey Russell, one of Hank's fellow pilots, and he was drunk as a skunk.

"Hold on there, Russell," Hallam said in a low voice, ignoring the man's question. "Where do you think you're goin'?"

Russell pointed at the bungalow. "In there," he said, somewhat belligerently. "Goin' to tell that gal a thing or two."

Hallam took a step toward Russell. He didn't know how Russell knew that Lorraine was inside, but the flyer might not know the identity of her companion. Hallam raised his hands and said, "Why don't we go find us a drink and talk about this?"

Russell shook his head obstinately. "Don' need a drink," he

said. "Had plenty already. Got to say something to that woman, though."

Hallam moved another step closer. He had to get Russell out of here before the man caused a commotion and drew the attention of Burke. He didn't want to do it, but he thought he could plant one on Russell's jaw and knock him out before he raised a yell.

Hallam's muscles tensed to do just that, but Russell must have sensed his intention. With surprising agility for a man who was drunk, he dodged to the side and lunged past Hallam's outstretched arm.

"Come out of there, you tramp!" he shouted at the bungalow. "Goddamn German whore!"

Hallam grabbed him around the shoulders and wrestled him back, but it was too late. Hallam thought about hauling Russell into the brush and making a run for it. Russell twisted around and tried to get loose, though, and before Hallam could get either of them out of sight, the front door of the bungalow banged open.

"Who's out there?" Burke yelled angrily. "What the hell's going on?"

There was a pistol in his hand.

Hallam saw the gun glinting in the light from inside and had to fight off the impulse to grab for his own Colt. Getting into a corpse-and-cartridge session in the middle of Hollywood wasn't going to help solve Hank's murder. He did shove Mackey Russell to the side, though, out of the way if Burke forced the issue.

Burke saw the two men and lined the pistol on them. "You again!" he spat, spotting Hallam.

Hallam held his left hand up, palm out. The right one he kept close to the butt of the Colt. "Hold on, Burke!" he called. "My friend's just had too much to drink. I'm tryin' to get him home."

"'S not true," Russell said, trying to push past Hallam. "Send that slut out here, mister. Got a few things to say to her!"

Hallam saw Lorraine peering past Burke's shoulder with a blend of fright and anger on her face. She couldn't help but hear what Russell was saying about her.

"Shut up, dammit!" Hallam hissed at Russell. "You don't know who that is."

"Don' give a damn," Russell slurred. "I know all I need to know about her." His voice twisted with anguish. "She and her kind helped get a lot of my friends killed. Wouldn't come out and fight us fair. Had to sneak around. Stinkin' spies . . ."

He swayed, caught himself, passed a shaky hand over his face.

Hallam thought he knew what had happened. Russell had been drinking, maybe ever since Hank's wake, and he had dwelt too long on the ambush that had wiped out his squadron except for him and the other three pilots. Alain Freneau, Lorraine's lover in Paris, had probably been behind that ambush, but Freneau was dead now. Russell couldn't strike back at him.

But Lorraine was very much alive. Not only alive, but working on the same picture as Russell and the other pilots. Her presence had finally been too much for him to stand. A lot of booze and brooding had pushed him over the edge. He had probably been following her and had finally decided to confront her.

To do what? Call her names? Hallam felt sure Russell wouldn't use violence against a woman. Revenge was really out of his reach.

But he could damn sure get himself killed.

Burke glared at Hallam and snapped, "I don't think I believe you, shamus. This is twice you've been poking around in my business." His lip lifted in a snarl. "The next time I'm going to put a bullet in you, you got that? Now get that drunken bastard out of here!"

Hallam dug his fingers into Russell's arm and nodded. "I'll do that," he said, pulling Russell toward the street. Russell still didn't want to go, but Hallam was set now, instead of being taken by surprise, and Russell was no match for his strength. Even as Hallam dragged him away, though, the pilot was screaming insults at Lorraine.

Finally, Hallam yanked Russell around a curve of the road and got out of sight of the bungalow. He paused and whipped his left hand across Russell's face. The man's head rocked on his shoulders from the force of the blow.

"Shut your goddamn mouth!" Hallam grated. "You could've got us both killed back there, you infernal idiot! What the hell were you tryin' to do?"

Russell shook his head and lifted a hand to his cheek. For a moment, he tensed in anger, ready to leap toward Hallam.

"Don't try it," Hallam growled. The mood he was in, he was ready to hand Russell his needin's and enjoy every minute of it.

Russell relaxed after several long seconds. "All right," he said. "It's all over, I guess. I just had too much to drink, too much to think about."

Hallam nodded. "I know."

Slowly, a sheepish smile played over Russell's features. "I suppose I should say thank you. From the looks of things back there, you saved me from getting shot. What the hell were you doing up here anyway?"

"Gettin' more confused by the minute," Hallam answered distractedly, thinking about what he had overheard in the bungalow. The unfortunate incident with Russell hadn't made him forget about the bearded man called Lowell and his mysterious conversation with Burke.

"You and me both, chum," Russell said. He rubbed his jaw again. "That's quite a wallop you pack."

"Better'n gettin' shot."

"That's for damn sure. Say, who was that little guy with the gun back there, Billy the Kid?"

"Just as bad," Hallam said, thinking about Jocko Burke.

THIRTEEN

Mackey Russell's car was parked on the street not far from Hallam's. Hallam wasn't sure the pilot was in any shape to be driving, but Russell insisted he was all right.

"I just need to go get some coffee," Russell said as he climbed into his car. In the glow from a nearby streetlight, his face looked pasty.

"You do that," Hallam told him sternly. "And maybe you better think twice before drinkin' that much again."

"Don't lecture me, Hallam. I know what I'm doing."

Hallam wasn't sure of that. Russell was damned lucky he wasn't dead now. Hallam knew what would have happened if he hadn't been there to stop Russell from barging in on Burke and Lorraine.

He watched the aviator drive away, Russell's car weaving slightly. Maybe he would get back to his home, or wherever he was going, without running into another vehicle. Hallam just hoped he didn't double back and try again to get into the bungalow.

If he was that stupid, then it was his own lookout. Hallam had done all he felt like doing to save Russell from himself.

He headed home.

It was too early for Liz to be back from the theater, so he went up to his own apartment and tried to read some of the stories in the issue of *Argosy* he had bought earlier. He couldn't concentrate on the words, though. His mind kept going back to the conversation between Burke and Lowell.

Hallam was sure they had been talking about Orville Cooke, but the more he considered it, the less likely he thought they had been talking about morphine. Cooke just wasn't the type. Hallam thought back to what he had learned in the newspaper morgue about Cooke, his personal life, his business, his charities, his art collection. There didn't seem to be anything there to indicate any possible connection with Jocko Burke, even less to indicate that any of this was tied in with Hank's murder.

Hallam fell asleep in his battered old armchair, trying to make some sense of the whole mess . . .

He woke up sometime in the middle of the night, stiff and sore from sleeping in the chair, and got up just long enough to limp to the bedroom and strip his clothes off. Then he threw himself down on the bed, and the answer came to him just before he drifted back to sleep.

It was time to pay a visit to Mr. Orville Cooke.

Hallam felt the same way about the decision when he awoke the next morning. He'd been poking around in this case for several days now, and while he had uncovered a lot of information, none of the pieces wanted to fit together.

The time had come to start making them fit.

Liz was up and about and more than willing to share a cup of coffee with him, Hallam found when he knocked on her door a few minutes later. There wasn't much conversation between them this morning, however. Hallam's mind was full of the events of the last few days, and Liz seemed preoccupied, too. She said that the job at the Egyptian was still going fine. Hallam nodded, glad to hear it.

"Reckon I'd better be goin'," he said a few minutes later. "Got a lot to do today."

"Anything I can help you with?" Liz asked.

Hallam shook his head. "Don't reckon there is. It's all to do with the case."

"What happened last night?"

Hallam shook his head. "I ain't sure yet." He settled his hat on his head and said, "Thanks for the coffee, Liz." He walked out of the apartment, the door slamming behind him, and Liz sat for a long moment staring after him.

Hallam had checked with his contacts the day before about Jocko Burke, but he hadn't asked anyone about Orville Cooke. Now he spent the morning putting the word out that he was interested in anything anyone knew that might tie Cooke into local criminal circles—especially Jocko Burke's circle.

It was nearly noon before he did any good. But then he asked the right question in the right place.

He was in a pawnshop run by a fellow named Snider, a man whose belly strained the dirty white shirt he always wore. He had a large cigar in his mouth and talked around it rather than remove it.

"Yeah, I know this guy Cooke," Snider said in answer to Hallam's question. "He's a customer of mine."

Hallam glanced around the dirty, cluttered shop and had a hard time imagining a rich man like Orville Cooke coming to a place like this. He knew, though, that the pawnshop was only a front for Snider's real operation. The big man was one of the city's busiest fences, dealing primarily in small, less expensive items. It took a lot of volume to make the kind of profits Snider wanted.

Snider must have seen the skepticism on Hallam's face,

because he shifted the cigar from one side of his mouth to the other and said, "Hey, even a rich guy can run a little short now and then."

"You tellin' me that Cooke comes in here and hocks things?"

"Well . . . I don't remember exactly. I just know I seen him here in the store once."

"Maybe he was buyin', not pawnin'," Hallam guessed.

"Could've been, I guess. My memory ain't so good these days."

Hallam grimaced and went to his pocket for a bill. He laid his hand on the shop's counter, the money underneath his big palm. He never had liked paying off informants, but he had learned to live with it in his years as a detective. A part of him still wanted to draw the Colt and do a little convincin' with it, but what the hell, the Wild West was gone. At least Hallam kept trying to tell himself it was.

Snider glanced at the bill and grunted in pleasure. "Seems like Cooke was buying something from me," he said. "Yeah, that was it. He bought a painting."

"Didn't know you let folks pawn paintings, Snider."

The man shrugged. "Don't remember for sure how I got hold of it, but I had it and Cooke wanted it. Paid a good price for it, too."

Hallam nodded thoughtfully and took his hand off the bill. It disappeared in one quick movement of Snider's paw.

"That the only time you did business with Cooke?" Hallam asked.

"Yeah. Like you said, what would a guy like that be doing in a hock shop?"

In this case, Hallam thought, Cooke had probably been buying a piece of artwork that had been stolen. And that was damned interesting. It was unlikely that a fence like Snider would have items like that on hand very often, but someone like Burke, who only dabbled in hot property and only moved expensive items . . . That could be the connection between Burke and Cooke, all right.

Hallam had the information he wanted. Now he could pay that visit to Orville Cooke.

Cooke had an office on Broadway in downtown Los Angeles. A telephone directory told Hallam that much. He drove over there and ran into a brick wall. Cooke was not in his office, a severe-faced secretary told him. He was at home and was not to be disturbed. And no, Hallam could not have Mr. Cooke's home address.

"That's all right, ma'am," Hallam said. "Reckon you've got a job to do, just like everybody else."

He didn't tell her that he knew from his newspaper research that Cooke's home was up in the Hollywood Hills. After leaving the office, it took only a telephone call to a *Citizen* reporter he knew to get the exact address. The gal wrote for the society pages, and Cooke threw an occasional party to benefit one of the charities he supported.

He headed back to Hollywood and took Beachwood Drive north toward the hills. Ahead of him, atop Mount Lee, the HOLLYWOODLAND sign showed up brilliantly in the noontime sun. Cooke's house was on Beachwood, not far before the road itself played out, in a neighborhood of large estates.

A high wall of pink stone ran around the place. There was a big gate of wrought iron, and through it Hallam could see the house sitting behind about a quarter mile of lawn. It was white stucco, but it lacked the tile roof to give it a Spanish look. In fact, despite its size it was plain and functional, and to Hallam, it looked more like a hospital than anything else.

There was a button set in one of the pillars to the side of the gate. Hallam checked first to make sure the gate was locked—it was—then pressed the button. He didn't know what kind of response he'd get, but he could always climb over the wall later if he had to.

The front door of the house opened a moment later, and a man in butler's livery stepped out. He started down the curving drive toward the gate, and as he came, Hallam thought about what he was going to say.

The butler came to a stop on the other side of the gate and peered at Hallam through the bars. "Could I help you?" he asked, though it was obvious from his expression that he didn't think he could.

"Need to see Mr. Cooke," he said brusquely.

"Do you have an appointment, sir?" The butler thought he knew the answer to that one, too.

"No, but he'll want to see me. Just tell him I work for Tom Rutledge, and I need to talk to him about business."

The butler's face took on a slight air of indecision. He had probably heard Tom Rutledge's name before, but he might not recognize it as belonging to one of the leading Texas oilmen. "Come with me," he finally said, unlocking the gate with a big key. "I'll see if Mr. Cooke wishes to speak with you."

Hallam gestured at his flivver. "All right if I drive up to the house? This leg o' mine gets a little stiff sometimes. Give you a lift if you want."

"Yes, certainly."

Hallam drove through the gate and the butler shut it behind the flivver. Then, when the man had climbed in the other side of the car, Hallam followed the drive up to the big house.

The butler led the way into an entrance foyer. "Please wait here, sir," he requested, then vanished through another set of double doors.

Hallam glanced around. The carpet underfoot was deep and soft. There were two paintings in the foyer, one to each side, both of them mountain landscapes. They were done well enough to make Hallam miss the Rockies for a moment. On one side of the foyer was a little table, so spindly-legged it looked to Hallam like it wouldn't hold up any weight at all.

The butler reappeared and said, "Mr. Cooke has just finished his luncheon, sir, but he said he would give you a few minutes in the study. If you will follow me . . . ?"

Hallam fell in behind the man and followed him down a long, wide corridor. There were more paintings on the walls here, all of them in heavy, ornate frames. Landscapes, portraits, battle scenes . . . There were all kinds, including some that looked like smears and globs of paint that didn't make any sense at all. In addition, there were small sculptures sitting on tables at regular intervals. Hallam had been in a museum or two, and he felt a little like he was in one now.

The butler opened a door and ushered him through into Orville Cooke's study. The man announced, "Here is the, ah, gentleman to see you, sir," then withdrew, closing the door with a gentle thump.

Cooke was standing in front of a tall, glass-fronted case, staring at something inside it. He turned around and came across the room, extending his hand to Hallam. "Orville Cooke, sir," he said.

Hallam returned the handshake. "Lucas Hallam. Pleased to meet you, Mr. Cooke."

If Hallam's name meant anything to him, Cooke didn't show it. He said, "What does old Tom Rutledge want with me, Mr. Hallam? Hasn't he got enough to keep up with there in the Permian Basin?"

"Yes, sir, I reckon he does." Hallam hesitated, unsure whether to try to stall or just to blurt out why he was really here, see what kind of reaction that got from Cooke. There were just as many paintings here in the study as there were out in the hall, and one of them caught his eye. "That's a Charlie Russell, ain't it?" he asked, gesturing at the canvas.

"Yes, indeed." A smile played over Cooke's leathery, creased face. "Are you familiar with art, Mr. Hallam?"

"Nope, but I knew ol' Charlie back in Montana. He was always sketchin' something. Could've been a pretty good hand if he'd've put his mind to it."

"We seem to have gotten off the subject, sir. I believe my man said you wanted to discuss business." Cooke pulled a big watch from his pocket and flipped it open. "I am rather busy today . . ."

"Yes, sir, and I appreciate you seein' me." Hallam cast around for something else to say and went on after a moment, "Actually, Tom didn't send me here, Mr. Cooke."

Cooke frowned. "He didn't?"

"No, sir. You see, I been workin' for Rutledge Oil for quite a spell now, and I was thinkin' it was time to shake that West Texas dust off my boots. I come to California to see about gettin' a job on a rig out here."

Cooke's frown deepened as he stared at Hallam for a long moment, then suddenly it disappeared. A smile began to tug at his lips. "What did you do for Tom Rutledge, Mr. Hallam?"

"Roughneck," Hallam said simply.

A laugh burst from Cooke. Hallam didn't think he was the kind of man who laughed often, but he seemed to be enjoying this. "Let me understand you, sir," Cooke said. "You came to California hoping to catch on as a roughneck in the oil fields, so you pay a visit to the president of an oil company?"

"I always like to go to the head man," Hallam said solemnly.

Cooke laughed again. "By God, man, I admire your gall, if nothing else."

"That mean you'll give me a job?"

"You'll have to see my personnel manager about that, Mr. Hallam, but I'll give you his name and a note to take to him. How's that?"

Hallam returned Cooke's grin. "That'd be right kind of you, sir."

Cooke went to his massive desk and sat down, drawing a pen and a sheet of paper over in front of him. As he picked up the pen and began to write, Hallam wandered over to the big cabinet where Cooke had been standing when he entered the room.

There were several shelves inside the case, and arrayed on them were at least two dozen porcelain figurines. Hallam leaned over to look more closely at them, impressed by the fineness of the detail work and the sheer amount of it. The figurines were of lords and ladies, soldiers and peasants and animals. All of the costumes looked European and hundreds of years old, like the getups actors wore in those pictures set in France and England in the days when people wrote with feathers. Hallam was no expert on art objects, but these were cute little statues.

"You like them?" Cooke asked as he got up from the desk. "I have almost the entire set now."

"Mighty nice, but they look like they'd break if you breathed on 'em wrong."

"That's why they're behind glass. They are very fragile." Cooke handed Hallam the note he had written. "You take that to the address on there and tell them I sent you. I make no guarantees that you'll be hired, of course."

Hallam stuffed the paper in his pocket. "I appreciate the help." He glanced at the other paintings on the walls. "Mind if I look around a minute more?"

"I think I can spare another minute for an art lover."

"Don't know about that, but I like a good picture."

Hallam walked slowly around the room, trying to commit to memory as many of the paintings as he could. He gestured at one of them and asked, "Where'd a fella go to buy something like this here?"

Cooke's smile was a bit superior this time. "I'm afraid collecting fine art is an expensive proposition, Mr. Hallam. You have to know where to find these items, and it's not a simple matter. You don't just go out and buy them. Many times, you find yourself bidding against another collector. Negotiations can be quite tricky. It can be more cutthroat than the oil business, in fact."

Hallam gave him a shrewd glance. "Reckon there are times you don't ask too many questions about where a feller got hold of something he's sellin'."

He knew immediately that he had stepped over the line. Cooke's pale gray eyes became frosty. "As I said, it's an expensive avocation, Mr. Hallam. Perhaps you should stick to something else."

"Yes, sir, I expect you're right," Hallam said quickly. "Like workin'. I'll go see your folks at the office right now. Thanks again, Mr. Cooke."

The butler appeared at the door again almost as soon as Cooke had pressed a button on his desk. "Good day, Mr. Hallam," the oil magnate said.

Hallam followed the butler to the front door of the mansion, then stepped out past him. "So long," Hallam said to the man, but the butler made no response.

The gate was still unlocked. Hallam opened it, drove out, closed it again behind him out of habit—when a man goes through another man's fence, he closes the gate behind him. Then he headed back down Beachwood toward Hollywood Boulevard.

He followed Hollywood Boulevard to Cahuenga and pulled around the corner to park in front of the Waterhole. There were several horses tied up next to the plain frame building that housed the favorite speakeasy of the movie cowboys.

After his trip inside Orville Cooke's sterile, museumlike home, Hallam felt the need of a good cold beer.

Hallam nodded to several of the men inside as he headed for the bar. A youngster in range clothes was standing there with a beer in front of him, and he grinned when he looked up and saw Hallam.

"Howdy, Lucas," he said. "Where the hell you been keepin' yourself? Ain't seen you in a coon's age."

"Howdy your ownself, Pecos," Hallam replied, leaning on the bar and nodding to the bartender. "Been workin' on a case most of the time," he went on.

"Hot damn!" Pecos exclaimed. "Tell me about it, all right?"

Hallam grinned. The boy's enthusiasm was nice to see. He was a riding extra and stuntman, and everybody just knew him as Pecos. Hallam didn't know his real name; nobody in Hollywood did. It was rumored that his daddy was rich, but Pecos didn't give a hang about anything except being a cowboy.

And he made no secret of the fact that Lucas Hallam was one of his heroes.

Looking at him now, Hallam was suddenly reminded of Hank Schiller. Hank had been full of piss and vinegar, just like Pecos.

Until somebody cut him down before his life hardly had a chance to get started.

"What's the matter, Lucas?" Pecos asked with a frown of concern. "You look like somethin's got you plumb worrified."

Hallam picked up the mug of beer the bartender had placed before him. "Let's go sit down, boy," he said. "I'll tell you all about it."

Hallam thought later that visiting the Waterhole was the best thing he could have done. Sitting down with Pecos and telling about everything that had happened over the last few days helped him get the events in order in his head. With what he already knew and what he had found out today, Hallam suddenly realized that he might have been looking at some things from the wrong angle.

The fog hadn't lifted yet, but it was thinning out.

"What are you goin' to do now, Lucas?" Pecos asked when he was finished with the story.

"Try to find out a few more answers, I 'spose."

"Reckon you'll need any help?"

Hallam grinned. "Not just yet, boy. I'll let you know if I do."

This wasn't the first time Pecos had wanted to help him out on a case. Hallam had put the youngster off so far, and he would continue to do that. Pecos had a lot of living to do yet. He didn't need that life cut short, as Hank's had been.

Hallam finished his beer and said *adiós* to the men in the speakeasy. He pointed the flivver back onto the boulevard.

A few blocks away he pulled up in front of a small storefront. A painted sign on the window said LONSBERG GALLERIES. As Hallam went in, a small bell over the door jingled.

The front room of the shop held quite a few canvases displayed on easels. The walls were also covered with paintings. A counter ran from one side of the room to the other, with a partition behind it dividing the building into two rooms. There was a curtain-covered door in the partition.

Sitting on the counter was as pretty a saddle as Hallam had ever seen.

Despite the fact that this was an art gallery, there was a decided Western feel to it. Many of the paintings had Western subjects, and there were spurs hanging on the walls between some of the frames. Hallam liked the place. Along with the Waterhole and Joe Posada's boot shop and Old Bob's Hollywood Guns, Lonsberg's was a reminder of home for Hallam.

A middle-aged woman pushed through the curtained doorway to the back room. Her face lit up with a smile as she spotted Hallam standing in front of a painting of a roundup scene. "Lucas!" she said happily.

"Howdy, Bea." Hallam nodded. "How are you and Axel?"

"Oh, we're fine." Bea Lonsberg came around the counter. "You're looking well, Lucas. Why haven't you been to see us in so long?"

"Well, I've been a mite busy. Makin' movies and bein' a detective and all."

Bea nodded. "I know. We saw you in Harry Carey's last picture. Axel got so excited."

Hallam grinned. He liked the Lonsbergs, had ever since he had wandered in here one day, drawn by the Western paintings, and met the middle-aged couple. They were from New York and had come to California hoping to improve Axel's health. He was an accountant at one of the studios, and Bea ran this small gallery. Hallam knew the gallery didn't make much money, but it gave Axel and Bea a chance to indulge a long-time dream.

They were in love with the West, maybe as much as he was. Knowing someone who worked in Western pictures, someone who was acquainted with Mix and Hart and all the other stars, was a source of great enjoyment for them. And Hallam liked coming to the gallery and looking at the artwork, especially the work of people like Russell and Remington, folks who knew what they were doing and who had some respect for their subjects.

Today, though, Hallam wasn't interested in Western art. He had some other kinds on his mind.

"I was wonderin' if you could help me, Bea," he said, turning his hat in his hands.

"You know I'll be glad to, Lucas. What do you need?"

"Do you have any books that show pictures of famous paintings and what they're worth?"

Bea frowned slightly. "I have some catalogues from galleries back East that have a lot of pictures."

"Older ones?" Hallam figured that Cooke had had some of the paintings for years.

"Some, yes. Would you like to look through them?"

. "I sure would, Bea, if it wouldn't be too much trouble."

"No trouble at all. They're in the office." She pushed aside the curtain. "I'll be right back."

Hallam spent the next hour going over the gallery catalogues with Bea Lonsberg. His hunch had been right; some of the paintings in Cooke's house were both famous and valuable. He pointed out the ones he recognized and got a rough idea of their worth from Bea.

Many of the paintings he remembered from his visit to Cooke were not in the catalogues, though. That didn't necessarily mean they had been stolen and sold through a fence, but as Hallam talked to Bea, he discovered that there was a flourishing market for such items.

"Oh, my, yes," she said in answer to a question. "There are a great many art collectors who will buy an item knowing that it may have been stolen. They don't care, not when it's something they really want. That's why Axel and I insist on verifying the provenance of everything we handle."

"Provenance? What's that?"

"Proof that the item being sold actually belongs to the person who is selling it, basically. It can get very complicated, Lucas. Dealing on the black market is really much simpler. There it all comes down to who has possession and who has the most money."

Hallam nodded thoughtfully. He wondered how many of the paintings in Orville Cooke's collection had been acquired from Burke and other fences.

"How about other things besides paintings? Like statues and little figures?"

Bea nodded. "It's just like with the paintings. There's a brisk traffic worldwide in art objects, and not all of them are sold legally."

Hallam remembered the glass-fronted cabinet in Cooke's study. "You recollect ever seein' some little figures, looked like they was made out of porcelain? Real fancylike, kings and queens and princes and princesses and like that."

"I've seen a great many figurines like that. They were once the rage in the courts of Europe."

Hallam frowned. "Courts?"

"Not like a court of law. Courts of nobility. Kings and queens, as you said. Many were specially made for royalty." Bea thought for a moment, then said, "Wait a minute. I think I have a book that shows some of them." She ducked into the back and returned a moment later with a thick, heavy-looking volume bound in leather. She placed it on the counter with a thump and said, "This is about the treasures of European royalty, and I'm sure it has some pictures of Dresden figurines."

She went on to explain about Dresden china and its beauty and fragility, but Hallam wasn't paying much attention. He was watching the photographs as Bea turned the pages of the book, and he suddenly stopped her by stabbing a blunt finger at a group of pictures.

"That's them," he said.

It was indeed the same set of figurines he had seen in Cooke's study. Judging from the pictures, there were a few more in the set that Cooke didn't have, and that agreed with the comment that the oilman had made. Hallam nodded in satisfaction at finding them, then looked up to see Bea staring at him.

"You saw these particular figurines?" she said, obviously finding that hard to believe.

"Yep," Hallam replied.

Bea shook her head. "You must be mistaken, Lucas. These are Mad Ludwig's."

"Not no more."

"No, you don't understand. King Ludwig had these made to his order more than fifty years ago, and then the molds for them were broken so that there could never be any more like them. He was called the mad monarch because of his obsession with art and his desire to have the most glorious collection in all of Europe. His castles are showplaces, Lucas. Why, one of them has a dome of pure gold in it."

"Sounds like he was a little touched, all right. With a name like Ludwig, this feller must've been German."

"Well, it wasn't called Germany then. I don't know that much about European history except as it relates to art, but I suppose you could call him a German. I believe he was actually the king of Bavaria. These figurines were in France, though, until they disappeared several years ago."

Hallam leaned forward over the counter, frowning. "What were they doin' in France?"

"They were in a private museum there. They disappeared during the war, though. It was always assumed that they were stolen. That's why you couldn't have seen them . . ." Her voice trailed off as she realized the significance of Hallam's claim.

He nodded, tapped the pictures of the figurines in the book. "Reckon these little fellers are worth quite a bit."

"They're priceless, Lucas. I don't have any idea what you could get from a collector for them, but I know it would be . . ."—she closed her eyes and nodded—"a lot."

Hallam closed the book. "Thanks, Bea. You've been a real help. Reckon I'd better be goin' now, though."

"Lucas." Her worried voice stopped him as he started to turn toward the door. "What are you mixed up in, Lucas?"

"I ain't sure just yet." A sudden thought occurred to him. "You know most folks in the art business around here, don't you?"

"Most of the legitimate dealers, yes."

"How about a feller about a foot shorter'n me, kind of round-faced, got dark hair and a beard. Name of Lowell, I think."

Bea nodded. "That sounds like Lowell Thorley. He has a gallery in downtown Los Angeles. What does he have to do with this, Lucas?"

"Reckon maybe I'd better go ask him," Hallam said with a grin. He waved and stepped out the door, closing it before Bea could stop him again.

Lowell Thorley had some questions to answer, all right, and so did Orville Cooke.

Hallam was going to do the asking.

FOURTEEN

Hallam looked up the address of Lowell Thorley's gallery and headed back toward downtown Los Angeles. He found the place on the bottom floor of a three-story building not far from the building where Orville Cooke had his offices. There were double doors made of heavy glass and tasteful gold letters above the doors said THORLEY GALLERIES—FINE ART. The doors were flanked by show windows, each of them containing a single painting on an easel.

Hallam pushed through the doors and strode into the place. The atmosphere inside was hushed. Hallam didn't like it much. The big room seemed rather underfurnished. There were a few pictures on the walls, some potted palms, a chair here and there. No people, though.

A door in the back wall opened and a man stepped through. Evidently opening the front door set off some kind of signal in the back. The man was thin, medium height, and had sparse brown hair combed over a large bald spot. He wore an expensive suit that was nevertheless starting to show signs of age.

"Yes, sir," he said, pale blue eyes taking in Hallam's craggy massiveness. "Can I help you?" Like Cooke's butler, he thought he already knew the answer to that question.

"I'm lookin' for Lowell Thorley," Hallam replied. "He around?"

"Do you have an appointment with Mr. Thorley?"

"Nope."

"Perhaps I can help you, then, if your business pertains to the gallery."

"It's personal," Hallam said. "Where can I find Thorley?"

The man spread his hands in a gesture of helplessness. "I'm sorry, sir, but I'm afraid I can't help you. Mr. Thorley isn't here at the moment, and I don't know when he'll be back."

Hallam thought he saw something lurking underneath the man's smooth exterior, some sort of concern he wasn't voicing. "Where does he live?" Hallam asked.

"I'm afraid I can't—"

"Reckon you *can*," Hallam growled. He was getting tired of people putting him off and outright lying to him. "This is police business, mister, and if you don't want to go interferin' in a murder investigation, you'll tell me where to find Thorley."

The man paled, and a few drops of sweat suddenly appeared on his high forehead. "Murder?" he asked.

"That's right," Hallam said. He wasn't lying; Hank's murder was indeed police business.

"Well . . . I really don't know where Mr. Thorley is. He hasn't been in today at all, and he doesn't answer his phone. I . . . I had thought about calling the police—"

"No need for that now," Hallam cut in. "Just tell me where to find his house."

"He lives on Beverly Boulevard. It's not far." The man gave Hallam the address, then added, "I'm afraid something may have happened to him. It's just not like him not to come in or call."

Hallam waved a big hand to indicate the gallery's wares. "He have much of this junk at his house?"

The clerk frowned, offended by Hallam's assessment of the artwork. "Some of the gallery's merchandise is stored at his house, yes. And some of it is quite valuable. That's why I suspected . . . well, suspected the worst."

Hallam nodded and said, "I'll check it out. Thanks."

"You'll let me know what you find?"

"If I get the chance."

Hallam drove north toward Beverly Boulevard and turned right on the broad street. It took him only a few minutes to find the address that the man had given him. The house was large, a red-brick Tudor-style that was not a mansion but was still bigger and fancier than a normal residence. Thorley had to be doing all right for himself if he could afford to live here. From the looks of his gallery, all of his money wasn't coming from there, either.

That fit in with Hallam's nebulous theory. Thorley, in partnership with Jocko Burke, was fencing stolen artwork, some of it to Orville Cooke.

There was a hedge along the street with a driveway turning in at the end of it. Hallam wheeled the flivver into the drive and pulled up behind an expensive roadster. It was the same car he had seen Thorley arrive in at Burke's bungalow in the Palm Court. The art dealer was probably home, then, and Hallam was curious why he wasn't answering his telephone.

Hallam suddenly thought that he might know the answer to that . . . and it wasn't a good one.

He went to the front door first, past colorful flower beds. There was a heavy lion's-head knocker in the center of the door, plus a button for a bell to one side. Hallam tried them both and got no response.

He followed a walk to the side of the house and around to the rear. Shrubbery grew close against the walls, and the side of the house had ivy climbing on it. Hallam turned the corner and headed for the back door. His right hand was just inside his coat, ready to grab the Colt.

There was a small covered porch on the rear of the house. Hallam tried the screen door, found it unhooked. He went inside, past some redwood lawn furniture, walked over to the door into the house. He expected it to be locked, but the knob turned under his fingers.

Hallam knocked again before pushing the door open. Still no answer. He swung the door back toward the wall and stepped in quickly.

The house was quiet, the air slightly musty, as if it had been closed up all day.

Hallam slipped the Colt from its holster and looked around. He was in a large kitchen with fairly new appliances and a big wooden cutting table in the center of the floor. There were large cabinets along the walls. Across the room was a swinging door, perfectly still at the moment.

He strode over and pushed through it, found himself in a dining room with a long table. This room had thick carpet and paintings on the walls, and a tall glass-fronted china cabinet sat to one side. There was no one in this room, either, and the pervasive silence still hung over the house.

In quick order, Hallam checked the living room and a couple of bedrooms, finding no one. The furnishings were consistently expensive, confirming his impression that Lowell Thorley had plenty of money. So far, he had seen nothing out of order, no signs of a struggle.

The hall leading to the bedrooms had one more door at its far end, and when Hallam swung it open, he saw that it led into a study. The bookcase-covered walls made the room dark, as did the heavy curtains over the French windows. He reached around the door, feeling for a light switch, found one, flipped it up.

There was a large desk on one side of the room, its top littered with papers. Several of the papers had fallen off the desk and were scattered on the floor. Actually, Hallam saw, they had probably been pulled off the desk when Lowell Thorley slumped against it on his way down.

Thorley was sprawled on the floor in front of the desk, facedown, the back of his coat marred by a large, dark, ragged stain.

Hallam's face was grim as he knelt beside the body. The tear in Thorley's coat confirmed that he had been stabbed. Hallam laid a hand against the man's bearded cheek. Cold, all right. Thorley had been dead all day, maybe since the night before.

Someone could have been here waiting for him when he got back from Burke's bungalow, Hallam thought. Maybe Thorley had interrupted a burglar. Hallam considered that, then shook his head. A thief would have taken something, would have messed the place up. It didn't appear that anything was missing, though Hallam couldn't be sure about that.

Thorley could have known his killer, could have let the person in. There were all kinds of possibilities. One thing was certain, though.

Lowell Thorley wouldn't be answering any of Hallam's questions.

Hallam stopped at the first drugstore he came to and went to the telephone booth in the rear of the store. He dialed the number of Los Angeles police headquarters and told the desk man who answered that there was a dead body in a house on Beverly Boulevard. Hallam recited the street address over the cop's excited babble, then hung up.

He knew some of the detectives who worked out of the downtown division, but none of them well enough to trust them not to haul him in for questioning. And he didn't want to be tied down right now. There were too many things to do. This case had become a maze of confusion and misunderstandings, but he felt like he was on the verge of making some sense of all of it—if he could stay on the loose a little while longer.

The cops would talk to the clerk at the gallery and probably get his description from the man, but it would take them a while to identify him and longer to catch up to him.

With all that had been going on today, he had forgotten to eat lunch. Hallam stopped at a tamale stand down the street and grabbed some supper, the fiery tamales burning his mouth and throat. He wished for some cold beer to wash them down, but a man couldn't have everything.

He headed back to Hollywood as dusk began to settle over the city. Night had fallen by the time he reached the movie studio. When he pulled up to the gate, he called to the guard, "Mr. McGinley still here?"

The guard glanced at his clipboard. "He's supposed to be. He hasn't left according to my records."

"Thanks." Hallam confirmed his name with the guard, then pulled over to the office building.

Sometimes filming went on at night, depending on the schedule for a picture, but judging by the number of cars in the lot, not much was going on tonight. Hallam didn't see anyone in the building as he went down the hall toward McGinley's office.

The glamorous secretary was still at her desk, though, and she looked up in surprise at Hallam as he asked, "Carl here?"

"I believe he's still on the lot somewhere," she said. "I know he had some work to do tonight, and he and Mr. Swan were supposed to have a meeting, I think."

"But he ain't in his office?"

"He's probably over at the aerodrome set. I believe that was where he was supposed to meet Mr. Swan."

"Thanks." Hallam nodded. "Guess I'll mosey on over there."

Swan's presence would be a bonus. He had intended to ask McGinley some questions, but Swan might be helpful, too. Hallam went to Building A, checked the big door, found it unlocked.

The lights around the set were burning. Hallam stepped over

cables and around equipment and headed for the set, looking around for McGinley and Swan. He frowned as he realized that they weren't in sight. The secretary had said they were probably over here, and Hallam didn't know where else they might be.

He stopped in his tracks at the edge of the set, his eyes narrowing.

There was a pair of feet sticking out past the end of one of the benches by the long table.

Hallam reached for his Colt as he stalked forward. His already grim face became even more bleak as he stepped around the table and saw Danby Swan lying on the sawdust-covered floor, an ugly lump on his head. There was a slight trickle of blood from a cut, as well. Somebody had clouted the director a good one.

Hallam knelt, saw that Swan was still breathing, felt for a pulse in the man's neck. His heart was beating a little rapidly, but it seemed strong enough. He was just knocked out cold. Hallam stood up and moved over to the bar, instinct telling him to check behind it.

Sure enough, Carl McGinley was behind the bar, sprawled there limply with an almost identical wound on his head. His pulse was steady enough, too.

Hallam grimaced. Both men were lucky they hadn't been hit harder. It didn't take much to cave in a man's skull. He'd have to go back over to the office, get the secretary to call an ambulance and the cops—

He heard the swish of movement in the air behind him and dove frantically to the side. Something slammed into his left shoulder.

Pain shot through Hallam, but he forced it to the back of his mind as he spun around. He saw B. W. Garrettson lunging at him again with a chunk of wood in his hand. Hallam recognized it as a piece of two-by-four like the studio carpenters used in building sets. He ducked to his right as Garrettson brought the makeshift weapon down.

Hallam started to lift the Colt in his hand. He didn't want to kill Garrettson, but a slug in the leg would sure as hell slow him down. Before Hallam could pull the trigger, though, Garrettson caught his balance and flung the two-by-four at him.

The board whipped through the air and slammed into Hallam's right knee. He grunted as agony blazed up his leg and slammed him in the belly like a fist. For a moment, everything turned red and then black, and before Hallam could do anything, Garrettson was on him.

Garrettson slapped the Colt aside, moving with the speed and strength of a lunatic. He drove his fists into Hallam's body, staggering the big detective.

Hallam felt himself going backward and tried to catch himself, but Garrettson hammered more punches into him. He fell heavily, landing on his back. With an exultant, savage cry, Garrettson lashed out with his foot. The kick hit Hallam in the knee again, and the pain was too much this time. He didn't lose consciousness, but the Colt slipped from his fingers and he seemed to drift off into a hellish crimson haze.

Through the red mist, he could see Garrettson retreating into the shadows of the big soundstage and then returning with some kind of metal can in his hands. The Klansman tilted the can and began slinging liquid all around the aerodrome set. Even in his dazed condition, Hallam could smell the pungent odor of gasoline.

Somewhere a tiny voice was crying out for him to do something, to stop Garrettson. But Hallam's body wouldn't obey. All he could do was lie there in front of the bar and watch as Garrettson got ready to burn the whole place down around their ears.

Garrettson tossed the gas can aside, fumbled in his pocket, took out several kitchen matches. He swaggered over to Hallam and bent down above him, confident now of success in his mission.

"Bastard!" Garrettson hissed, his foot thudding into Hallam's side. "Wake up, you son-of-a-bitch! I'll teach you not to interfere with one-hundred-percent Americans!"

He struck one of the matches, eyes glittering in the sudden flare, then waved it back and forth tauntingly over Hallam's face.

"It's all your fault. The cops are after me and you framed me, mister. Well, now you'll pay. By God, you'll pay! You'll be cleansed with the purifying fire of patriotism! This studio will never hire another goddamned foreigner!"

He flicked the burning match at Hallam's eyes.

Somehow, Hallam forced his brain to work enough to send a message to his muscles. Sluggish though they were, he turned his head just enough that the match missed his eyes, hitting his cheek instead and rolling down his face to the floor beside his head. Hallam's left eye jerked closed in reaction to the pain of the burn. The match went out when it hit the floor.

Garrettson turned away, still laughing. He struck another match and tossed it at the gasoline-splattered set. The fuel went up with a fierce glare as the match hit it. Garrettson lit another one, flung it away from him to start a blaze on another part of the set.

Behind him, Lucas Hallam climbed slowly to his feet.

Garrettson didn't know it yet, but he'd made one hell of a mistake.

Hallam embraced the pain radiating from his injured knee and his burned face. He gripped it tightly, using his hold on it as a brace to haul himself back onto his feet. He took one awkward step, his right leg almost useless—almost. Another step, and then Garrettson heard him coming. The Klansman started to whirl around as Hallam brought his right fist looping up from his knees.

Hallam hit him.

The fist caught him square in the jaw, sending him crashing back against the bar. Garrettson rebounded from it, took two steps, and pitched to the floor, smacking his face against the planks. He didn't feel it.

Everything still looked red to Hallam, but now that was from the fire. It bloomed all around him, licking fiercely at the wooden set. He knew he had only minutes to get the others out of here before the whole building was ablaze.

He staggered over to the bar, leaned on it as he went behind it. Bending, he got his hands under Carl McGinley's arms and lifted the producer's dead weight. Hallam grunted with the strain as he prodded his aching muscles into the effort. He draped McGinley over his shoulders and started for the door of the soundstage.

Hallam kept his eyes fixed on the exit, bumping into things as he put one foot in front of the other. His right leg started to buckle several times, but he stiffened it and went on. Finally, he saw the door directly in front of him. He stepped out onto the little landing at the top of the three steps leading to the asphalt. There was no question of putting McGinley down gently. Hallam turned around and released his hold on him, letting McGinley fall.

Better a few bumps and bruises than burning to death.

Hallam went back to the set, intending to repeat the nightmarish journey twice more if he could. Danby Swan would be next, and then, if there was time, B. W. Garrettson.

But Garrettson was gone.

Hallam knew the man must have come to and ducked back into the shadows away from the set. Maybe he was trying to find another way out. It was possible; there was a door at the back of the building, too. Hallam couldn't worry about that now. He still had to get Swan out of here.

The place was an inferno by now, the heat from the fire blasting at Hallam's face. He scooped his Colt from the floor and then picked up Swan as part of the set collapsed. The walls were ablaze now, and the roof was about to catch. It wouldn't take long for the whole building to go up. Hallam shouldered Swan and began to retrace his steps.

The fire was all around him, but Hallam found a way

through. Beams began falling behind him as he staggered out into night air that suddenly seemed blessedly cool. He couldn't negotiate the steps. He just fell down them, Swan going with him.

McGinley was moaning and starting to come to. Hallam got onto his hands and knees, then climbed the next mile to his feet. He hooked his fingers in Swan's collar and began to drag the director away from the side of the burning building. When he had Swan about twenty feet away, he let him go and went back for McGinley.

McGinley was sitting up and shaking his head, looking around in utter confusion. Hallam loomed up above him like some charred, smoky giant and extended a hand to him.

"Come on, Carl. We got to get out of here."

McGinley took Hallam's hand, and Hallam pulled him to his feet. With a long arm around him to support him, Hallam helped him over to where Swan was lying, still out cold.

"Lucas . . . ?" McGinley croaked. "Wha' happened?"

Hallam was too tired to explain now. He just held McGinley up as they watched the building go up in flames and listened to the wail of approaching sirens.

"I told you!" a voice howled behind him. "It's God's purifying flames!"

Hallam turned his head and saw B. W. Garrettson. The Klansman had gotten out, all right, and now he was coming to finish the job he had started. He had a long piece of metal in his hands. As he lifted it and started to charge toward them, Hallam recognized it as a piece of a light standard. It was heavy enough to be a dangerous weapon.

Hallam said, "Damn," and wrapped his fingers around the butt of the Colt where it was stuck in his belt. Still holding up Carl McGinley, Hallam turned and lifted the old revolver.

He triggered off two shots. The first bullet smashed Garrettson's right shoulder, and the second slug punched through his right knee. He screamed and flopped to the ground, the metal pole clattering away as he thrashed and shrieked.

Hallam slid the Colt behind his belt again and turned back to the flames. The sirens of the fire trucks were close now.

He hoped there were some ambulances, too.

FIFTEEN

The doctors managed to keep Hallam in bed until the next morning. By then, though, he was limping around the room looking for his clothes and demanding to be let out of the hospital.

"Raising a ruckus as usual, I see," Ben Dunnemore said dryly from the doorway.

Hallam glanced at the Homicide cop and glared. "They might as well give this room to somebody who really needs it," he declared. "Ain't nothin' wrong with me a little rest won't fix."

That was true. His knee was wrapped tightly, but the doctors thought that no bones were broken; it was just badly bruised. The burn on his face, painful though it had been, was only superficial. There was a small dressing on it, but that was all. And his lungs, seared by smoke inhalation, just needed a chance to recover.

"So you're all hale and hearty, eh?" Dunnemore said.

"That's good. Then maybe you won't mind explaining to me just what the hell happened out at that movie studio last night."

Hallam had already explained it to other cops what seemed like four dozen times. In fact, the doctors had finally had to run the detectives out so that Hallam could get some sleep. Dunnemore wanted to hear it again this morning, though, so Hallam obliged.

He told Dunnemore about going to the studio to ask Carl McGinley some more questions about the case. He *didn't* say anything about Lowell Thorley's murder. Hallam recited the story of finding McGinley and Swan in the soundstage, then being attacked by Garrettson. Dunnemore winced as Hallam told him about the burning match thrown at his eyes. Hallam finished by saying, "They tell me they've got Garrettson under guard here in the hospital. He ain't goin' anywhere for a while."

"Not with a busted shoulder and kneecap, he ain't," Dunnemore agreed. "I just came from talking to him. He tells the story a little different—according to him he's just a misunderstood patriot—but I don't think there'll be any question about which of you is telling the truth."

"He admit that him and Brownlow were behind all the other sabotage on the picture?" Hallam asked.

Dunnemore rubbed his jaw. "Well, now, that's the funny part. He's proud of what he did, couldn't wait to tell us about it. If you want my honest opinion, Lucas, the strain of being on the run for a couple of days has sent him round the bend. But he still insists he didn't have anything to do with that airplane nearly crashing or with that young pilot being shot later. If he's telling the truth about that, we've still got a murderer on the loose."

Garrettson was telling the truth. Hallam was sure of that. He had a pretty good idea who was responsible for the deaths of Hank Schiller and Lowell Thorley. Now it was just a matter of getting some proof.

And that was something he couldn't do from a hospital room.

"How about it, Ben?" he asked. "How about you pullin' some strings and gettin' me out of this here place?"

Dunnemore looked dubiously at him. "I shouldn't. This is probably the safest place for you. You can't get into too much mayhem in here." He shook his head. "Ah, hell. I'll go talk to the doctor."

The fire had completely destroyed Building A. All that was left of it was a gutted shell. Before the fire department could bring it under control, it had spread to the other buildings, damaging them. They weren't ruined, but they would need some cleaning up and repair. Only the studio offices had been spared.

That's where Hallam found Carl McGinley later that morning. McGinley was sitting behind his desk, his chair turned around so that he could stare out the window at the devastation Garrettson had caused. There was a bandage on his head, also courtesy of B. W. Garrettson.

"Mornin', Carl," Hallam said as he came into the office. "How you feelin' today?"

"Morning," McGinley grunted. "I suppose I'm fine, Lucas. A little headache, but not bad."

"Could've been a lot worse."

McGinley turned his chair back around and clasped his hands on the desktop. "That's right," he said. "I owe you my life, Lucas. I hope you know that. Anything you ever want from this studio, you've got it." He pushed a piece of paper across the desk toward Hallam. "There's a start. Your fee for settling the Garrettson case."

Hallam glanced at the check, saw that the amount was higher—a lot higher—than his usual rates would justify, and shook his head. "You hired me to stop the trouble, Carl," he said. "I may have caught Garrettson, but not until he damn near ruined the whole studio, not just one picture. I don't collect on a job like that."

"Then consider it a fee from me personally. Bodyguard

duty, if you like. And your hospital bill is already paid, by the way."

Hallam nodded. "I know. They told me when I checked out." He pushed the payment back across the desk to McGinley. "But I still can't take this."

McGinley sighed. "You're a stubborn old coot, you know that."

Hallam grinned and said, "So they tell me." He waved a hand at the window. "What's going to happen about all that?"

"Naturally, production's shut down on all of our pictures. We should have a couple of sets back in order in a week or so, so the delay won't kill us. Building A will have to be completely rebuilt, though. Until it is, Danby is shooting the rest of the location footage out at the ranch."

"Is he goin' to be able to do the rest of the picture with only five pilots?"

The producer nodded. "Oh, yeah, no problem there. It just makes things a little more difficult not to have Hank. But we've got a lot of footage that the Army's provided, whole squadrons taking off, troop movements, things like that. The only thing we're really using the pilots for are individual takeoffs and landings and dogfight scenes. In those, there are never more than a couple of planes on camera at one time, anyway." McGinley sighed. "I guess we've been lucky. There's not much left of *Death to the Kaiser!* to shoot. We should be able to get it in the can all right."

"Reckon Swan can manage, then. He doin' all right after last night?"

McGinley touched the bandage on his head. "He's got one of these," he said. "But other than that he's okay. We were both real lucky you came along when you did, Lucas."

"Garrettson came in through the back lot, I reckon, figured he'd burn the place down. Findin' you and Swan on the set was just coincidence."

"That's one more thing we're doing while the studio is

closed down," McGinley said. "We're putting up a better fence around the back lot. People won't just come waltzing in anymore."

"Good idea." Hallam looked thoughtful. "Carl, do them flyers have any lockers or dressing rooms or anything like that here?"

"No, they don't do enough studio work to warrant anything like that." McGinley peered narrowly at Hallam. "What's on your mind, Lucas?"

Hallam hesitated a moment, then said, "You know Garrettson didn't kill Hank or sabotage that airplane that day. Somebody else did that."

"You don't still think that Danby had something to do with that, do you?"

"I ain't got proof of anything just yet. I'm tryin' to lay my hands on some, though." Hallam nodded. "Maybe I'll take a *paseo* out to the location shootin'."

"And stir everything up again? Come on, Lucas, we nearly got killed already. The case is over, let the cops handle all the rest."

"Nope." Hallam shook his head. "This case ain't over. Not yet."

Hallam felt like the case had traveled a big circle. He was back where it had started, the studio's location ranch where Danby Swan was putting the finishing touches on the exterior scenes of *Death to the Kaiser!*

As Hallam drove up, he could see the planes looping around in the sky high above the fields. There were four of them aloft at the moment. Two bore German markings and were closing in on a ship with the Indian's-head symbol of the Lafayette Escadrille on its fuselage. Off to one side was another plane, this one a D.H.4 like the one Hallam had ridden in with Hank Schiller. Maybe it was the same plane, for all Hallam knew. The man in the rear cockpit was holding a bulky something and aiming it at the other three airplanes.

A camera, Hallam suddenly realized. There was a camera-man in the D.H.4.

He parked near the equipment trucks and got out of the flivver. A couple of cameras were set up on the ground, as well as the airborne one, their operators crouching awkwardly behind them. The cameras were tilted back as far as they would go.

There weren't a lot of cast members on hand today, Hallam saw as he scanned the group of people standing around watching the filming. The scenes being put in the can today must be all flying sequences, he thought. He spotted Simon Drake standing not far from one of the cameras and ambled in that direction.

Drake saw him coming and shook his head. As Hallam came up to him, he said, "I certainly didn't expect to see you here today, Mr. Hallam. I supposed that you were still in the hospital."

Hallam grinned. "Hospitals and me don't get along any too well. Too much like being in the hoosegow." He jerked a thumb at the planes roaring overhead. "The rest of your bunch is up there, I reckon."

"That's right." Drake nodded. "Art and Pete are flying the Fokkers, and Mackey is piloting the Nieuport."

Hallam looked around the location, searching for Danby Swan. When he didn't spot him, he asked, "That's Swan up there in that airplane with the camera?"

"Yes. He said everything would look more authentic with aerial photography. He's right, of course, though keeping a camera even halfway stable isn't easy."

"And von Ottenhausen's flyin' it for him?"

Drake nodded again.

Hallam was silent for a moment as he watched the planes maneuver. Bursts of machine-gun fire chattered from the Vickers guns mounted on the Nieuport as it tried to fight back against the two-to-one odds.

That was interesting, the fact that Swan and von Ottenhausen were up in the same plane. Considering the enmity between the two men, it was surprising that they would trust each other. Under these circumstances, though, there wasn't much one could do to hurt the other without endangering himself in the process. So maybe it made sense after all.

"We heard about what happened with Garrettson," Drake said. "We're all glad that madman is finally in custody. Now perhaps we can put all of the tragedy he caused behind us."

"You mean Hank gettin' killed?"

"Of course."

Hallam shook his head. "Garrettson didn't kill Hank."

Drake shot a surprised glance at him. "He didn't? We just assumed that since he was behind the sabotage . . ."

"Hank was killed because he found out about something he shouldn't have. We already suspected pretty strongly that Garrettson and the Klan were behind them problems that had cropped up earlier. It was possible that Hank actually caught him at the studio about to try something. That's the theory the cops were goin' on. But they were wrong."

"You mean someone else killed Hank, someone not even connected with Garrettson?"

"Reckon that's the way it was, all right."

Drake's hand closed on Hallam's arm. "My God, man," he said urgently. "Do you know who?"

Hallam nodded. "Reckon I do." He didn't say anything else.

After a moment of staring at him, Drake said, "You don't intend to tell me, do you?"

"Don't have any proof yet," Hallam replied. "I ain't one to go makin' accusations I can't back up. I'm goin' to get proof, though . . . tonight."

The four airplanes were coming in for a landing now, their wheels touching down smoothly as each craft descended in turn. The D.H.4 was the last one down.

Hallam and Drake didn't say anything else as the pilots leaped down from their craft and strolled over. Mackey Russell grinned and called, "How'd it look, Simon?"

Drake nodded as his three friends came up. "Excellent," he told them. "I don't know what Swan thought of it, but I thought you performed flawlessly, as usual."

Pete Goldman looked at Hallam and asked, "What are you doing here, Mr. Hallam? I thought the case was all wrapped up."

"Mr. Hallam believes someone other than Garrettson killed Hank," Drake said tightly. "He won't say who he suspects, though."

The other three pilots stared at Hallam. "Is that true?" Art Tobin asked.

Hallam nodded. "Reckon it is. I'll tell you boys the whole story, soon's I got the killer and the proof the cops'll need to hang him."

"Need some help?" Russell asked. "If Garrettson didn't murder Hank, I'd like to get my mitts on the skunk who did."

Hallam remembered how Russell had been ready to tear into Jocko Burke. That incident had been brought on because Burke was with Lorraine von Ottenhausen, and Russell held a grudge against her because she had been a German agent during the war. The man held a grudge, all right, and had a temper on top of it. Hallam didn't think he'd be too helpful when it came to catching a killer.

"I can handle it," he said. "Just wanted you fellers to know that Hank's killer is goin' to be brought to justice. You can count on it."

Swan and von Ottenhausen had left the D.H.4 by now. Swan came over to the flyers while von Ottenhausen walked off by himself, as aloof as ever.

"Superb, gentlemen!" Swan greeted them. "That was some beautiful flying, and I've captured it all on film." He tapped the heavy camera he was still carrying. "Thanks to the miracle of Mr. Akeley's invention and my own sure hand." He seemed to be in a good mood this morning, considering what he had gone through the night before. He looked at Hallam and smiled. "I certainly didn't expect to see you here, Mr. Hallam. I owe you a great debt of gratitude. You saved my life, you know."

Nobody seemed to expect Hallam to be anywhere this morning. Hell, he was just bunged up a little bit, and everybody was acting like he was on his deathbed. He grunted, "Was just tryin' to get the hell out of there myself. Nothin' to worry about."

"Well, no matter what you say, sir"—Swan stuck his hand out—"I thank you."

Hallam shook his hand, returning the hard grip. Swan could be a stiff-necked so-and-so at times, but he was sincere now.

"Hallam thinks somebody besides Garrettson killed Hank, Mr. Swan," Russell told the director. "What do you think about that?"

Swan's eyes narrowed. "You mean this whole dreadful affair isn't over?"

"It will be soon," Hallam promised. "After tonight, the whole story'll come out."

With a dubious look, Swan said, "I'm not sure about this, Mr. Hallam. I was convinced that Garrettson was our culprit."

"He caused all the problems up until the day that oil line was cut," Hallam said. "Way I figure it, somebody took advantage of all the trouble you'd been havin' to try to get rid of Hank."

Swan smiled thinly. "Well, at least you don't seem to suspect me anymore."

Hallam grinned, but the expression didn't reach his eyes. He didn't say anything.

After a moment, Swan said, "I'd best get busy setting up the next shot. Gentlemen, if you'll come with me we can discuss the maneuvers you'll be required to perform." He turned and walked away, clearly unsure what to make of Hallam's attitude. Was he still a suspect or not?

Hallam wasn't saying. In fact, he wasn't saying any more than he already had.

If his speculations were right, it had been enough.

The pilots followed Swan, nodding their farewells to Hallam. "Go get 'em, Mr. Hallam," Mackey Russell called.

Hallam nodded. "I intend to," he said.

Hallam had some time to kill, so he picked up a newspaper and headed home. It seemed like a long time since he had seen Liz, and she was going to be angry that he hadn't let her know when he was in the hospital. But he hadn't intended on staying cooped up there for long, and while he was there, he had been busy talking to cops.

Maybe she wouldn't be too angry. He'd take her out to dinner before she had to go to work.

Before he had to go solve a murder or two . . .

Liz wasn't home, though. At least she didn't answer his knocks on her apartment door, and when he listened, he couldn't hear anyone stirring around inside. She was probably out shopping, he thought. There were several markets and stores within walking distance. He'd see her later.

He went on up to his place and settled down to read the newspaper. Lowell Thorley's murder had a prominent place on page one. LOCAL ART DEALER FOUND SLAIN, the headline read. Hallam scanned the story and found out that Thorley had been fifty-seven years old, that he had been born and educated in England, and that he had lived in Los Angeles for the past fourteen years. There were quotes from several people in local art circles mourning his death and commenting on what a fine person he had been.

Hallam noted wryly that there was no quote from Jocko Burke. Evidently the link between the respected art dealer and the little gangster wasn't common knowledge.

According to the story, the body had been discovered by a clerk from Thorley's gallery who had come to the house to check on his employer when Thorley didn't show up at work. The clerk had told the police that someone had been asking at the gallery for Thorley, and the cops were regarding that someone as the primary suspect for the moment. Hallam read the description the clerk had given and had to grin. The man wasn't much of a witness. The description had him several inches taller and about fifty pounds heavier than he was in real life. It was close enough that he could expect a visit from a Homicide detective sooner or later, though.

Unless he handed them Thorley's killer before then, and that was one of the things he intended to do.

Liz didn't show up all afternoon. Hallam began to worry and called the Egyptian Theater. The manager told him that Liz wasn't there. She had been at work the night before, and everything had seemed normal.

Hallam hung up as the man was asking him if anything was wrong. Damn right something was wrong, Hallam thought. He reached into his pocket and found the key to Liz's apartment. He hadn't planned on ever using it, but now he thought it was probably justified.

He knocked again and called her name several times before giving up and sliding the key into the lock. The door opened easily, the slight creak of its hinges the only sound in the silent apartment. Hallam wished there were other sounds in the place. Too many times in his life, he had gone into rooms that were hushed and quiet and found things he would have rather not found.

In this case, though, he rapidly discovered that there was nothing to find. Everything was in place in the apartment.

There was just no sign of Liz.

Hallam stood in her living room and took a deep breath. All right, he told himself, she had gone somewhere but there was nothing to worry about. Her shopping trip had taken longer than expected, that was all. Or she had taken one of the Hollywood tour buses and was out seeing some of the sights that he had been too busy to show her. He knew he had neglected her since she had come to Hollywood. That hadn't been his intention, but that was the way it had turned out, nonetheless.

Maybe she was just mad at him and was out cooling off. She had been to the Waterhole with him before; maybe she had gone there.

A phone call from his own apartment eliminated that chance. No one at the Waterhole had seen her all day.

"Well, hell!" Hallam said aloud as he stood at the railing of the little balcony outside his apartment, looking out at the city. She had to be there somewhere.

But he had a couple of killings to clear up, and he had already laid most of the groundwork. If he delayed, there was a chance that Hank's killer would never be caught.

He had to carry through with his plan.

Then he would find Liz if he had to turn the whole damned town inside out.

The sun was beginning to drop out of sight below the western horizon as Hallam drove the flivver through Hollywood and turned onto Beachwood Drive. His face was set in hard lines, and anger smoldered in his eyes, along with a touch of urgency and worry. His knee hurt, but he didn't even pay any attention to it now.

He turned at the gate leading into Orville Cooke's estate, getting out of the flivver to lean on the call button. A moment later, a light came on illuminating the portico over the front door of the mansion. The same butler who had admitted him the day before stepped out, looked toward the gate, and then went back inside, shutting the door behind him with finality.

Hallam waited a couple of minutes, then hauled out his Colt.

Two shots busted the lock on the gate. He shoved it open angrily, then got back into the flivver and drove through.

The butler was back outside by the time Hallam reached the portico. He stepped forward with his hands up, palms out. "Please, sir," he said. "Don't force me to call the police."

"If you were goin' to call the cops, you should've done it afore now," Hallam said, shouldering him aside. The butler clutched at him, but Hallam bulled on, tearing out of the grip.

He still had the Colt in his fist, and he lifted it as he slammed open the study door with his other hand.

Orville Cooke was seated at his big desk, and he stared at Hallam in alarm as the private detective strode into the room. "See here!" Cooke exclaimed. "What's the meaning of this?"

Hallam leveled the Colt at the old oilman. "Come for some straight answers," he grated.

"You never worked for Tom Rutledge," Cooke accused, as if lying to him were worse than pointing a gun at him.

"Reckon that's right, but I knew him a long time ago. Less'n he's changed an awful lot, he's a good man. He ain't the type to buy stolen goods from a cheap mobster."

Cooke was already pale. Now an even deeper pallor set in. "I don't know what you're talking about, sir," he said, but his voice carried no sincerity.

Behind Hallam, the butler said, "I've called the police, Mr. Cooke. Should I disarm this ruffian?"

Hallam heard the double click of a shotgun being cocked. He grinned. "My thumb on the hammer's all that's keepin' this hogleg from blowin' a hole in you, Cooke. Maybe you best tell that feller behind me to go away."

Cooke stood up slowly, his face twisted in a frightened grimace. "For God's sake, do as he says!" he ordered. "Can't you see the man's insane?"

"Shut the door behind you," Hallam added.

After a long, tense moment, Hallam sensed as much as heard the butler move out through the door and shut it behind him. He risked a fast glance over his shoulder and saw that the man was really gone.

"This won't take long," Hallam said. "You just tell me the truth." He stepped over to the glass-fronted cabinet and gestured with the Colt at the Dresden miniatures inside. "These little fellers once belonged to a German name of Mad Ludwig, ain't that right?"

Cooke nodded shakily.

"They was stolen from a museum in Paris durin' the war. You knew that, didn't you?"

Once again, the oilman nodded.

"You've been buyin' 'em, a piece or two at a time, from Lowell Thorley for a couple of years."

"Thorley said that eventually he could get me the whole set. There are only a few pieces missing now." Cooke stepped around the desk and moved a pace toward Hallam. "Please. I don't know who you are, but I meant no harm. I . . . I knew the figurines were stolen, of course. But I thought that so much time had passed that it didn't really matter anymore."

"Do you know where Thorley was gettin' the figures?"

Cooke shook his head. "I didn't ever ask him. I didn't want to do anything to disrupt our relationship."

"Reckon you heard that Thorley was killed."

Cooke swallowed nervously and said, "I know. But I swear I didn't have anything to do with his death."

Hallam nodded. "Know that. You helped set it all in motion, though." He moved toward the door, keeping an eye on Cooke. "I'm leavin' now. Your butler best not try to stop me. When the cops get here, you can tell 'em what happened. Reckon they'll be a mite interested in the whole story."

He turned and walked out of the study, watching carefully for the shotgun-wielding butler as he left the house. The man had evidently decided not to risk his life, though. Hallam didn't see him anywhere as he got in the flivver and drove rapidly away from the mansion. As he pulled away down Beachwood and then cut through on some of the other residential streets, he heard sirens behind him, loud for a moment and then receding. Looked like he had finished his talk with Cooke just in time.

Cooke had confirmed his suspicions about the figurines, though. Someone had stolen them from the museum in Paris during the war, and they had made their way over several years and thousands of miles to Hollywood, passing through several sets of hands along the way.

And at least one of the people who had handled them was a killer.

As Hallam looked out over the lights of the city, he told himself that soon he would know who the hands belonged to.

SIXTEEN

Night had fallen by the time Hallam reached the Palm Court. An earlier call to the Pimlico had told him that Jocko Burke wasn't at the speakeasy. Hallam had expected that. Burke would be at the bungalow, trying to salvage a situation suddenly gone bad.

Hallam parked on the street and approached the bungalow on foot, as he had on his previous visit. Before he left the flivver, he checked the loads in the Colt and strapped the bowie onto his belt. With a tight grin, he wished he still had the old Greener he had carried during his brief stint as a stagecoach guard in New Mexico. A scattergun might come in handy tonight.

A sporty little roadster was parked in front of Burke's bungalow. The car could belong to Burke himself, or he could already have visitors. Hallam slipped up to the window he had used before in his spying, raising up just enough to peer over the sill and through the gap in the curtains.

Burke was inside, pacing restlessly back and forth. He had a cigarette dangling from his lips and a drink in his hand. He wasn't talking to anyone, and Hallam could tell from his attitude that he was alone.

Time to change that.

Hallam went to the front door, the Colt in his right hand, and lifted his left to rap sharply on the panel. It was an impatient knock, and Burke must have mistaken it, thought it belonged to whoever he was expecting. He jerked the door open.

"It's about time!" he barked. "Everything's gone to—"

He broke off abruptly as he looked up and saw Hallam standing there on the little porch. His eyes widened as he stared down the barrel of the Colt.

"Hell, Jocko," Hallam finished for him in a soft voice. The muzzle of the gun thumped into Burke's chest as Hallam went on, "Get in there!"

Burke backed up quickly, Hallam following him into the bungalow and kicking the door shut behind him with a booted foot.

"Hallam!" Burke exclaimed. "What are you doing here, you bastard?"

"You know why I'm here, Jocko," Hallam said. "Your pard called and told you I was onto your little scheme."

Burke shook his head. He had his hands partially raised in response to being covered with the Colt. "I don't know what the hell you're talking about," he said.

"I'm talkin' about the way you got hold of them little statues so that Thorley could sell 'em to Orville Cooke and make a fortune for the both of you. Already been to see Cooke, and I figure he's goin' to tell the cops everything he knows. He ain't fond of the idea of bein' tied in with a killin'."

That was speculation on Hallam's part, but he thought Cooke had been shaken up enough by his visit to tell the police as much as he knew. Cooke had to know as well as Burke that the game was up; he would want to come out of it with as little personal damage as he could.

Burke shook his head. "Cooke doesn't know anything

except that the figurines were stolen. The only person he could incriminate is Thorley, and Thorley's dead."

"You're admittin' that you and Thorley were in it together, then?"

"Why the hell not? You can't prove a damn thing, Hallam. All we have to do is keep our heads and let you look foolish."

Hallam heard the soft sound of the door opening behind him. He knew the man standing there probably had the drop on him. He could whirl around, take the man by surprise, maybe get off a couple of shots. That would give Burke a chance to go for his gun, though, and Hallam's back would be a big target. Anyway, the last question was just about to be answered. Hallam didn't want any gunplay yet.

"I'll get the proof," he said quietly, as much for the benefit of the man behind him as for Burke. "You ain't got as much to worry about, Jocko. You didn't pull the trigger on Hank Schiller. You didn't kill a boy who looked up to you, a boy who thought you were his friend."

A gun barrel dug hard and painfully into Hallam's back. "Shut up, you old son-of-a-bitch!" Mackey Russell grated. "Just shut up and drop your gun!"

Hallam grinned savagely. "Howdy, Mackey," he said evenly.

He sensed Russell stiffening behind him. "How the hell did you know?" the flyer asked.

"I didn't for sure," Hallam told him. "Knew it had to be one of the four of you. Reckon you were my leadin' suspect, though. That was quite a show you put on when you were here before. Maybe you should've been an actor instead of a stunt pilot."

"It was stupid," Burke spat. "He could have just left when he spotted you, instead of trying to make you think he was drunk."

"I wanted to know what Hallam was doing here," Russell said in his defense. He shoved the gun barrel harder into Hallam's back. "You haven't dropped that pistol yet, pal."

"No, and I ain't goin' to. You can shoot me, Russell, but you can't stop me from blowin' a hole in Burke there. Then how'll you get rid of them other figurines?"

"I'll bet I could find a way," Russell said thoughtfully.

"Russell!" Burke exclaimed. "We're partners, remember?"

Hallam saw the opening, knew he had to drive a wedge in there and widen it. "You know how much him and Thorley was makin' from Cooke, Russell? I ain't sure, myself, but I'd be willin' to bet it was a hell of a lot more than your cut. And you was the one who sold your soul to get the damn things in the first place."

"Goddamn you." The words were soft, deadly quiet. Russell's voice shook with emotion as he went on, "You think I haven't thought about that every day and every night since the war?"

Burke still had his hands up. He frowned and said, "What the devil are you two talking about?"

"You never told Burke the whole story, Russell?" Hallam asked.

"He didn't need to know. All that was important was that I had the figurines and he could find a buyer. If you want to tell him, though, you go ahead."

That would take some more time, and that was what Hallam wanted right now. And he wanted to be sure that all his guesswork was correct. The mere fact that Russell was here, sticking a gun in his back, confirmed some of his speculations.

"Reckon I can spin the yarn, all right," he said. "I figure it all goes back to the war, to a feller named Freneau. He was a German spy in Paris, and the way it looks to me, he must've been a thief, too. He stole them figurines from the museum that had 'em on display. He planned on usin' 'em to help him get information he needed. He used one of 'em to pay off an American pilot who gave him the flight plans for the feller's squadron. That was you, Russell."

Hallam knew he was taking a chance laying it all out like

this. Russell could decide he had heard enough and pull the trigger. Hallam knew how guilt could eat on a man, make him more than a little crazy.

Russell just grunted, though, and said, "Go ahead."

Speaking to Burke, Hallam went on, "Russell's squadron was ambushed, and him and three other pilots were the only ones to make it back alive. Russell went on the flight because he knew that it would look too suspicious if he didn't, once it came out that the squadron had been ambushed. But he knew the attack was comin' and was able to get out of the dogfight with a whole skin. Once it was over, he got to thinkin' that maybe it would look better if the blame for sellin' 'em out fell on somebody else. I ain't sure of this part at all, but I figure he planted some evidence to tie another pilot named Jack Norton in with this Freneau feller, make it look like he was the traitor and that he was killed in the battle because of the remorse he felt over it."

"That's a good guess, Hallam," Russell admitted. "Nobody liked Norton to start with. He made a perfect scapegoat."

"Russell must've decided after it was all over that he hadn't been paid enough by Freneau, though. Maybe Freneau gave him one of them figurines, maybe he gave him cash. Ain't important. What's important is that Russell went back to Freneau and demanded a bigger payoff. Freneau turned things around, though. He threatened to reveal that Russell was a traitor unless Russell paid *him* off. Russell didn't figure to be blackmailed, so he killed Freneau and took the collection of figurines. He knew they was valuable and would probably get to be worth even more if he hung on to them until after the war. He couldn't get too rich too fast from them. That might look fishy to the other pilots." Hallam turned his head slightly. "How'm I doin' so far, Mackey?"

"Right on the money, Hallam," Russell said. "You're pretty smart for an old cowboy."

Talking it out had been a help, Hallam thought. The theory had been a little vague, even in his own head, but now that he had explored it, he saw that it all tied together. He had filled in the holes with guesswork, and it had turned out to be right. There was still more to be covered, though.

For one thing, he had to get out of here alive.

"So after the war, Russell and them other three pilots stayed together, barnstormin' around the country and windin' up in Hollywood doin' stunt flyin'. Once he was here, Russell tied up with you somehow, Burke, and through you and Thorley started disposin' of the booty he had brought back from Paris. The whole bunch of you had sold off most of the figurines and probably piled up a pretty good stack of *dinero*. Russell had to live with the memory of sellin' out his pards, though, and it got hard to swallow over the years. He had to worry all the time about the other fellers findin' out what kind of man he really was."

"The respect of a man's friends is important, Hallam," Russell said tightly.

"Reckon I know that. So Russell had to keep it a secret that he had the figurines. Not only would it maybe foul up sellin' 'em to Cooke if anybody else found out, but Drake and Tobin and Goldman might realize how he had got hold of them little statues. That's what Russell really couldn't face. That's why he let his true nature out again and killed Hank Schiller."

"He found one of them in my duffel bag one day," Russell said. "The kid shouldn't have been rummaging around in there, and he sure as hell shouldn't have unwrapped it." Once more, his voice threatened to break as he went on, "God, I didn't want to kill him. I tried to pass the figurine off as just some gimcrack I'd picked up, but Hank was curious. He thought it looked German, and he was going to ask von Ottenhausen about it."

"So you decided to gimmick that airplane, figurin' that Garrettson would get the blame, just like he did for a while."

"I thought it would just look like an accident, and if the sabotage was discovered, everyone would think Garrettson was responsible."

The pretense of talking to Burke was over now. Hallam was speaking directly to Russell as he went on, "You grabbed the opportunity when Hank took over the job of flyin' that Spad at the last minute. You and him went over the engine together before he took off, and he finally figured out that you must've cut that oil line. He didn't want to believe that of you, so he come face-to-face with you and asked you to explain. When you couldn't, he went to the studio—reckon he needed a place to think—and called me. You followed him there and got to him first, though. You couldn't worry anymore about makin' it look like an accident. Hank had to be got rid of 'fore he could tell anybody else about you. You wore a helmet and flyin' goggles in case anybody got a look at you, like that guard at the gate."

There was an ominous bleakness in Russell's voice as he said, "You've got it all worked out, all right. But now that you know, you'll have to die, too, Hallam."

"What about Burke?"

"Well, you started me thinking. Maybe I could dispose of the rest of the figurines myself. Why should I keep splitting the take?"

"Russell!" Burke said warningly. "You'd better get your head screwed on right. You need me, mister."

"What for?" Russell snapped. "I've been dumb for too long, Burke. I let this old cowboy flush me out with his talk about knowing who the killer was, but that's the last mistake I'm going to make."

"You're damn right!" a new voice cracked from the door on the other side of the room. "Both of you, drop those guns!"

Hallam's eyes flicked to the doorway, saw Nate Farraday standing there with a gun in his hand. So Burke hadn't been alone when he came in, after all. Farraday had been hiding, waiting for the right moment to show himself.

The gun barrel in Hallam's back was jerked aside as Russell spun to face Farraday. Hallam dove forward, seeing out of the corner of his eye that Burke was grabbing frantically for his own gun. As Hallam hit the floor, two shots blasted out, one from Farraday, one from Russell.

Hallam heard Russell grunt in pain, and the gun in Farraday's hand started to track toward him. Hallam squeezed the Colt's trigger. It roared and bucked against his palm as the heavy slug smacked into Nate Farraday's chest, driving him back through the doorway. He dropped the gun as he fell.

A bullet plowed into the floor next to Hallam's head. He rolled desperately to the side as Burke fired again, the little .32 in his hand spitting flame and noise. Hallam surged up into his knees, putting his left hand down for balance as he triggered twice. Both bullets caught Burke in the body, spinning him around and sending him crashing back against a little table. He fell over, sprawling lifelessly to the floor.

Hallam stood up slowly, keeping the Colt pointed toward Burke as he did so, then turning to check Nate Farraday. The henchman seemed to be as dead as his boss, but Hallam went quickly to both men and prodded them with a boot toe to make sure. He nodded grimly. They were done for, all right.

Then he turned his attention to Mackey Russell.

The pilot was curled up on the floor, clutching at his middle and groaning. Blood welled between his fingers. The gun he had poked in Hallam's back was lying a couple of feet away, forgotten in his agony.

Hallam grimaced. There wasn't anything much worse than being gutshot.

He knelt beside Russell, ignoring the twinge of pain he felt from his knee as he bent it. "Take it easy," he told the wounded pilot. "I'll get an ambulance, get you to a hospital."

Russell tilted his head back and opened his eyes, which had been squeezed shut in pain. Beads of sweat stood out on his forehead as he choked out, "Too . . . too late . . . for me . . . Let me . . . die . . . Hallam . . ."

"You'll be all right," Hallam told him. As he looked down at

Russell, he felt like a part of him should be glad that the man was suffering. Russell was a murderer. He had killed Hank, an innocent kid who could have grown into a fine man.

But Hallam couldn't watch this and be glad. He'd seen too much death and suffering over the years to enjoy any of it, no matter how well deserved it was.

"You ain't goin' to die," he said to Russell now. "You just ain't."

A step from the front door of the bungalow made his head jerk up. Russell hadn't completely closed the door behind him when he came in, and now it swung open to reveal two people standing there. A man and a woman, and each of them had a heavy automatic—German-made, of course—pointing at Hallam.

"You're right, Mr. Hallam," Count Wolfram von Ottenhausen said. "Russell can't die yet."

"Not until he has told us where the rest of the figurines are," Lorraine von Ottenhausen added, her voice like the hiss of a murderous cat.

SEVENTEEN

Hallam didn't move for a long moment as he looked up at von Ottenhausen and Lorraine. Then he said, "This man's hurt. He needs a doctor."

"It's too late for a doctor to do him any good, and you know it," von Ottenhausen said. "Step back away from him, please."

Hallam slowly stood up and stepped back a pace. He glanced down. Russell's eyes were closed again. The pilot didn't seem to know what was going on, the pain of his stomach wound blotting out everything else around him.

Lorraine came forward as her brother continued to cover Hallam. Bending over Russell, she said urgently, "The figurines! Where are they?"

Russell moaned. His mouth worked, but nothing intelligible came out.

Hallam's eyes darted back and forth between the count and Lorraine. The woman's gun was pointed toward the floor now, but von Ottenhausen's weapon was still aimed directly at Hallam, and his dark eyes never moved. There was a thin smile on his lips as he said, "Please, Mr. Hallam, do not attempt anything foolish. I would not like to have to shoot you."

"Gotten kind of particular, ain't you?" Hallam asked. "Stabbin' Lowell Thorley in the back didn't seem to bother you."

Lorraine glanced up. "I did that," she said coldly. "The man was a fool. He would not tell us what we needed to know."

"Cooke already has most of them figurines," Hallam pointed out. "How many more of 'em could Russell still have? Enough to make it worth murder?"

"If it was only one, I would still have a debt of honor to avenge," Lorraine snapped. "Russell stole them from Alain and then killed him! Alain was my lover. The figurines must be mine!"

Hallam shook his head. Her eyes were flashing with an insane fire. "Reckon you've been after them little statues for years."

"Ever since the war, actually," Wolfram von Ottenhausen said. "My dear sister is a bit obsessed with them, I'm afraid."

"They're mine, I tell you!" Lorraine spat. She reached down and grabbed Mackey Russell's hair, jerking his head back. She put the barrel of her weapon against his jaw and ground it painfully against the flesh. "Wake up! You cannot die!"

Russell's eyes fluttered open, but he couldn't seem to focus on her. "Wh . . . what . . ."

"Where are the figurines?"

The intensity of Lorraine's question seemed to get through to him. He licked his lips, said, "D-duffel bag . . . in locker . . . airfield . . ."

"He must mean the airfield where the planes for the film are kept," von Ottenhausen said eagerly. "All of the pilots have lockers there."

Hallam grimaced. His own search for the remaining figurines had taken him to the studio and to Lafayette's, but he hadn't thought about the airfield.

"F-figurines . . . rich man . . . so sorry . . ."

Hallam heard those words, breathed faintly by Mackey Russell, and then the pilot stiffened suddenly for a moment. A hideous rattle came from his throat, and then he went limp and his head thudded against the floor.

There were three dead men in the room now instead of two.

Lorraine stood up, looked pleased. "At least he told us where they are before dying, the treacherous swine." She glanced at her brother, then nodded toward Hallam. "Kill the old man."

Hallam was ready to make a play. The Colt was still in his hand, and he knew that no matter how fast or good Von Ottenhausen was, he'd get off a shot or two, at least. But the count was hesitating, seemingly unwilling to pull the trigger, and Hallam gambled his life on waiting.

"Why kill him?" Von Ottenhausen asked. "He cannot harm us, Lorraine. We will get the figurines and be out of the country before he can convince anyone to stop us."

"He knows I killed Thorley," Lorraine snapped.

"How can he prove it?"

"Reckon that's right, ma'am," Hallam spoke up. "I know the whole story, but with Burke dead I can't prove a damn thing."

Lorraine laughed contemptuously. There was no hurry now, now that she knew where the rest of the figurines were. "The whole story," she said mockingly. "How could you know?"

"I know you and your brother suspected one of the pilots who survived that ambush was the one who actually sold out to Freneau. You tracked 'em to Hollywood and came here yourself to try to find out which one. You worked with Freneau, you knew he set up that ambush and paid off one of the pilots with a figurine. You figured that whoever the traitor was, he was the one who killed Freneau and stole the rest of the figurines. When you got here, you found out who in town might be movin' goods like that, and that led you to Burke. You started carryin' on with Burke to find out what he knew about the figurines, and that led you to Thorley. You probably went to Thorley's house the same night you saw me and Russell here, but Thorley couldn't tell you anything. He didn't know where the figurines were. You must've lost your temper with him, or he got mad and tried to throw you out, or something like that. He got a knife in the back for his trouble."

"It was a very unpleasant scene," von Ottenhausen said. He cast a disapproving glance at his sister. "I told Lorraine there was no need for violence."

Lorraine sneered. "For a Prussian nobleman, brother, you have an awfully delicate stomach. Now are you going to kill this American dog, or shall I?"

Hallam smiled. "I'd listen, was I you. Hear them sirens? Somebody must've reported those gunshots to the cops."

Hallam had heard the sirens while he was talking and had plunged ahead with the story to keep the two Germans distracted. Now von Ottenhausen's head jerked toward the door as the wail of approaching police cars became plainly audible. He barked a curse in German, then said, "Come, Lorraine, we must leave!"

"Not until the cowboy is dead!" she cried, whipping her gun up and firing.

Hallam wasn't there anymore. He had thrown himself backward, toward the window he had looked through earlier. His shoulder hit the glass and shattered it as Lorraine's bullet whined through the air where he had been a second before.

He didn't want a shootout. He wanted the Germans alive, so this mess could be cleared up for the cops.

As broken glass showered around him, he fell to the ground outside, landing gracefully and rolling away. He had been lucky this time; he hadn't banged his bad knee against anything. He surged up onto his feet and ran toward the front of the house, trying to cut the von Ottenhausens off and pin them inside.

He was just a little too slow. They came bursting out of the front door as Hallam reached the corner of the bungalow. The count flipped his gun up and triggered off a shot that made Hallam duck back. Hallam returned the fire, but hitting moving targets in the dark was next to impossible.

Car doors slammed, and an engine roared into life. The count's Bugatti leaped away from the curb with a squeal of tires.

"Dammit!" Hallam growled. He needed those two if he was ever going to make sense of this for the authorities.

There was only one thing to do. He knew where they would be heading. He just had to get there before they could get away with the figurines.

He ran through the shadows, back to his flivver.

The old car was slow but steady, and Hallam knew the back streets of Hollywood like he knew the game trails and mountain passes of his home. As he slewed the flivver around corners and down alleys, he figured that he could reach the airfield not too far behind von Ottenhausen and Lorraine.

As he drove, he opened the cylinder of the Colt, punched out the empty shells, thumbed in fresh ones.

The gate in the fence around the airfield had been closed, but now it was smashed open. There were lights on in the little office building, more lights out by the runway itself. Hallam drove past the damaged gate and skidded the flivver to a stop next to the office. The Bugatti was parked there, its grill bent and twisted.

Hallam plunged out of the flivver and through the door of the building, the Colt ready in his hand. He spotted movement to his right and wheeled in that direction. A man was sitting on the floor, holding his head and swaying back and forth. There was blood on his head where someone had clouted him.

Hallam recognized him as the manager of the airfield, recalling him from his visit here with Hank Schiller. The man must have been working late when the count and Lorraine came bursting in. Hallam dropped to a knee beside him and said, "Which way'd they go?"

"Oh, my head . . . Who're you?"

Hallam ignored the question. "Them two that was just here, where are they?"

"They were headed for the hangar last I saw of 'em. Lordy, they didn't have to hit me like that!"

"They take something from a pilot's locker?"

"Hell, I don't know . . . They could have, they had to go right past the lockers on their way out—"

The window in the office was open, and the abrupt cough and rattle of an airplane engine starting up came to Hallam's ears. He got to his feet as the engine smoothed out. "Damn," he bit off as he ran out of the office, down the hall, and out the rear door of the building.

The D.H.4 was rolling out of one of the hangars onto the runway. Hallam could see two people in it, but they both wore helmets and goggles. He couldn't tell which one was Lorraine and which was her brother. But he knew what they intended to do. They were going to take off and fly away from here, taking the remaining figurines with them.

He had to stop them.

He broke into a run again, heading out onto the runway as the plane began to build up speed. It would have to come past him on its takeoff. Hallam hauled up when he reached the center of the broad, grassy strip, lifting the Colt and lining it on the rapidly approaching plane.

Muzzle flashes flickered from the front cockpit of the D.H.4, but he couldn't hear the shots over the roar of the engine. The nose of the plane was starting to lift as Hallam aimed the Colt at it and began squeezing the trigger.

The boom of the Colt blended with the thunder of the plane. Hallam fired all five bullets in the cylinder, then threw himself forward to the ground as the D.H.4 soared over him, missing him by only a few feet. Noise and prop wash slammed into him, driving his face against the runway. Then in an instant the airplane was past him, still climbing like a bird of prey—

And trailing flame from the underside of its fuselage . . .

Hallam rolled over and pushed himself up in time to see the wings suddenly tilt. The plane dipped crazily toward the ground, and one wing tip scraped the runway. The craft straightened up for an instant and came down on its landing gear, then bounced back up. There was a sudden burst of fire around the engine, and the wings tilted the other way. Again the fragile construction plowed into the earth, and the plane began to tumble. It hit, bounced, hit again, came apart in a disastrous shower of flame and debris, a hundred yards past where Hallam was slowly getting to his feet.

He started walking toward the wreck, the Colt hanging loosely in his hand at his side, when he saw movement there. Shocked that anyone could have survived such a fiery crash, Hallam kicked himself into a run again.

The fire burned fiercely but quickly, and the blaze was already dying down by the time Hallam reached the plane. He saw the figure in the front cockpit, slumped forward over the controls. Memories of escaping from the burning movie studio came vividly to him as he darted forward and reached out to grasp the jacket of the aviator. Hallam hauled the figure out of the cockpit, sprawling to the ground with the effort. Then he got to his feet and pulled the limp body away from the burning wreckage.

In the garish light, Hallam knelt beside the body and reached out to grasp the helmet and goggles. Even before he stripped them back, he knew who he would find underneath them. He had known as soon as he felt the weight.

Lorraine von Ottenhausen's head lolled limply to the side as Hallam pulled the helmet and goggles off it. Hallam could tell from the angle of her neck what had happened. The crash had broken it, probably killing her instantly.

He had to know if any of the shots he had fired had hit her, though. He ripped open her jacket.

No wounds. The crash had killed her, not his bullets. Somehow, that made him feel a little better.

He did find something inside her jacket, though. A cloth bag filled with little shards of what looked like porcelain, brightly and intricately painted.

The last of Mad Ludwig's legacy, smashed into a million pieces, shattered just like Lorraine's obsession had broken her.

Hank Schiller's killer was dead, and now so was Lowell Thorley's. And Lucas Hallam was tired, damned tired.

He stood up and limped away from the dying flames.

The eastern sky was getting light as Hallam pulled the flivver to the curb in front of his apartment building. He had been talking to cops all night again, and it wasn't getting any easier.

Ben Dunnemore had believed his story. Hell, Hallam thought grimly, there was no one alive anymore to argue with it.

That might not be true, though. There was one person involved in the case still unaccounted for.

Count Wolfram von Ottenhausen's body had not been found in the wreckage of the D.H.4. Hallam had told Dunnemore about seeing movement at the downed plane. It was hard to believe that anyone could walk away from such a crash, but it looked like von Ottenhausen had done just that. The cops would turn him up, though, if he was still around Los Angeles.

Hallam got out of the flivver and softly shut the door. As tired as he was, he wanted to see if Liz had returned. His worry about her had been overwhelmed by the explosion of events the night before, but now it was back in full force. He limped toward the building, looking up at her windows. There were no lights there, but he wouldn't expect her to be up at this hour of the morning.

Dunnemore had read him the riot act, tearing into him about withholding evidence and going out to trap a couple of killers by himself, not to mention shooting up the town, shooting down an airplane, and generally raising one hell of an uproar. "You may save your license, Lucas," Dunnemore had told him, "but I'll be damned if I see how."

Hallam wasn't going to worry about that. He was getting too old for private-eye work, anyway. And he could get plenty of jobs as a riding extra. He seemed to remember that Art Acord was starting a new picture in a couple of days . . .

He climbed the stairs to the second-floor landing, knocked heavily on Liz's door. He waited, then knocked again. Twice was enough. When there was still no answer, he used his key and unlocked the door.

Dawn light came in through the windows, giving the place a reddish-gold glow as Hallam stepped inside. His eyes scanned the room, narrowing as he saw the bare walls, the empty floor. For a moment, his brain refused to accept the fact that the place had been cleaned out.

The apartment was deserted. Liz and all of her belongings were gone.

The only thing left was an envelope lying in the middle of the floor.

Hallam stepped forward and bent to pick it up, aware that his heart was beating heavily, painfully. He ripped it open and took out a sheet of paper, his blunt fingers wrinkling it and making it crackle loudly in the hushed apartment. As he looked at the words, he recognized Liz's handwriting.

The message was simple. Phrases like *finally made up my mind* and *out of place here* and *no time for me* leaped up at him. Hallam read the letter once, then again. It was still the same the second time. He took a deep breath, not sure what he should do.

Then he crumpled the letter in his knobby fist and stood there in the empty apartment for a long time.